When the Smoke Clears

C. N. JOHNSON

Happie Face Publishing Company

ISBN: 978-1-953181-02-2

Dedication

In loving memory of:

Barbara J. Brown

Jerry P. Wilkins

Darrell S. Johnson

John O. Brown

Marcel L. Johnson

Contents

Acknowledgments

Thank you to God first, for there would be no me without his loving grace. To all my family and friends who've supported me along the way, to the ones that understood my creativity and never let me stop dreaming and reaching for my goals, thank you all for believing in me even when I didn't believe in myself.

1
Starting Out

Sean

"Best Trucking has the potential to make the next Forbes Fortune 500 Company list. The question is, how are we going to make it there? Our goal over the next year is to push the sale and get the client. I need this marketing team to put your blood, sweat, and even your children's tears into boosting our account status. Any new ideas, bring them to my attention immediately. Also, we will be introducing a whole new human resources team since we've been having problems with the old one. Be prepared for ongoing meetings over the next few months. We will meet again next Monday. That is all. Thank you for your time, and enjoy your weekend," my manager, Sarah, ends with. She always wants us to push out so much for her and make her look good, but she never pushes for us when we are trying to get ahead.

We get called into meetings almost every other day. I am a Digital Marketing Specialist here, but I'm always looking for a way out. I want to stay in the company and grow, however, every time I try to spread my wings, Sarah always ends up clipping them. *Fuck this place,* is my daily attitude. I walk out and pretty much fly down the hall. I don't want anyone stopping me to talk, so I have to move fast.

"Aye, Sean, wait up!"

Damn, spoke too soon. Just as I could taste the freedom on the outside and feel the fresh air and the sun on my face, Cody, my coworker, yells my name from the other end of the hall. He is a very slim and dapper brother; a sharp dressed brown-skinned dude, no taller than 5' 9" at the most, has a bald head like Mr. Clean, and wears these Malcolm X-like glasses. He runs down the hall to catch up to me. Something is really up with this guy; he needs some friends, I swear he does. Maybe, if he didn't brown-nose and act like he knows everything, someone would hang out with the guy. Instead, he finds me, the only one that keeps to their self around here and wants to connect.

"Sup man," I say.

"Damn, you walk fast, bro. What's the hurry? You got a hot date this weekend?" he asks. Did I mention he's always trying to get the 411 on my personal life? Maybe he wants some pointers on how to bag a lady or something.

"Nah, just going to hang out with my son. You?" I ask, as if I really cared.

"I'm going to come up with a couple of these ideas for Sarah for Monday. You know, get a head on things," he smiles and hits my shoulder. "I think we should get togeth-"

"Cody, my man." I hit his shoulder back. "I really gotta go. I'll see you on Monday. I gotta go pick up my son." Already annoyed that he stopped me, I make a fast break to the door.

"Oh, okay. We'll talk later," he says.

"Yeah man," I say back and walk off. I step out into freedom and hop into my red Jeep Wrangler, fully loaded with black leather seats that match my tints and rims. Working at Best Trucking will steal your joy, but it has brought me this dope ass ride. The only thing that can ease my soul after a long week is to bump Nipsey Hussle in the ride. That's my guy. I didn't even know him personally, but if you ask me, we were friends for years, so his death really hit hard for me. He's forever my favorite rapper. I blast my shit and skirt out the parking lot.

I pull up to my sister's house at 6:30 p.m. to pick up my son. Luckily, my sister is a teacher at his school. She teaches first grade, and he's in Pre-K, so I don't have to worry about who is picking him up since I get off so late–she just brings him home with her. Since the school goes to third grade, they will share a few years together, which gives me great comfort.

I'm kind of like a single father. Where is his mother? I'm sure she will pop up sooner or later.

I knock on the door.

"Open up big head, it's me!"

After 10 mins, which felt like years, Twin opens the door. Twin is my sister. I call her Twin because she is my twin. Get it? Born the same day and kind of even share the same name. I'm Sean Anthony Johnson, the great, and she's Seana Andrea Johnson, the other. Since everyone calls me Sean, I started calling her Twin to separate us from each other. People say we look alike, but besides our brown skin tone, she looks nothing like me. She's short, a little thick, and has these gorgeous hazel eyes, but I'm not really sure where she got those. I guess that gene skipped me. Our father was Cherokee and black, so she got his straight hair, but she keeps a short Toni Braxton type haircut. She is the number one lady in my life. I love her more than life itself. She's my heart beat and without her, I couldn't live.

"Damn, Twin, what took you so long? It's cold out here!"

"Well I'm trying to wash clothes, cook, and help your son learn his colors. What took you so long?" Twin asks.

"Another meeting at the office. Last minute tings ya' know mon!"

"Hey dad!" my son, Lil Sean, yells from the kitchen table.

"Big Man! How was school?" I ask him. I walk into the kitchen and I kiss him on the head.

"Good!" he says.

"Oh word? Learn anything good?" I ask.

"No!" he replies. I laugh because he is one of the most honest kids I know. He reminds me of myself. That's my guy. I call him Big Man because he's so tall for his age. If you didn't know he was three, you would think he's at least five. He's kind, funny, and has an old soul. I swear he's been here before. He's so chill. Most kids his age are all over the place and into everything, but give him a good toy or put on a good movie and he is relaxed. He even two steps with me when I play the oldies. Besides my curly hair and perfect hair line, he looks just like his mother.

"What do you mean no? You didn't learn nothing at all?"

"No, I knows did," he says, causing both me and Twin to laugh.

"You knows did?" I ask and I laugh again because I know what he is trying to say but can't find the right words. This kid is adorable.

"Yes," he says and shakes his head.

"Well, that's because you 'knows it' all like your auntie," Twin says.

"Or maybe, if we are being truthful, you're just smart like your father," I add.

The front door opens and in walks Twins' husband, Joe. Joe is a 6'5" dark-skinned brother and built like a wall, has the heart and body of a giant, but is a big teddy bear on the inside. He is the only man that I ever trust my sister with.

"Smart like Uncle Joe!" Lil Sean screams out.

"Uncle Joe?!" Twin and I say at the same time.

"Ya' damn right you're smart like your Uncle Joe," Joe says as he walks into the kitchen and kisses Twin.

"Hey babe," Joe says to her. He then reaches over the counter and gives me a handshake, high fives Lil Sean, and whispers, "We are the smartest people in this entire family," before walking into the living room. Lil Sean agrees.

"Daddy, Mommy coming?" Lil Sean asks me in his soft, innocent voice. Twin turns away from the stove and stares at me.

"I don't know, man," I tell him. It breaks me down sometimes because I just don't know how to explain to him that his mother is an asshole.

"Text mommy," he tells me. Little does he know that I've been texting her all day.

*

Yesterday
10:30 p.m.
Me: hey just want you to know that we miss you, gn

Today
9:00 a.m.
Me: GM

10:45 a.m.
Baby Mom: GM

10:46 a.m.
Me: you coming over tonight?

12:06 p.m.
Baby Mom: I'll let you know

12:30 p.m.

Me: What you mean you'll let me know? This that bullshit Kay. You're here one second, then gone the next. Why do I have to beg you to come see your own son? You need to stop walking in and out his life, calling him once in a blue moon, telling him u going to come and you don't show. He looks forward to seeing you and it upsets him when you don't come.

12:45 p.m.

Baby Mom: He's upset or are u upset?? Lol, boi get a life, don't you got work to do? Stop texting my phone, before I block you again!!!!

12:46 p.m.

Me: Ur son, dumbass. Every time you find a new dick to suck you start acting goofy.

6:58 p.m.

Me: you are coming past the crib tonight or Nah

So, here's the thing about his mother. She is my on-again, off-again girlfriend. We met our senior year of high school. My sister became a cheerleader the last year of school and she met my son's mother, Makayla Adams. The two were like peas in a pod. They went everywhere and did everything together, and as I started seeing her around more and more, I became heavily attracted to her. Kay was sexy and all the dudes wanted to tap that. She was short, had light brown eyes, ass and titties like a full-grown woman, and long, wavy hair that was all hers. She never knew her father, but I knew she had to be mix with something because her skin was caramel and smooth like Melanie Fiona.

The thing that attracted me the most was her smile; it was as adorable as a care bear and as soon as you saw it, it was like your body warmed from the inside out, but get her mad, and she had a mouth like a sailor. She was my first and my everything. By the end of the school year, we were so deep in love that we couldn't stay away from each other, so we all went to the same college. Things were perfect. My sister had her best friend, and I had my girl. In my heart, I believed nothing could ever go wrong.

-ding ding- Text from Baby Mom

7:00 p.m.

Baby mom: NAH

My stomach dropped the same way it does when you're driving and you hit a dip in the road. I was so pissed but sad at the same time. As my heart ached, I kept a straight face for my son's sake.

"Mom's not coming tonight, kid. She said she has to work and that she's sorry. She will make it up to you." Lil Sean hangs his head. I hate that she does this to my boy. I can take it, but he doesn't understand why his mother keeps walking out on him.

"When work over?" he asks.

"It's going to be too late, buddy."

"Tomorrow?" he asks as he looks at me with his light brown puppy dog eyes he got from his mother. Damn, this shit really hurts my heart.

"Yeah, buddy. Maybe tomorrow," I tell him.

My sister looks at me, then says, "Lil Sean, go in the living room with Uncle Joe."

"Okay." He jumps down off the stool.

"Here, take your puzzle too. Have uncle Joe help you since you two are the geniuses of the family." Twin smiles and Lil Sean laughs.

"We da smarties!" he says. For a three-year-old, his vocabulary is amazing, thanks to his personal teacher, his auntie Twin. He takes his stuff and runs into the living room. Twin looks at me like a pissed off mother whose child brought them back a diet Coke from the corner store when she asked for a Pepsi.

"Give me your phone, Sean." She holds out her hand.

"Why?" I ask.

"Give me the damn phone, Sean!" she yells.

"Okay, mom." I hand over my phone. Watching her read my texts makes me so nervous because I know she is bound to say any and everything her lips could spit out in judgement. She shakes her head.

"Exactly what I thought. What the fuck is the matter with you?" she whispers.

"What you mean, what's the matter with me, Twin?"

"Oh, don't talk that twin shit with me because right now the stuff you are doing, I wouldn't," she says. Twin turns back to the stove, then turns back and looks at me while she tastes her sauce off the spoon.

"Why are you even texting that girl? She doesn't want to be a mother and she damn sure don't want to be somebody's wife."

"I text her for Sean and nothing else," I say.

"We miss you," she says, looking back at the texts. "Really, Sean? Fool must have been on both of our birth certificates if you think I didn't read the texts before just now?" she says.

"All right, last night I missed her a little. What's wrong with letting people know how you feel?"

"People, yes. Your son, yes. Your friends, fine. But not that hoe. She's in and out of both your lives, here for two weeks and gone for two months. She's doing more damage to you then she is to Lil Sean. I don't know how many times I have to tell you. She is no good for you. She is toxic. The devil in disguise. She only comes around when she thinks you're talking to someone else and tries to play that 'I wanna be a family again' bullshit."

"Twin, relax. I hear you." I rub my forehead. She is about to make this in to something bigger than it already is.

"No, you don't, because even after all these years, she is still hurting you and you're hurting your son by letting her do it."

"All right, all right already! Damn, this is too much for a Friday. Shit," I say playfully as I smile at Twin.

"I'm not playing, Sean. Everything is a damn joke to you."

I get up and try to hug her. It seems like my problems stress her out more than they do me. She grabs my arms as I go in for my hug and looks me in the eye.

"Sean Anthony Johnson, you are my soul and that little boy in there is my whole heart. He is hurting, but not as bad as you. You smile, joke, and laugh, but deep down she has torn you apart. You may fool everyone else with this cover up, but I am you and you are me. When you hurt, I hurt and the pain you feel, I feel that same pain. You're a Taurus, so I know you're going to do what you want, but I'm only telling you this because I love you beyond belief and something has just got to give," Twin says before she pulls me in for a hug. I feel like she's trying to bring out an emotion that I just wasn't ready to give. Before she got me all misty eyed, I pulled away and smiled.

"All right, nigga, enough with the mushy stuff," I say. She pushes me and smiles.

"You're such a dick, you know that?" she declares.

"It takes a dick to know a booty hole, nuts, and butts," I say.

"Ew, boy, why can't you ever be serious? Sean, look at me." I look at her and she looks back at me in a daze as if she knew that I knew that everything she just said was all true.

"Ugh. Why are woman always trying to open you up and get you all in your feelings?" I say, throwing a dish towel at her face. "I'm outta here. Big Man, come get your stuff. It's time to go," I call out. Lil Sean comes running in the kitchen.

"No, he hasn't even eaten yet. Just leave him here since you're ready to run out so fast. You go out and have some fun, drink, do something–it's Friday. Get your mind in order, and I'll bring him home in the morning," Twin says.

"You wanna stay with Auntie tonight?" I ask. Lil Sean jumps up and down.

"Yes, yes, yes! ICakes, Auntie Twin?" He gets so excited. ICakes is his favorite pancake place.

"I didn't know that this sleepover was going to cost me money," Twin says as Lil Sean runs up to her and grabs her legs.

"Please, please, please!"

"All right, how can I say no to that?" Lil Sean does a little spin move combination dance of some sort and his face just lights up. I love that he can just bounce back from his mom's bullshit. I wish I could.

Joe walks into the kitchen, walks behind Lil Sean, covers his ear and whispers into Twin ear, "Please, please, please can I get some ass tonight?" Twin bursts out laughing.

"Now that's something I can say no to," she laughs again.

"All right creeps, it's getting too freaky in here. I'm heading out. Big Man, come give me a hug, I'm leaving." Lil Sean runs over to me and hugs me.

"Be good for your aunt and uncle tonight," I say and high five him.

"Okay, daddy" he replies.

"Holla at the kid," I say as I walk out the door.

Twin

Joe leans on the kitchen countertop and pops a few of my grapes in his mouth.

"He still soft on M-a-k-a-y-l-a, huh?" Joes spells out her name since Lil Sean is in the room. I tell Lil Sean to watch TV in the next room while I make his plate so me and Joe can talk.

"I just don't understand it, Joe, I really don't. He bags girl after girl, and yet, he's still stuck on this dog chain waiting for her to return home. She has nothing, and she is nothing, but this goofy fool stays pressed.

I take my grapes from Joe. "Okay, enough."

Joe stands up and starts walking back past me and says, "It's because he's a damn Taurus. Y'all stingy and stubborn." I feel offended by his Taurus comment, even though it is very much true, so I throw the dish rag at him as he walks back into the living room.

2

The Crew

Sean

All I could think about on the drive home was what my sister said. I know she's right, but I can't get the idea of Makayla, Lil Sean, and I becoming a family out of my head. We were together off and on for 13 years now and I still don't want to give that up. The girl has my whole heart. My father gave up on our family when me and Twin were five. The last thing he said before he walked out the door was, "I can't take this shit no more!"

We didn't understand. We just knew that our parents were fighting. I don't know how Twin felt at that moment, but I just thought he would be back. He always came back. Foolishly, I waited for him to return until I was nine.

I never wanted to be like him, so I stayed with Makayla through all the ups and downs to work on us for the sake of my family. I always wanted a family. That moment my father left, my mother went to her room and came out an hour later. That hour seemed like forever. Me and Twin cuddled up on the sofa and watched TV, and I remember Twin putting a blanket over us. Twin has always been my safe place. I never worry about anything when she's around. Our mom walked into the living room, smiled at me and Twin, and simply asked us if we were hungry. She never looked upset, and we never saw her cry, but Twin knew she was hurt, and she did everything she could to keep her smiling. The crazy part is that I'm just now realizing I'm just like my mother, and Twin is doing for me what she did for her. Our mother passed away almost three years ago from cancer, just six months after Twin married Joe and three months after my son was born. Damn, I miss her.

-ding ding- Text from Mally Mal

My heart always skips a beat when I get a text; I guess part of me wishes for it to be Makayla.

8:15 p.m.

Mally Mal: Bro we out tonight or you on daddy duty

8:17 p.m.

Me: Nigga every night is daddy duty Tf you mean

8:20 p.m.

Mally Mal: U right, ma bad, well are you able to take your apron off for a while and come out tonight?

8:23 p.m.

Me: Lol, Fuck you, nigga

Where at tho, Twin got Sean for the night so im in.

8:30 p.m.

Mally Mal: Twin the bid fr meet me at shakes at 10

8:31 p.m.

Me: ard

I meet up with Mally at Shakes around 10:45 that night. Shakes is our go-to bar out in northeast Philly, close to the Tacony-Palmyra Bridge that goes over to Jersey. There's always a great mixed crowd, just like the bars we used to go to in college. I think that's why we love it so much. When we ain't got much to do, that's where you can find us. We are all in our 30s now, so beyond drinking here, bowling, chilling at someone's house, or singing karaoke, we don't do much.

"Well, it's about damn time, playboy," I hear Mally scream from the other end of the bar.

As I walk down, he says to the bartender, "Give my mans a shot.

He's a single father." I laugh, call him an asshole, and take the shot.

"My mans done put down the sippy cup and picked up a shot glass. The Gods are on our side tonight, baby," he says. I can tell

Mally is already lit.

I met Jamal, aka Mally, in band class and he was and still is the loudest guy. Tall, dark and skinny, he's the only brother I know that can play the saxophone like Kenny G. Now, he uses his talents as the music director at MazeTown University, our alma mater.

"Nigga, we just got here and you already on one," James walks up behind me and says.

James is a football guy. Everything about him is football. The man even has Philadelphia Eagles bed sheets and a shower curtain. He's short and stocky now, but he was the quarterback for our college team back in the day. His name was "Irish Husky" on the field because he is light skinned with red hair. We started hanging out after we met at the university bookstore; we were both pissed that the textbook we both needed was out of stock. Now, he's a teacher and a high school football coach for Cheltenham High, where Twin and I went to school. I introduced him to my homies after we met, and he introduced us to Joe, who was also on the football team.

"My nigga," I say embracing James who walked in with Kelly, another one of our friends.

"Hey, beautiful," I say to Kelly as I kiss her on the cheek.

Kelly is now a stylist for up-and-coming artists. She has the dream job; all she really does is shop for clothes using other people's money and gets paid to dress them, but she came into the picture our sophomore year when Makayla and I started falling apart. We met in English Lit. and she became one of my best friends. We started sleeping together after Makayla cheated on me and left MazeTown. She knew everything about me, helped me with my breakup, and she gave the best head, which honestly helped me with my break-up the most. She sucked me dry and made my toes curl every time. We fell out when Makayla came back our Junior year. I knew that I would end up breaking her heart, so I was honest with her and told her Makayla wanted to work out our relationship, and I had to break it off with her. Kelly said she understood and was cool with us just being friends, but to this day, I still think she's hurt by it. She has always kept her cool, even when the group would hang out and I was there with Makayla. However, even now, she will make it known she still has some feelings for me. Every time Makayla goes missing, she hits on me. I will admit, I flirt with her here and there, but it's never serious. Everything with her is cool until I bring another female around the group who isn't Makayla and then she acts flaky. Sometimes it's too much, but hey, at the end of the day, that's my friend, dance partner, and I will love her to the death of me like all the rest.

No one really dealt with Makayla after she cheated the first time. Twin tried to give her a chance for the sake of me but after Makayla got pregnant the first time and demanded that I leave school to be with her and the baby, her and Twin got into it, and they haven't been friends since. Unfortunately, Makayla miscarried at six weeks and it was devastating to the both of us. That was the only thing that pulled her closer to me. After that, we stayed together for five years until Lil Sean was born.

"Shots, shots, shots!" Mally yells to the group.

"Bro, can we get a table, sit down, and relax before we get wasted?" I insist.

"Yes, can we? I'm not standing up at the bar all night in these heels," Kelly says. As we get seated at our table, in walks Tiffany, her younger sister, Tam, and another girl who looks familiar. The whole crew is there minus Twin and Joe, who really don't go out much since they got married.

Tiffany is our African goddess. She is as woke as woke can be. She lets us know on a daily basis how black we are not. Mixed with African and Jamaican, she's tall and skinny with a rich, dark chocolate skin tone, has mad sex appeal, and can make a mean oxtail. If you ever wanted to date someone that reminded you of Naomi Campbell, she's your girl. Men fall at her feet and she just walks right by them. The crew thinks she might be a lesbian because we catch her checking other women out. She hasn't come out yet, but we don't judge her. Shit, I think it's sexy. She teaches African-American studies at Philadelphia Community College.

It always feels good getting with everyone, and it's amazing that our group outlasted our college days. After 12 years of friendship, I consider them family. Sadly, we lost one of our friends, Mike. Now, Mike was my best friend. We were like night and day; while I was studying and focusing on only being with Makayla, Mike was running through women like water and doing every hustle you could think of to make money. He was a tall, light skinned dude with a curly afro and a chipped tooth. When you saw me you saw him, but he was a hothead and got kicked out of school his freshman year for fighting a security guard when he got drunk. That didn't keep him away, though. He was always on campus and lived in my room for about a year.

Mike was gunned down just months before my son was born. He called me the day of his murder and told me he was coming over and that he had something important to tell me, but he never made it. I gave my son his name as a middle name–Sean Michael Johnson, Jr.– so he will forever live on.

Tiffany, her sister Tam, and the other girl walk over to the table. I say hey and kiss Tiff and Tam on the cheek. As I look at the third girl, I can't shake the feeling like I've seen her somewhere before.

"Look at all my beautiful black kings and queens. Black lives matter!" Tiff says as she raises her fist. We all do the same and repeat.

"Y'all already know Tam, but this is her friend, Brittany," Tiff says, going around the table introducing Brittany to everyone. When she gets to me, Brittany says, "I know you. You work at my job. Sean, right?"

"Yeah, that's me. I thought you looked familiar. You look diff-"

"Different, I know. Everyone says that when they see me out." She smiles.

"Small world," Tiffany adds with a smirk.

I knew I had seen her before, but I never really noticed her. She works in our shipping department and always wears these thick ass coke-bottle glasses and loose-fitting clothes, but tonight she is looking like a snack. Her heels are high, her dress is tight, her hair is up in a bun and there are no coke bottles in sight. She sits to the left of me and she smells so good. Like *really good*–like peach cobbler on a Thanksgiving morning. Even though my heart calls for Makayla, tonight I want to put my vanilla ice cream on top of that cobbler, if you know what I mean.

Kelly will act goofy if I take notice of this girl, so I keep it cool. The night is perfect. I laugh, joke, and drink with my friends like I don't have any cares. I have fun and it really keeps my head off Makayla. It's not until around 1:30 a.m. that Kelly's drunk ass goes to the bathroom which is a relief because she has been crowding me all night. Brittany is at the bar with Tam, so now's my chance to get up and talk to them.

"Ladies," I address them.

"Yo! I'm litty bro, like litty litty, bro!" Tam says. I know when

Tam is drunk because she starts speaking slang. Any other time, she uses her 50 million-dollar words she learned from Harvard. Yes, Tam is a smart kid; she didn't end up at MazeTown like the rest of us.

"I hope you didn't drive, baby girl." I look over at Tiffany, who can barely stand up straight. "I know Tiff ain't drive; she's never the designated driver." We laugh.

"Y'all need a ride? I'm about to call it a night," I ask them.

"Yes please! Tiff would stay all night if she could," Tam says as she throws her arm around me and sips my drink in my other hand. I laugh as she pretends like she isn't drunk.

"All right, I got you," I kiss her on her forehead as she breathes out about 10 long island iced teas in my face.

"Can you drop Brittany off too?" Tam asks.

"Tam, I can take a taxi. I'm fine, you don't have to," Brittany says.

"No, no, no. He's going to take you home. He's a good guy, he's like family." She grabs my face.

"He has sweet cheeks, y'all work together, and the best part, get this, he won't rape you."

I look at Brit, a bit shocked and embarrassed that she'd even think of that. I shake my head and say to Tam, "Yeah, it's time to get you home. Come on, let's get your stuff."

"Nope, not until Brittany agrees. I'm not moving," Tam says. Brittany smiles.

"Sure, if that's okay with you." She stares directly at me. "I don't want you to go out your way," Brittany explains.

I smile at Brittany and say, "I got you."

While helping Tam back to the table and her drink spilling all over the place, she whispers in my ear, "She likes you. She's been talking about how fine you are all night."

"Who?" I ask.

"Brit, fool. She wanna fuck," Tam whispers in my ear. I immediately start thinking about all the things I could do to Brit's body. Brittany walks over to grab her things and helps me get Tam's stuff.

"Aye yo'! Im'a take them home," I say to the crew.

"Damn, Tam, you stay getting lit fast. It's only like 10:30," Tiff stutters through her drunkenness.

"Tiff, it's almost 2 a.m.," I say.

"Shit. I gotta go to work in the morning. Can you take me home too?" Tiff asks as she gathers all her things.

I nod. "For sure. Let's go."

"What about me?" Kelly asks. "Can you take me home too, daddy?" Here she goes with the bullshit.

"No," I say coldly.

"You ain't never had a problem with taking me home before," she says in her sexy voice.

"Sorry, car's full. We out. See y'all later," I call to everyone. I say my goodbyes, dap up my homies, and as I go to give Kelly a hug, she grabs my face and kisses me on my lips, and I immediately push her back.

"Kels, you gotta chill," I tell her.

"You love it," she says, as she smiles and sits.

"Not tonight." I touch Brittany's lower back and open the door for her as she helps Tam out the door. I look back at Kels, sticking my tongue out at her and she gives me the middle finger.

3

What A Ride

Sean

For the entire ride, Tam is knocked out in the back, Tiff is grooving to the music in the front, and Brittany is on her phone. As we get closer to Tiff's house, she asks, "Are you hitting Kels again or something?"

I roll my eyes and shake my head. "Hell nah. I haven't hit that since college, you know that," I mumbled. I knew this would come up, but it was a conversation I didn't really want to have with Brit in the car.

"Oh, okay…"

I look at her with suspicious eyes. "Why you ask that?"

"I don't know, she just been real handsy. Y'all do the little flirt thing here and there, but she's been coming on real strong lately. I don't know, maybe it's just me," Tiff explains.

"Nope," Tam says as she sits up. "I see it and I don't even hang with y'all often." Me and Tiff laugh.

"She's just mad," Tiff laughs at Tam slurring her words.

"Mad at what, boo?" Tiff asks.

"Mad because Brit thinks Sean is fine, and she overheard us talking about him." Brit looks shocked and hits Tam.

"What? Sean's been feeling you all night too, girl. If you ask me, the crazy bitch is blocking," Tam adds.

I massage my forehead. I can't believe this conversation keeps going left.

"Wow," Tiff and I say as Brit smiles. We pull up to Tiff's house.

"Well, I feel sorry for y'all on the rest of this car ride," Tiff says as she eyes Tam, who is still too drunk to function.

"Thanks, bro. Call me and let me know she got in safe," Tiff says as she exits the car.

"I got you," I reassure her. She looks through the passenger window and says, "Tam, call me in the morning, okay? You hear me?"

"Yeah, yeah," Tam responds waving her hand.

As soon as we pull off, Brittany says, "So you and Kelly are not dating?" Before I could say no, Tam's drunken ass sits back up and says, "No, that girl is irking, she gets goofy any time there is another female around Sean. She's jealous of anyone he's attracted too."

Confused, Brit asks, "So, why would she be jealous of me?"

"Why not you? You're beautiful," I add. She says thank you and looks back into her phone. I look through my rearview mirror and the light of her phone shows her face; she smiling and bites her lip a little.

Jackpot! I think to myself.

"Sean, take me home next, I gotta get out this car. I'm getting sick… if that's cool with you, B," Tam says.

"Yea that's fine, as long as he won't rape me," Brit laughs.

"Whoa, what the fuck? See what your drunk ass done started Tam?" I say. Brit laughs and says she's only joking. She catches my eye in the rearview looking at her, she smiles, and looks back in her phone and I can see her biting her lip again.

Double Jackpot. Is it me, or is Tam being my wing-woman right now?

"I got you, babe, just don't throw up in my car, all right?" A short 10-minute drive and finally, we pull up to Tam's house. I get out the car to help her out and to make sure she doesn't fall flat on her face.

Tam says, "Brit, babe, can you get my bag and open the door for me?"

"Sure, honey. You want me to help you up the steps?" Brit asks as she collects Tam's bag.

"No, Sean got me."

As I help her out the car and walk her up the steps, her ankles wiggle in her heels so she leans on me then whispers, "You owe me."

I chuckle after seeing how well Tam had my back, even in her drunken state. After we get Tam in the house, Brit and I walk back to the car. She goes to get in the backseat, so I ask her if she would like to sit up front, and she smiles and agrees. After five minutes of silence she speaks with very up front and forward questions.

"So you got kids?" she asks.

"I have a kid, yes," I respond, a bit confused as to why this is her first question.

"How old is he or she?

"He's three."

"Nice," she says.

It's a little awkward, but if this is how we will start off, then I'll do the same thing.

"You have any kids?" I ask her. She shakes her head no.

"You want any?"

She looks at me and smiles. "One day. Not now, though. I'm still in school," she replies.

"School?" I ask with my eyebrow raised.

"Yeah, I went back to college to finish my bachelor's degree in art," she adds.

"Oh okay, I see you, working and going to school. Do your thing," I say, and she laughs.

"What's funny?"

"Because you said 'school' like I was going to say high school or something."

"Well, I gotta make sure," I laugh.

"So, how old are you, since you're worried about my age? Are you like 40 or something?" she asks.

"Your mother is 40," I joke.

"My mother is dead," she replies as she lowers her head and looks out the window.

"Oh damn, my bad." I look to the road. I think to myself, *Way to go Sean, you just fucked that up. I'm not getting no ass tonight.* "Hey, yo, I'm sorry. I didn't know."

"Well, you wouldn't have known because if you did, you would know that I was joking," she says and laughs.

"That's fucked up you know." I smile, but try to figure out if she's a little off. Who jokes about shit like that? I take my focus off the weird shit, since I just really want to fuck.

"Yeah I know," she giggles. "So, how old are you, though? All jokes aside."

"I'm 30. I'll be 31 on May 13th."

"A Taurus baby, huh," she mentions.

"Yup, through and through."

She directs me to slow down and pull up right in front of her place.

"You live by yourself?" I ask. She stares at me with big eyes.

"That's a little creepy to ask, don't you think?"

I realize how weird it sounded and I laugh. "Yeah, I guess so. My bad."

"No, I live with my mother."

"The dead one, right?" I quip.

"Yup."

We sit in the car for another hour talking about work and agreeing on all the stuff we hate about it. I'm getting bored, and if she's not trying to fuck, she needs to dip. Before she gets out the car, she stops and turns to me.

"So, you're attracted to me, huh?" she asks.

"Yeah," I shrug.

"Why didn't you ever say anything to me at work?"

I look down at the wheel, thinking of the best line I could give her because I hadn't paid much attention until now.

"Honestly, I hate it there and I don't pay anyone any mind. I just do my job, and get the fuck outta there."

"I feel you," she says. "Well, maybe we can have lunch some time?" she insists.

"Sure," I agree. She looks at me and bites her lip for the third time and now I have to have her. It's 3 a.m. and I'm already lit, so I lean in and kiss her. She leans into it, starts touching my chest, and instantly I feel a hard-on coming. Her lips are so soft and juicy, and her touch was easy like a Sunday morning. I knew right then that we were going to fuck. She unbuttons my pants and starts touching on me. I see her eyes light up when she feels how big it is. I ask her to come take a ride home with me, and I would bring her back when she's ready.

She says, "No," and stops. She takes me by surprise and I can't help but think to myself, did she just get my mans up and then stop? Then she says, "No, I'll get in my car and follow you, if that's all right?"

"Cool with me," I say. She quickly jumps in her car and she

follows me all the way to my place. With the way I have been feeling lately, I'm about to blow this girl's back out. I hope she can handle all this dick. Makayla is always in the back of my mind, but in a way, sleeping with other women makes me feel like I'm getting her back for everything. It really is the best feeling. I keep looking in the rear-view mirror to make sure she is still following, and we pull up to my crib around 3:30 a.m.

When we walk in, she looks at me, and I look at her. She bites her lip, I throw my keys down, pin her up against the wall and kiss her. I haven't even started fucking her yet and she's already moaning. We shuffle through the hallway, ripping each other's clothes off. She smiles as my face lights up when I see how big her titties are. God D, and the D is for damn. When we get down to our underwear, I pick her up and take her to my room. I push her on the bed, reach over to my nightstand, and pull out a condom. As I'm putting it on, I can tell that she wants it so bad by the way she's biting her lip and moving her hips, and it is turning me on even more. As soon as I slide in, she gasps for air. I asked her if she's good and she lets out a quiet "yes."

Any blood I had left in any part of my body is all in my dick and I'm rock hard. I kiss her as I softly stroke. Even with the condom on, I can feel how soft, warm, and wet she is inside. She is so wet that now and then, I pull out just to make sure the condom isn't broken. Surprisingly, it isn't, and it turns me on more. She bites my ear softly as I stroke harder and harder. Her legs shake, and they open wider. She breathes heavily and moans in my ear. She yells out my name and calls for the Lord as she digs her nails into my side. Either my dick is good, or my dick is damn good.

I go deep, her legs wrapped around my back, and she pulls me in deeper. She scratches my back and bites my shoulder and five minutes in, she tells me she's about to cum.

She screams out, "Baby, I'm gon' cum! Oh shit, I'm about to cum!" I open her legs wider and stand in it. I bend my head down and suck on her nipples. I can feel her juices pouring out on my nut sack and now my inner thighs are just as wet as hers and she starts to cum. I flip her around mid-climax while she's still on the dick and she yells, "Oh yes!"

I'm hitting it from the back now with longer, deeper, and harder strokes. Her being so wet makes it so easy to rotate her without ever pulling out. The sound is like making mac and cheese, and I'm mixing all up in her insides. She cums again and again and again. I pull her hair, bringing her closer to me. I rest back on my knees while she sits on my dick.

She screams out, "Damn!" She moves in a circular motion, and then rocks back and forth, holding on to my thighs for dear life. I play with her clit and kiss on her shoulder until she cums again. Her head falls back on my shoulder and her eyes roll back. I push her back up on the bed, arch her back and stroke harder until she cums again.

"What are you doing to me?!" she yells out as her hands slide down the headboard. I let her get one more nut before I cum. I'm so ready for it, and I give her harder, faster, longer, and deeper strokes. She ends up coming two more times back to back before I let off.

Hot, sweaty, and sticky, I pull out and she falls face first on to the bed. I lay beside her and look over, her face still in the pillow.

I laugh and say, "You good?"

She picks her head up while biting the pillow and says, "What the fuck?"

I laugh as she drops her head back down. I get up to drop the condom off in the bathroom trash and I get us some water. The clock reads 5:15 in the morning and I can already see the light peeking through the blinds as I walk back to the room.

"Brit, you want some water?" I ask.

"Nah I-I- I'm cool. I just need to go to the bathroom," she says. I tell her where the bathroom is and while she gets herself together, I sit on the side of the bed and drink my water. I check my phone for any texts from Makayla. None. I put my phone on the charger and Brit walks back into the room. She stands in the doorway for a while with her head on the door and her hand on the knob. I laugh and tell her to come to me. She gets back into bed, scoots closer to me, and lays her head on my chest.

"Wow, that was–shit, that was what it was," she says.

"Oh, so you liked it, huh?" I ask.

"Shit, I loved it." We lie there and fall asleep. Around 9 a.m., I wake back up and I check my phone for a text from Makayla and still got nothing. Damn, I need to relax and stop checking for her.

"Are you texting your hoes, apologizing for not being with them last night?" Brit asks as she sits up in bed and fixes her bun.

"As a matter a fact, I am. How did you know?"

"I had a feeling," she says, stretching out. "So, what are you telling them?" she asks as she crawls over to me.

"I just stated that I had to blow some girl's back out last night and maybe we could reschedule to meet up another time."

"Oh really," she says now inches away from my lips. She leans in and kisses me, her lips still so soft.

"So, what are your plans for today, sir?"

"Well, my sister is about to drop my son off soon, then I'm going to hang with him. You?"

"Your sister or your baby mom?" she asks suspiciously.

I look at her and reassure her that despite the jokes, I'm not playing her.

"My sister."

She nods and keeps her eyebrow raised, but she gets off the subject. "Well, I have to go home and get dressed for work."

"You work on weekends?" I ask her.

She nods. "Yes. Packages never stop, office boy. Some of us still got to work." She reaches for her phone.

"Shit, my phone's dead," she says.

"Aww, is Mommy going to be mad you didn't come in last night?"

"Ha ha ha," she mocks me. "No, she's dead, remember?" She quickly looks around for the clock and when she notes that it's now 9:30, she rushes out of bed.

"Fuck, I gotta go," she says, jumping up and gathering her stuff. I gotta be at work at 11 and I still have to go home and get dressed. Have you seen my bra?"

"Check the hallway," I say. She throws on her clothes and I walk her to the door, only half dressed. As I open the door, my sister and son are standing there.

"Dad!" Lil Sean greets me.

"Hey!" I say, completely shocked. I have never introduced my son to anyone I have slept with or hung out with. For all he knows, I'm just waiting around for his mother.

"Well, hello," Twin says. She eyeballs Brittany and waits for a proper introduction.

"Twin, this is Brittany. Brittany, this is Seana, my twin sister. We call her Twin. The little guy is my son, Lil Sean. Say hi, Sean," I tell him.

"Hi Ms. Brittany."

"Hi Sean and Seana. Nice to meet you both, " Brit says.

I can tell she is caught off guard just like I am. My son and my sister caught her doing the walk of shame, and she is definitely embarrassed. She quickly walks past them and rushes out the door.

"I'm going to walk her to her car, and I'll be back," I tell them. When we get to Brit's car, we notice that we were way more lit than we thought we were just by the way we parked our cars. I open her car door for her.

"Thank you for a wonderful night. I hope we can do it again some time," she says with a smile.

"Oh, no doubt. Maybe we should have that lunch date, too," I say.

"Definitely. Oh yeah, maybe I could have your number, too?" she adds. I laugh.

"Yeah, that might help." I say. I wait for her to get settled, but then she remembers her phone is dead.

"I guess if you really want to talk to me, you'll get in contact with me," she says.

"I will." I lean in the car and kiss her.

"Damn, your lips are soft," I comment.

"Both sets," she says, which makes my dick jump. We smile at each other and I close the car door. She puts on her coke-bottle glasses and drives off. Confused by if she could see anything last night, I walk back in the house.

"So, who was that?" Twin asks with a smile on her face.

"Yeah, who was that, daddy?" Lil Sean asks as he comes running in the living room.

"A friend," I look at Twin, hoping she will drop the subject, at least in front of Lil Sean. She notices my look and tells him to play so we could "talk."

When the coast is clear, she asks me, "Who was that, Sean?"

"Brittany," I reply dryly.

"I know the god damn girl's name. You told me that at the door. Who is she and don't you dare say she's a friend." I look over to her and smile and sit on the sofa.

"I met her at Shakes last night. She's friends with Tiffany's sister, Tam, and small world, she works at my job."

"You must like her if you're walking her out at nine in the morning. What happened? You hit?" Twin asks.

"Yeah, I hit. What do you think she was doing here?"

"Wow," Twin says

"What you mean, wow? I always hit," I say with a smile. I call to Lil Sean to grab my phone off my bed.

"But she just met your son."

"That was your fault. I didn't know y'all were coming by so early."

"Well, she met your son and your sister, she's cute, has a job, and by the smile on your face, she left you satisfied."

"She was all right," I reply. Lil Sean trots in with my phone in hand and gives it to me. I kiss his forehead and tell him to go back and play.

"All right enough to get escorted to the car?" she asks as I check my phone to see if Makayla texted me. Again, nothing. "Maybe she's the one to finally get your head off Makayla."

I looked up at her and then back down at my phone. "Maybe."

4

Going Backwards

Sean

It's been three months, and Brit and I are still hanging out. Nothing is official yet, we just do us. We don't even make anything public at work; for all anyone knows, I don't know her, and she doesn't know me. We both feel it is best to keep everyone out of our business. Our "dates" have been a lot of Netflix and chill, Chick-Fil-A and chill, work and chill–basically we have been doing a lot of "chilling," if you know what I mean.

She has also spent time with Lil Sean, which is big because I have never let him know about any other female besides his mother. He really takes to her too. He asks for her when she's not around and runs to her when they haven't seen each other in a while. Brit has also been chilling with the group, even without Tam. She even started ignoring Kelly like the rest of us do. We talk all day and fuck all night. She even had me come to the job while she was working overnight a few times for a quick smash in the back of a delivery truck. I couldn't even begin to tell you how freaky Brittany is. Sometimes she just asks me to go to lunch with her so she can top me off in the car on the side of our building.

Besides sex, I have learned a lot about her, like the fact that she is 24, which explains her high sex drive and she wants to be an art teacher. I met her "dead" mother, who is very sweet and reminds me of my mother. It's been a great time so far; she makes me happy, I make her happy, and it has been a while since I thought about

Makayla.

-ding ding- Text from B

7:00 p.m.

B: Open the door sweet cheeks

7:00 p.m.

Sean: coming now

I open the door for Brit. "Sweet cheeks?" I say with a big smile on my face.

"Yes, sweet cheeks," she says, as she walks in and slaps my ass.

"I didn't know we were giving out nicknames now."

"I didn't give you that nickname. Tam did."

"Tam?" I asked, confused.

"Yes, that night at Shakes, when she was trying to convince me to let you drive me home, she called you sweet cheeks." I laugh and shake my head. I pull her close and we continue our banter back and forth as we walk to the kitchen.

"Hi, Ms. Brittany." Lil Sean walks in, and Brit and I break apart.

"Hey! There's my guy!" she picks him up and swings him around as Lil Sean giggles and hugs her back.

"You make food?," Lil Sean mentions.

"Yes, I am! Guess what I'm making?"

"Pizza!?" Sean yells with so much joy and Brit laughs.

"No, I'm making your favorite!" Lil Sean stops and puts his finger to his chin, tapping it as if he is thinking. This kid, I swear, is too much.

"What does Auntie Twin always make?" I say, helping him out.

"Spaghetti?"

We both nod and, with a smile, Brit says, "Yes, and I'm making it just for you."

"Daddy have none?" he asks.

"I don't know, let's ask him." She turns to me.

"Daddy, would you like some of my spaghetti?" Brit asks as she touches my face.

"Oh yes, daddy wants spaghetti," I say. She bites her lip and puts Sean down.

"Sean, go pick up your toys in your room and put on your PJs, dude," I tell him.

"Okay, captain!" he replies and Brit laughs.

"I swear, I don't know where he gets this stuff from," I tell her. When Lil Sean is out of sight, I push Brit against the sink and start sucking on her neck. She tells me to stop, but she's not stopping me. She moans and grips the back of my shirt.

"Okay, okay, stop," she demands as she pushes me away.

"I have to make the food. It's already 7:30 and Sean has to go to bed soon."

"Fine, I'll leave you to it, but I want extra spaghetti after dinner."

She winks and says, "Oh yes, captain"

Walking out the kitchen to go to Sean's room to make sure he's cleaning up, I see my phone light up from the sofa, so I double back and grab it. As I'm walking back to Sean's room, I open my phone.

Text from Baby Mom

7:36 p.m.

Baby Mom: I miss you

My heart drops to my feet and I'm stuck in the hallway, unable to move.

Brit yells from the kitchen, "Bae, where's your strainer?" I hear her but cannot speak right now.

She yells again. "Bae…" Finally, words come out and I tell her where to find what she needs, but I'm way too distracted. I scurry into my room and sit on the bed.

-ding ding- Text from Baby Mom

7:40 p.m.

Baby Mom: Bae we need to talk, I miss you. I miss my lil man

7:41 p.m.

Baby Mom: Can we meet up tomorrow somewhere

7:41 p.m.

Baby Mom: Please Anthony I need you

She only calls me by my middle name when she really wants to talk. I stare at the phone as I fight so many thoughts and try to make sense of what's happening right now.

7:41 p.m.

Baby Mom: I love you, and if you don't want to see me ill understand, at least let me come pick up Sean and spend some time with him Bae. xoxoxo

I close my phone. I sit there going back and forth in my mind on what I should do. Do I text her back? Do I agree to meet up with her to hear what she has to say, or do I just let her come pick up Sean? Shit, it's been three months since I've talked to her and four since she's been gone. I had rehearsed over and over in my head what I would say to her when I see her and now, I'm at a loss for words.

After dinner, I want to go straight to sleep. I don't want to have to explain my sudden change of mood to Brit. I put Sean in his bed while Brit cleans up the kitchen, and I head to the room and lie down before Brit gets in there. When Brit walks in, she closes the door behind her, takes off her clothes, and crawls in the bed with me. I want to tell her I have a headache or something so we wouldn't have sex, but she is wearing my favorite pink panties, the ones with the opening in the middle, where I didn't even have to take them off her or pull them to the side. I can slide in her while she is still wearing them. I can't contain myself and I get hard just at the thought.

She comes closer to me. "Bae, are you okay? You didn't eat much at dinner… was it nasty?" she asks.

"Nah, not at all. It was good, I just got a headache, that's all."

"Aww, my baby. Let me rub your head and make you feel better."

She puts her hand down my boxers and begins massaging my other head. She leans in close so I can smell the perfume I love that she wears and starts licking on my chest and around my nipples, and I can't resist. I go up like a flag on a pole and she moans at the sight of it. I get up to flip her on her back and she pins me down.

"No, Daddy. I'm the one giving out the extra spaghetti tonight, remember?" she says. Damn, I love it when a woman takes charge. I reach over to grab a condom and put it on. She gets on top and slowly puts me inside her. She has a tight grip on me as I ease right in. I can already feel that's she's extra wet as soon as the tip touched. Fuck it. I'm ready. Let's do this.

She's starts riding and as soon as I start to enjoy it, my phone light flashes bright. The room is dark, so the flash on my phone is blinding. We ignore it and she rides some more, but then the flash lights up again. The more she rides, the more my phone goes off. She stops.

"Damn, who's blowing you up?" she asks.

"Nobody important. Come on, why you stop?"

"If it's no one important, then why do they keep texting and calling you?"

"Don't worry about it," I tell her. She gets off of me and sits next to me on the bed.

"We not gon' finish?" I ask.

"Finish with the bitch who is texting you," she says with her arms crossed.

"Who even said it was a bitch?"

Brit gets up, puts on my robe, and walks out the room. Annoyed and still horny, I get up and grab my phone.

5 Missed Calls from Baby Mom
10 Text Messages from Baby Mom

Brittany comes back in the room, sees me checking my phone and starts putting on her clothes.

"Where you going?" I ask.

"Home. Whoever is calling you needs you more than I do."

"B, stop it. Can you sit down for a minute?" She ignores me and continues putting on her clothes. I walk over to her and take her shirt from her just as she puts it on and I throw it on the floor.

"Brittany, sit," I demand, and she sits.

"B, it's my baby mom. She wants to see Sean and keeps pushing the issue, but I haven't responded yet."

"Are you lying to me right now?" she asks. I shake my head no, knowing I wasn't telling her the whole truth, but I definitely wasn't flat out lying. I pick up my phone and showed her all the missed calls.

"So, what are you going to do?" she asks.

"I'm not sure yet. The only thing I'm sure of right now is that I don't want you to leave tonight." I lean over to kiss her, start undressing her, and push her back on the bed. I open her legs, grab her thighs, and pull her to the edge of the bed. If this was going to be it for me and Brit, I wanted her to feel like the time we shared was appreciated. I wanted to make it all about her tonight. I lick down each side of her thighs and lick from her navel to her toes. Then, I open her legs wider and suck on her clit. I use my tongue and slowly lick on the outside of her entrance right before sticking my tongue in and out. I sex her with my tongue as her legs shake and suck on her clit, licking her lips until she starts to cum.

While she cums, I put my thumb in her ass and my pointer finger in her pussy. She holds the pillow over her face and screams into it and starts squirting at the same time. After she cums, I flip her over and start eating her ass and pussy while I jerk off to the sounds of her moans. She cums over and over as I tongue her down and finger fuck the shit out of both her holes. I want her orgasms to be intense, so I make sure to keep hitting her g-spot. When she screams out, she can't take anymore, I give her one more nut before I slide in. I stroke her until her body shakes uncontrollably, almost seizure-like. The last time she cums, I cum with her. I lie next to her in the bed and I can see that she has tears running down her face but tries to wipe them before I can see. She lays her head on my chest and for some reason, I know that this would be our last time, and I wonder if she feels like that too.

The next day after Brittany leaves for work, I call Makayla. She asks me if she can come over tonight and spend the rest of the weekend with me and Lil Sean. She says she wants to apologize to the both of us for the way she's been acting, but to be honest, I'm just happy to hear her voice.

Makayla shows up around 1 p.m. I open the door and there she is, looking as good as always. She got a little thinner, but nothing to be alarmed about. She cut her hair, and it's the first time I've ever seen her with a bob cut and not her wavy long hair flowing down her back. Her natural beauty is something I love, but today, she has on makeup. I must say, I could get used to her new look. It kind of turns me on. As soon as she walks in, she wraps her arms around my neck and I pull her in close, holding onto her hips. I cannot resist her. She tells me that she wants to be a family again and that she will try harder.

"You do want to be a family again, don't you?" she asks me. I tell her yes and she asks if we could try it again for the sake of our son and our history and, of course, I agree. My heart couldn't have been happier. Nothing in this world would make me happier, and there is no one I would rather be with than her. She is my whole heart and my everything.

We spend that whole day with our son; we take him out to eat, to the movies, and then to the Jumping Jack Trampoline Park. We play, we laugh, and everything just seems to fall right back into place like we were never broken. My son is loving being with both of his parents. Once we get home, I realize we were having so much fun that I didn't check my phone all day. I immediately notice that I have three missed calls from Brittany and five text messages. While Makayla puts Lil Sean to bed, I go to the bathroom to read Brittany's texts.

2:30 p.m.

B: Hey I Just want to say sorry for last night I was tripping, maybe I can come over and make it up to you later?

3:15 p.m.

B: Hope you're not mad, you're not picking up when I call

3:30 p.m.

B: Guess you don't want to see me tonight??

3:45 p.m.

B: Your phones not dead so why won't you respond

6:45 p.m.

B: ok Sean, fuck it

I feel bad. I don't know how to respond. Should I text her and tell her I'm getting back with Makayla or should I just not say anything at all?

9:28 p.m.

Me: Hey sorry, I been out with Sean all day. Took him to the movies, out to eat and then to Jumping Jacks.

9:30 p.m.

B: oh ok, I was getting kinda worried. You wanna meet up tonight or maybe for breakfast in the morning? I kinda missed you today sweet cheeks.

9:31 p.m.

Me: lol, but nah I'm super tired, I'm going to just put Sean to bed and go to sleep myself. And tomorrow I'm taking him out again, boys' weekend, ya know. But I'll see you at work on Monday.

9:45 p.m.

B: yea sure..........Monday

Hopefully that will buy me some time, and she won't try to hit me up until then. Honestly, I just don't want her to call and Makayla get wind of it because she will answer my phone and say some smart ass shit to B, and B doesn't deserve that.

Later on that night, Makayla and I make love. No wild shit, no extra positions, just her body touching my body, my skin wrapped up in hers. It feels good, as always. I don't know what spell she has me under, but making love to her gives me peace. However, in the middle of us making love, all I can think about is how I didn't change the sheets from last night. Call me an asshole, but fuck it, I got off on just knowing that fact. After that, we have a deep conversation.

She talks about how she wants to change and be different. She claims she never wants to lose me and that she would go crazy if she does. Since losing her mother and our first child, she says things just don't make sense, and every time we fight or on the days she doesn't feel like a good mother, she can't help but to run away.

"Well before you leave, how about you try talking to me about how you're feeling," I utter.

She shakes her head no. "I have so many demons I'm living with, you wouldn't understand. If you found out who I really was, you wouldn't love me."

"I'll always love you, Kay, no matter what."

I beg her to talk to me, but she just lays her head on my chest and tells me she loves me. The mystery of her makes me want her even more. I wish she could open up to me, but for now, I'll take all I can get. I tell her I love her, that I'll always keep a place for her to run back to, and we will work everything out. She says I am her safe place and with me is where she wants to be.

Monday comes quick. I dread running into Brit because I know I have to break things off with her and it'll hurt, but it has to be done. I haven't heard from her since Saturday night, so I'm even worried about how she will react when I see her. To avoid walking into her, I text her as soon as I get to work and try to read her feeling through her texts.

9:15 p.m.

Me: Hey

9:30 p.m.

B: Hey I can't really talk now, what's up

9:31 p.m.

Me: Wanted to know if you wanted do lunch?

9:32 p.m.

B: Yea sure, I am going on break at 12 got a meeting at 1:30

9:35 p.m.

Me: Ard, I'll meet you at my car

I went on about my day. Just thinking about how this conversation could go was driving me crazy. I keep getting the sweats. I don't know what to say to her. She is more than just a one-night stand. I normally would never even call other girls back, but I honestly care for B, not to mention, she met my son. Damn, this is going to be hard.

Brit meets me at my car around 12:15.

"Hey, you," Brit says as she hops in the car. I greet her back and give her a hug before pulling off to head to lunch. We make small talk for a bit.

"So how was your Sunday?" she asks.

"It was good, yours?"

"It was fine."

"Nice." Things become more and more awkward the more we try to force a conversation. I want to just come out and say we're done, but I can't take hurting B.

"So, you and Lil Sean did a lot of guy stuff, huh?"

"Yup," I say pulling up to our favorite cheese steak spot, which is about a block away from our job.

"So, what y'all do?" she asks.

"Just chilled and stuff," I said.

"So, you were having so much fun that you couldn't text or call me?" she snaps and her mood completely changes. I can hear the frustration in her voice. I quickly try to change the subject back.

"B, I'm hungry. Can we get out the car, order, and talk inside?" I ask her nicely.

She breathes heavily, sits back in the seat and bites her full bottom lip, and not the sexy half bite she does when she's turned on. Her hands are tightly clasped together on her lap and she stares straight ahead, shaking her head. After a few moments of silence, she turns and looks at me.

"No, because what you're not going to do is play me," she says, getting louder and clapping her hands while she talks.

"What are you talking about?"

"You're not going to sit here and act like everything is cool, Sean. First, your ex blows up your phone, and then you don't answer my calls and texts. Then, you text me back late at night and give me some fuck boy ass excuse that you were hanging out with your son, when for the past three months we have done nothing but talk and text if I'm not with you. You push me off through the text and tell me, 'hey yeah I know its Saturday night, but I don't want to talk to you until Monday.' What the fuck, Sean?! What up? What's good?"

I wasn't ready for all this. I felt a little scared. She went from nice Brittany to bitch Brittany in a matter of seconds. "Can we just go inside?" I ask again.

"No, I'm not even hungry now. Just be honest with me."

I'm nervous and begin to sweat a little. It's never been this hard to blow someone off. I think to myself, *Will she cry? Will she try to fight me in the car?* I've never seen this side of her before. I feel bad, but I have to be honest with her. I take her hand and hold it.

"Okay, I'll be honest with you, B. My baby mom came by the house on Saturday and wanted to hang out with me and Sean."

"And why wouldn't you just tell me that?" she asked.

"Because I want to work it out with her, but I didn't know how to tell you. Everything is just happening so fast and I don't even know how to deal with it," I say. Brit sits quietly as she stares out the window, but she still lets me hold her hand.

"So, Friday when she was blowing up your phone…"

"She kept texting me about how she wanted to be a family again, but I didn't reply until you left," I explain.

"I kind of figured that you were acting different because of her," she says with a sigh. "I guess I was right."

"Listen B, I'm so sorry. Believe me when I say I never meant to hurt you, but-"

"You have to do what is best for your family, I know. I understand." We grow silent. I look out the windshield and B stares out the passenger window.

"Can you take me back to work?" she asks. I nod, bust a U-turn, and in a few minutes, we're back in front of the building. As she gets out the car, I say, "I hope we can still be friends."

Without a word, she closes the door. I wait for her to respond, but I don't blame her for not wanting to have anything to do with me right now.

She takes a few steps towards the doors, but then turns around. She's keeping a strong face, but I can tell she's broken up inside.

"We're cool," she says before turning her back on me.

5
Same Old Mistakes

Sean

It's been a month since I have talked to or seen Brittany, which is crazy since we work at the same place. I hope that she didn't quit because of me. I have tried contacting her once or twice just to see how everything is going and to see if she is okay, but I never get a response. I truly liked B, but I can't help that I will forever be in love with Makayla. She is the mother of my son.

Besides my sister being pissed at me about Makayla getting back together again, everything is going pretty damn well. I'm happy, my girl is back, my son is happy that his mother his home, and Makayla and I haven't had one fight since she has been back. Our sex is even back to the way it was when we were in college. It will work this time, I just know it. The whole world can turn their backs on me, but I will never turn my back on her and this family.

My alarm clock goes off at 6:30 a.m. and I hardly feel like I've gotten any rest. I look over at Makayla and I'm just so happy she's there. I kiss her on her head, which causes her to wake up. I continue to kiss her and she asks if it was morning or did I just wake her to finish what we started last night as she turns over and runs her hand over my chest. Before I could respond, she sits up and starts kissing my chest. I lose focus for a second when she slides her hand down and touches on me. I tell her don't start nothing she can't finish, and she turns my head to the side, licks my ear, then whispers to meet her in the shower. She pulls back the covers and hops out of bed. When she gets to the door, she turns back and smiles. I jump up and we head straight to the shower for a morning quickie. Back in college, this was our daily routine. We would wake up early in the morning and sneak to the showers for a quickie if we didn't stay in each other's dorm room. I would hold her up and keep my hand over her mouth, so if someone came in, they wouldn't hear her moan.

After our shower, I get dressed, and she gets Sean up and ready for school. My family is finally how I always hoped it would be.

"Hey, Bae," she called to me from Lil Sean's room. "Would you mind if I take the Jeep today and run some errands while you're at work? I can take Sean to school and pick him up." She walks into the room. "I have a lot to do today."

"All right, yeah, I'll just take the motorcycle out. It's supposed to be in the 70s anyway," I say.

"Thanks bae," she says, kissing me.

"Just make sure you're on time to pick him up," I tell her.

"I know. He is my son too." Annoyed, she leans her head to the side and rolls her eyes.

"I'm her son too!" Lil Sean yells from his room.

I yell back, "I know that, thank you, son."

Makayla laughs, kisses me again, and fixes my tie.

"Don't you look so handsome," she tells me.

"Why thank you, my love. You must want another round?" I flirt as I pull her closer.

She pushes me, "You better get your ass out there and make momma that money." She slaps me on my ass.

"Tonight then," I say.

"Tonight," she replies. I kiss Lil Sean on the head and head out to work. What a beautiful day, and I've got to be the happiest man alive. I get to work on time, and no one even bothers me. The lady that sits behind me and talks all day long isn't even here today. I'm feeling so good, I even have lunch with Cody, who has a lot of insight on how bias the company is and the reason for so many changes. He told me which managers are on their way out the door, and who all the racists are. I'm not one for gossip, but today I am here to listen.

-ding ding- Text from Wife

2:30 p.m.

Wife: I love you bae, hope you're having a great day
2:33 p.m.

Me: I love you too..
2:34 p.m.

Me: Tonight right
2:35 p.m.

Wife: lol yes tonight and every night, xoxo
2:36 p.m.

Me: you the bid xoxo

Around 5:30 p.m., my manager calls for another time-consuming meeting with information that she could have sent in an email. Luckily, Makayla will pick up Lil Sean today, so I'm not that pissed. Hopefully, we get in and get out fast so I can go home to my family. I laugh at that very thought, but it keeps me going.

"Hey, Sean!" Cody waves me over to his desk from all the way across the room. I'm not even bothered by him, and I casually stroll over to see what's up.

"So, I heard that we are getting the new HR team today. That's what the meeting is about."

"Oh word?" I say. I'm starting to believe Cody is an inside man because he really knows everything and I wonder what he knows about me.

"Yeah man, I'm about to go in, but I'll save you a seat next to me," he says.

"Cool. I'll be in there in a few, just sending off this last email."

I am the last one to enter the meeting room and all eyes are on me. Our manager, Sarah, shoots me a look and checks her watch, so I apologize and rush to the seat Cody saved me.

"As you all know, we said last week that there will be some changes. We have decided to bring in a whole new HR team since the last team wasn't working out for us."

"Told you, bro, they got all those racist bias HR workers out of here," Cody whispers to me.

"Please welcome one of our new HR supervisors, Tiera Anderson, who will introduce herself and the new team." We all clap out of courtesy, but it's the end of the day and I couldn't care less about anything other than getting home.

"Thank you all for coming to the meeting. I know its late and everyone wants to go home. My name is Tiera Anderson, and I am taking over for Betty Jones. I am one out of five new HR supervisors for the region, and will oversee the shipping and receiving department. Even though I won't be interacting with this department, I just wanted to introduce myself and the team since you'll be seeing me around. I have been with the company for 11 years now, working at the main office in New Jersey…" she explains. She continues to rant more, introducing the other members of the HR team.

-ding ding- Text from Twin

5:36 p.m.

Twin: Where are you

5:37 p.m.

Me: At work in a meeting

5:38 p.m.

Twin: When were you going to tell me Lil Sean was coming with me?

5:38 p.m.

Me: He's not Makayla is picking him up

5:39 p.m.

Twin: Well she's not here, where is she

5:39 p.m.

Me: Idk, hold on ill hit you back

6:00 p.m.

Twin: Figures

*

Text to Makayla

6:00 p.m.

Me: Bae where u at?

6:01 p.m.

Me: Its 6 Sean got out of school at 5, you're an hour late

It's 6:15, and I still have no response, so I leave the meeting to go call her. I call her almost 10 times and still nothing. Suddenly I get a bad feeling and my heart skips several beats. I drop everything and leave work, completely forgetting the meeting. I am happy to have

Twin because I know she wouldn't leave my son at school nor would she wait for Makayla to arrive. Since I rode the bike today, I go straight home since I can't pick up Lil Sean without my car, anyway. Speeding in and out of lanes, popping back and forth between cars, I get home in 25 minutes. As I pull up to our apartment, I notice my Jeep sitting out front in the lot. I'm relieved that my Jeep is there, but worried about where Makayla could be.

As soon as I walk out in the house, I yell out her name.

"Makayla! Makayla!" I look in the kitchen and then walk back to our room, and I am in shock. She's asleep.

"Makayla!" I yell. Now that I know she is okay and still here, I'm pissed.

"Oh, hey bae," she says as she wakes up.

"Kay, why didn't you go pick up Sean?" She sits up, completely groggy.

"Shit babe, I'm sorry. I forgot and fell asleep."

"You forgot? What the hell you mean you forgot Kay? That's your son! You don't forget your son, but I guess I should be used to that, huh?"

"Used to what?" she asks.

"You not showing up for your son." I walk out the room, and Makayla runs out the room after me.

"What the fuck is that supposed to mean, Sean?"

"It means exactly what you think it means. You always forget about your son, me, everything! Now where are my god damn keys?" I scream. As I look around the house for them, throwing stuff out the way, tripping over shoes and all, I'm getting more pissed off as she stands in the hall looking dumb.

"Fuck you. You act like I put him in harm's way. Your sister is there, and I know she took him home with her."

"That's beside the point, Makayla. You're his mother; no one else should have to pick up your slack, and even if something was wrong, you wouldn't know because you weren't even picking up your damn phone!" I yell, still looking for my keys. I walk past her in the hallway, and immediately can tell something is wrong with her. I stop and walk up to her, examining her eyes and how unbalanced she is and I know something is wrong.

"You been drinking?"

"I had a few glasses a wine at my sister's house. What's the big deal?" I step back, shake my head, and laugh. How can I love her so much when she always makes me want to put my hands on her? If I was a woman beater, I would square up with her right now in this hallway. The inner me wants to choke her out so bad right now.

"So, let me get this straight: You got drunk and went to sleep and this is your reason you couldn't go pick your son up from school?"

"I was never drunk! I said I had a few glasses a wine. You act like I'm an alcoholic!" she says as she flings her arms around looking more like a crack head.

I can't even take it. I back walk into the room, spot the keys on my bed, and head out to pick up my son.

"So, what, I can't drink now? Shit, do I have a curfew too?" she asks as I open the door.

I walk right up to her face and as calm as I can, I say to her, "You can do whatever you want to do as long as it doesn't involve my son."

"He's my son too!"

"Well act like his fucking mother!" I yell, slamming the door behind me.

I arrive at Twin's house around 7:45 p.m. As soon as I knock on the door, Twin opens the door and comes outside as if she's been waiting for me so she could give me a piece of her mind. She stands in front of the door with her arms crossed.

"Look Seana, I don't have time for your BS right now. Where is my son?" I ask.

"Where was she, Sean?" Twin asks.

"Yo, what did I just say? Damn, I can't come in your house now?"

"I don't give a damn about what you just said! My nephew was waiting for someone to pick him up! Jesus Christ, he's only three years old, Sean. What if I wasn't there? What if he walked off with someone else?" she says. I knew she was right but I'm so annoyed and on fire about all this, I wasn't going to give her the satisfaction of being right.

"Well you were, and he didn't," I reply. I'm just as angry as she is–in fact, I'm more angry. The last thing I need from anyone is to be told off about something I'm already upset about.

"Wow. Are you hearing yourself right now? How dumb are you going to let this girl make you, because you sound stupid," she yells.

"She made a mistake, okay? She was running errands all day, and she fell asleep. It was an accident."

"Forgetting to put the milk back in the fridge is a mistake. Forgetting your wallet at home, that's a mistake, but forgetting to pick your child up from school is irresponsible!" she yells.

"She's had a hard life. You just don't understand." I try to push past her and walk in the house, but she blocks the door and gets in my face.

"Are you really going to stand here in my face and make excuses for her now? You've got to be kidding me!" Twin says.

"Are you going to let me get my son or you just gon' stand here in my face? It's getting late." I take a step back. We stare each other down for a few moments. She wants to say a lot, and so do I, but I can't care about any of it. I just want to get Lil Sean and go home.

"What hard life has she had? Please enlighten me," Twin says.

"She's still dealing with her mother dying."

"Your mother died too. In fact, our mother died after hers did and you were closer to your mother then she was to hers, so next."

"She still messed up about losing the baby. Nigga, it's a lot, what you want me to say?"

Twin balls her fists, throws her head back and closes her eyes. After about 20 seconds or so, she relaxes her stance, and looks right into my eyes.

"I had three planned pregnancies and three fucking miscarriages with my husband. That's three children lost, and you have the audacity to say this bitch has it hard because she lost her unplanned child in college with her boyfriend she had already cheated on? Not to mention, she lost a child she didn't even want until it was gone." By this time, Twin is right back in my face again.

"You and I both know Makayla was intoxicated when she miscarried. That never seem strange to you? Why would someone who knows their pregnant get drunk? Let's be honest here, Sean. She got pregnant because she wanted to keep you around after she cheated! She thought you would leave school for her." I try to interject, but she keeps speaking her mind.

"She kept you there, and she got rid of it when you rejected her request. If you haven't figured it out by now, you're as foolish now as you were before. You've been getting played. Stop acting like a little boy and grow up."

She walks back to the front door and yells inside, "Sean, baby. Get your stuff. Your father's here."

She immediately closes the door, turns around, and stares at me. I don't know what to believe; she doesn't know what really happened, she only thinks she knows, but all I can do is just stand there. I have no words. I'm numb.

"If she leaves my nephew at school again, I'm taking him because obviously your irresponsible too." Lil Sean comes running out the door, and I couldn't be happier to see him.

"Hi, Dad!" I throw a smile on my face, so he won't notice the hurt and confusion I'm feeling.

"Hey, Big Man," I say as he walks over to me. I pick him up and hug him tight. I can tell he is tired by the way he put his head on my shoulder and doesn't say much. I hold him tight as we head to the car. My back is to Twin, but I can feel Lil Sean use the rest of his energy to wave goodbye, and as I turn to look back, I see Twin waving back before walking in the house.

As soon as I pull off, my baby boy is knocked out. I thought he would be up to talk to me so I didn't have to think about all this, but I guess I was wrong. Shit, have I been wrong about a lot of things? Did Makayla really kill our baby? She couldn't be that spiteful, could she?

We get home in no time and it doesn't even seem like I was driving because my mind was too far gone. I walk in the door holding Lil Sean, who is still asleep. I go straight to his room, put his jammies on, and lay him down without waking him. I softly caress my boy's curly hair and smile.

"How could she not care about you as much as I do? You're perfect," I whisper to him. I don't know what I would do if something ever happened to him. After I close his door, I walk around the apartment and notice that Makayla's stuff is gone. Her clothes are gone and hangers are all over the bedroom floor. Once again, she has walked out our lives. How did this happen again? I can't help but think it was my fault.

I walk into the kitchen and reach to the back of the fridge to the coffee can where I keep my "in case of emergency" weed and wrap. For me, this is an emergency. I go into the living room, open the window, put on my favorite album, Lenny Kravitz's *Mama Said*, turn to my favorite track, "It Ain't Over 'til It's Over", and spark up. Once again, I am in my feelings. I start feeling sad about our first child not making it into this world. I think about losing my mom and how just maybe if she was here, she would help me figure things out better. I'm pissed at Twin for not understanding and threatening to take my son, my only true love in this whole world. I'm furious that Makayla put me in such a tough spot, yet again. Just how did we go from making love this morning to her leaving is the question that sat on my heart like a ton of bricks. Somewhere around two and a half blunts, seven shots of whiskey, and 15 rounds of that song on repeat, I fall asleep right where I am.

The next morning, I wake up to my alarm clock going off in my room. Lenny is still playing. I notice that my son's comforter is on top of me, and then I pull back the comforter, there he is curled up on the other end of the sofa.

"My boy," I think to myself. For a three-year-old, he is smarter than most. Covering me up is the sweetest thing he could do. How could his mother just leave him all the time? I get up, turn the record off, and then I go to turn off the alarm. Once back in the room, the reality of it all hit me again. Feeling confused, hurt, sick, and betrayed once again, I call out of work. I just can't bear to deal with the outside world right now. Thank God I have five weeks of vacation.

I decide not to take my boy to school today; today, we will forget the outside. I sit on the edge of the bed trying to remind myself that I've been here before, that I'm strong, and I will not let this hurt me, but in reality, I feel like crying. Even though she has left so many times before, it always feels like it's the first time. Staring at the wall in a daze, Lil Sean walks in.

The first thing that comes out his mouth is, "Mommy gone?" and that shit just breaks my heart even more.

"Yeah, buddy," I say.

He looks at me, climbs up on the bed, gives me a hug, and says, "It's okay." I swear this kid is ahead of his time and his sweet, kind soul warms my heart.

"Okay," I say and kiss him on his head.

"Hey, what do you want for breakfast, Big Man?" I ask him.

"A steak."

I laugh. "A steak?! What you know about a steak?!" He cracks up as I tickle him, and his laugh only makes me smile.

"How about some bacon and eggs?" He shrugs and says okay and I get to cooking with Lil Sean by my side. All day we eat, sleep, snack, and watch TV. Even though I am hurting inside, I will not let it show for both his and my sake.

Around 4:30 in the afternoon, my sister comes walking in the door.

"Sean," she calls out to me. She has her own keys for emergencies, but she never uses them for that–she comes and goes as she pleases. I yell from my room to let her know where we are, and Lil Sean jumps up out of bed.

"Auntie Twin!" he yells, running to her.

"Hey boo. I missed you today," she says.

"I stay with daddy."

"I see," she replies as she makes her way down the hall to my room. She stands in my doorway and Lil Sean runs into his room. I stare into my phone.

"I see you didn't go to work today," Twin says. I say nothing.

"Why wasn't he at school?" I stay quiet and stare at my phone.

"So, you're not going to answer me?"

"If you came all the way over here to start your shit," I begin, putting the phone down, "You can exit," I say as I get up and leave the room. She follows me out as I clean up the mess me and Sean have been making all day, and Twin stands in the walkway.

"What happened," she asks.

"Why does it matter? So, you can tell me how foolish and stupid I am for letting her come back, or tell me I'm a bad father for letting her walk in and out of my son's life? She left. Happy?!" I yell.

"No, I'm not happy." Lil Sean runs into the kitchen, and before he can get into the room well enough, Twin snaps her fingers and says, "Room," and Lil Sean runs right to his room.

"I'm never happy when you're upset. I tell you these things hoping you will stop hurting yourself. Look, right now, you're hurting, and I would never say you are a bad father. You're the best father in the world. Listen, I'm sorry about yesterday. I over stepped. I was just so upset, but it's not my place to dictate what goes on in your home. I know that you have Lil Sean's best interest at heart," she says. I walk into the living room to clean up, and Twin follows me. Things are quiet for a while; as I clean, she stands there, waiting for me to say something.

"I flipped out on her about not getting Sean from school before I came and got him and when I came back…" I stop cleaning and stand there with my back toward Twin and drop my head. The thought of this happening once again weakens me.

"She was gone." I feel my eyes water, but my pride won't let me cry. Twin walks up behind me, wraps her arms around me, and lays her head on my back. As we stand there, my phone vibrates in my pocket. As Twin lets go of me, I take it out and see that it is a text from Makayla.

5:55 p.m.

Wife: Yo stop texting and calling me, Im waking up to 5000 texts and calls, WTF, I don't wanna be with you, I never wanted to be with you. I been fucking another nigga the whole time I was with you. Yea I was tired yesterday. Tired from him fucking me in your Jeep lol Your whack your boring and I can't let you tie me down anymore. Find someone else.

I feel the heat from hell rise from the ground up into my body and I am on fire. I am so fucking hurt that I am past crying–I'm angry. I squeeze my phone so tight that my screen cracks and I can no longer move.

I can see Twin saying, "What's wrong? What does it say?" but I can't hear her. I can feel her trying to get my phone out of my hand, but I can't let it go. Then a rage comes over me I never felt before; it is so dark and disturbing that it puts fear in my own soul. I kick over the coffee table and drop my phone into Twin's hand, walk to my room, and then I completely black out. I don't snap back until my sister is standing in front of my front door pushing me back crying and yelling saying, "Think about your son! Please! Please!"

On the third please, I hear her, and then I hear my son calling my name and banging on his room door. Twin managed to lock him in before stopping me from making a horrible mistake.

I can't even recall going in my closet and getting it out my safe, but I stand in the hallway with my gun loaded, ready to walk out the door to go kill both Makayla and whoever she fucked in my Jeep. I look at my gun and drop to my knees. I cry for the first time since my mother passed. My sister takes my gun, slides it into the living room, holds me, and cries with me.

After about five minutes, Lil Sean starts crying and bangs on the door. I get up to let him out as Twin takes my gun and puts it back in my safe. I pick him up and wipe his tears.

Not worried about his own self, he asks, "Daddy, you okay?"

"Yeah, Big Man. I just hurt my foot," I tell him, which isn't a complete lie because I am just starting to feel the pain in my foot from when I kicked the coffee table over. I lie on his bed with him in my arms and hold him tight until he goes to sleep. When he's sound asleep, I walk into the living room and overhear Twin talking to Joe on the phone, saying she is going to stay with me tonight.

"You don't have to stay. I'm good. Really," I tell her.

"I'm staying. You need me now and I'm not going nowhere." I walk over to the sofa, sit down next to her, and put my head on her shoulder. I notice she picked the coffee table up and all the stuff that was on it.

"Thank you," I say pointing to the table.

"No problem. I put your gun in the safe too." I thank her again and we sit in silence for a few more moments.

"You really scared me. I've never seen you like that before."

"I'm sorry… I've never felt like that before," I say.

"So, were you really going to kill her?"

I think for a second. "I don't know. In my head, she is already dead." She lays her head on top of mine, and we both sit there in silence.

6
Changes

Sean

Days turn into weeks and weeks turn into months. I haven't spoken to Makayla in six months, and I'm finally getting back to my old self. Twin made me get rid of my gun because she didn't feel safe with me having it in the house. So, to ease her mind, it's now at her house in the basement, locked in my safe.

A month after everything happened, I tried to reach out to Brit, but the number was disconnected. I had a few one-night stands, but other than that, I don't feel like I can ever reconnect with someone again. All I need is my boy, my family, and my friends. Cody convinced me to join this leadership program at my job. There's a lot of meetings and problem solving for the company, but I hate the current position I'm in now; I'm just in it to see who I can meet that can help me move my way up. Plus, I'm looking to make more money so I can get me and Lil Sean a house–that's my focus. Since me and Twin are back to the usual plan of her taking Lil Sean home with her after school, I end up staying to do overtime or to attend some of these meetings.

"Hey bro, guess what?" Cody asks as he sits on my desk.

"My man, get your ass off my desk. What I tell you about that weird shit?" I ask him playfully. I have become quite fond of Cody; I thought he was just a kiss ass, but the man knows a lot about growing and becoming successful.

"Sorry man, but guess what?"

"What?"

"I heard one of the new HR ladies has a thing for you," he tells me.

"Man, I don't want no old ass lady."

"She not old," Cody says with a smirk.

"Well, I'm not messing with no chick that can determine my career. I'm cool. You holla at her."

"I married with three kids. Plus, I'm gay."

I stare at Cody in complete shock. Damn, I have been working with Cody for four years now, and I never knew he was married and to a man at that.

"Well, if you change your mind, she's right there," he points to the front of the room. I look up from my computer and my eyes find who Cody is pointing to.

"Damn, she bad," I say.

"I know, right? How haven't you noticed her? Almost every guy in here wants her just like every girl in her wants you," he tells me.

"I don't notice anyone at this fuck ass job, but she looks stuck up as hell anyway, so I'm good."

"She's a businesswoman."

"Yeah, I'm cool." I look back down at my computer, thinking to myself, That's why me and Cody never talk about chicks. He's gay.

"Suit yourself, but I hear she's very interested in you," he says and walks away. I take another look at her, we lock eyes, and she smiles. I think nothing of it and keep going on about my day. When lunch time comes around, I'm not that hungry, so I sit in the café for a while and watch TV. About a half an hour into my break, the HR lady walks in the café and goes to get something out of the vending machine. As she stands there with her back to me, I check her out. She is very tall; I don't usually do tall women. She has light brown skin and long, black hair pulled back into a ponytail. She wears glasses, and has on a white collared long sleeve fitted button up dress shirt with a gray skirt and black heels. She's thin with a little booty and absolutely not my type. Just looking at her, I can tell that we have nothing in common. I'm not looking for anything anyway, so it doesn't matter to me.

When lunch is over, I head out the café, and just as I'm leaving, the HR lady comes back in and somehow, we run right into each other. She grabs my arm and I grab her shoulder, both of us trying to keep our balance. We both casually say excuse me and go about our ways.

For the next few weeks, I see her around the office more and more. Either she has always been around, and I never noticed her, or what Cody said is true–she really is interested in me and wants me to notice her. When I think about it, her office is not on my floor and she's not even the HR supervisor for my department. Am I her reason for coming up here every day? She doesn't say anything to me, and she just walks by me like I'm not even there. Then again, I don't say shit to her either, and I do my best to make myself unknown. She must be playing some game. Maybe she wants me to ask her out or start talking to her just because. Whatever it is, I'm not here for it.

After work, I go to Twin's house to pick up Sean and to talk about the plan for our birthday in three and a half weeks. When I walk in, I see that Sean is already knocked out.

"What job did he work at today?" I ask Twin.

"Right," she laughs. "He ate and went right to sleep."

"I want that feeling. What you make? You made some for me too?" I ask as I look around the kitchen for my plate.

"I made meatloaf, mashed potatoes, and string beans, and you already know I made extra for you," she says with her hands on her hips, wearing sweat clothes and a bonnet. Twin really is like me and Lil Sean's mother. Twin hands me my plate and sits at the table with me while I eat.

"So, what's the birthday plan and who you gon' get to watch Lil Sean?" she asks.

"I got Aunt Ruby on standby; she said she would. I was thinking, us and the crew should go out to Atlantic City, stay at a hotel, go out to dinner and club hop a little."

"That sounds cool, but no ratchet ass club, though. Something nice and classy where we can sit in VIP somewhere," she adds.

"Oh, fo' sho. There's this spot called The Waters. It's connected to a casino and hotel. It's supposed to be a five-star type jawn. I figured we can go there on Saturday night and bring our birthday in. What you think?" I ask her. Twin takes out her phone and searches.

"Yeah, this looks dope, and the rooms are nice. I'm in, but damn, VIP is $600 for three hours," Twin states shaking her head.

Joe walks in the kitchen smelling like outside, covered in dust and dirt from working on the garbage truck all day. "What's $600?" he asks. Twin smells him as he gives her a kiss.

"Ew, you need a shower. Here stinky." She gives him the phone. "Sean thinks this would be a good place to bring in our birthday. What you think?" He scrolls through.

"Yeah, this is hot," he says and hands her back the phone. We keep discussing the price and how we can pay for it. Twin suggests that we split the cost 50/50, and just as I go to agree, Joe jumps in.

"I got it," he says. "It's my gift to y'all."

"My gift? I don't want that as a gift," Twin says as Joe laughs.

"You gon' get something else, Bae," Joe says. "This D!" Joe laughs as he walks upstairs to go shower.

"Well, it better last longer than five minutes," she yells back to him. My stomach turns as I avoid picturing Twin and Joe getting it in.

"All right, ew! I'm trying to eat over here," I finally say.

"Shut up boy," Twin laughs. So, AC it is?" she asks.

"Yup, I'll text everyone now."

8:45 p.m.

Me: Aye, so me and Twin have decided to go to Atlantic City for our Birthday. We are going down Saturday May 12th and bring in our Birthday that Sunday. Y'all in?

8:46 p.m.

Tiff: Im there

8:48 p.m.

Mally Mal: you already know, there better be some hoes

8:49 p.m.

James: this guy smh…..im in tho

8:53 p.m.

Kels: lol… Hell yea, I need a ride tho… Sean you got me

8:54 p.m.

Me: Im sure the bittys will be up in there, but Bet and yea Kels

8:59 p.m.

Twin: I'll send everyone the full details tomorrow

"You driving Kelly? This should be interesting, " Twin says.

"Why you say that?"

"It just is. Y'all have such a love/hate relationship." I roll my eyes because I'm already tired of talking about Kelly and our "unique" relationship, so I change the subject.

"Any who, there's this new HR lady at my job an-"

"Nope," Twin says rolling her eyes.

"You haven't even heard what I was going to say," I say.

"I don't need to. She works at your job and she's HR, don't do it," she tells me. "Look at what happened with you and Brit. Now you can't even find her. The poor girl done up and quit."

"She didn't quit," I say avoiding eye contact with her.

"Sean, you're playing with fire. You can't risk your job, and you know damn well you're going to break things off with her as soon as she falls for you."

"God damn it, woman, just listen to me! All I'm saying is that I think she likes me. She's been trying to get me to notice her without making it obvious," I explain.

"But you notice her," Twin points out.

"Exactly."

Twin laughs. "If you're asking if she likes you, she most likely does. Should you go after her? No, but you're going to do what you want, so baby boy, do you, and take the bait," she says.

"Maybe I will." We both laugh and put my plate in the sink and prepare to head home.

"You need to be chasing a wife, so I can retire," she replies.

I shake my head. "Never that. You're too good to me, girl," I say as I carefully pick up Lil Sean. We say goodbye and Lil Sean and I call it a night.

At lunch the next day, I sit in the café again, and on my way there, I see HR lady. She is talking to the boss of all the bosses at this location, Mrs. Tracey Patterson, the flyest old head ever. Her dress game is fire, and she never misses a beat. She always sports heels and fly ass pants suits, her makeup is always done, and her hair always did–she's just sharp and has crazy swag. She's a powerful black woman who runs our entire building. When she walks in a room, the room shuts the fuck up. I want that "you better know who I am, bitches" energy. If she wasn't my boss, I would smash.

I'm texting Mally as I walk past them and hear, "Hello, Mr. Johnson." I turn around, shocked that Ms. Patterson even knows my name; she is like the Beyoncé of the whole Best Trucking Company.

"Mrs. Patterson," I say as I nod my head. I don't know why I nod, but she makes me nervous, and I really don't know what else to say.

"I hope to see you at tonight's meeting," she says.

"Sure thing. I'll see you there," I reply with a smile.

"Good." she smiles, and I give her another head nod and walk away. The whole time I speak to Mrs. Patterson, the HR lady didn't lift her head once. She didn't speak, she didn't smile, nothing. She keeps her head down, looking at her iPad. Come to think of it, she didn't even come upstairs today to my floor. Maybe she's not interested after all. Who knows, but she is looking kind of good with her pant suit on today.

"Hey, Sean!" someone calls me from down the hall just as I am about to walk in the café. I turned to see who called me and to my surprise, I catch the HR lady staring at me. Did she completely ignore me when I was in her face but watch me walk away? Yeah, she's feeling me.

I finally see that it was Jaz, another chick who works in my department and is always throwing the ass at me on the low who called me. She walks down the hall with a huge smile on her face. She's not a bad looking jawn – short, brown and thick, and has a nice ass, but ol' girl got five kids by four guys and she's only 29. Every nigga she fucks knocks her up, which means she's fertile as a motherfucker. Nah, I'm cool.

"Hey, I'm about to go grab something to eat. You want to ride along?" Jaz asks. Now I've been on a few lunch dates with Jaz before, so it was nothing out of the norm. I really didn't want to go, but today, since this was going to play out right in front of the HR lady, I accept to see if I notice a reaction from her.

"Yeah, where we at with it?" I ask.

"Don't matter to me, I just gotta get outta here. I hear it's 70 degrees out," she says. While I talk to Jaz, I can feel the HR lady staring at us off and on. By this time, Big Boss Patterson has left, and HR lady is still standing in the hall acting like she is looking at her iPad. We finally agree on a place and when we head out, I don't look back, but something tells me she watches us walk out.

Later that night, I drive all the way to Delaware for this meeting. It's a big event at Delaware University. I arrive around 6:30, and it's cocktail hour. They have food, an open bar, and a lot of managers speaking. I've never even seen the company put on like this. Back at the office, we get a few donuts here and there, but this meeting's set-up lets me know they have money. They do it real big for the higher ups. Waiters were walking around handing out hors d'oeuvres, there's an ice sculpture with shrimp under it, they got a live band playing jazz, and everyone suited and booted. I'm glad I wore a suit to work today since I came here right after. There's only going to be about 10 of us regular workers here from the leadership group, so the others back at work don't even get a chance to experience this.

I don't know anyone, so I am happy when I find Cody.

"Damn, look at this place!" I say.

He looks around and says, "I know, right."

"Come, let's get you a glass of wine." We walk over to the bar.

"We got wine and beer, what would you like?" the bartender asks. I ask for a Yuengling, which was my go-to drink during my college days. I grab my drink and tip him before turning back around to see all the upscale spread of food we have to eat.

"Open bar and shrimp? Who is paying for all this?" I ask Cody. If anyone knows, it would be him.

"That lady right there," he points to Mrs. Patterson, who was accompanied by her sidekick, the HR lady.

"She came out of pocket for this or the company paid for it?" I ask.

"Out of pocket. You know damn well the company isn't treating us this good," he says.

"You right," I laugh. "So, why is she doing all this?"

"It's for us."

"Us? What do you mean?" I ask.

"Yeah, everyone in the leadership program. She's making us into leaders, helping us grow within the company, meet new people and network."

"Wait. So, this is her program?" I ask.

"Yes sir. You want to grow, don't you? Why do you think I told you about it?" he says as he sips his wine.

"Oh, that's how she knows my name," I say.

"Yup, and she pays attention too. Remember Luke, the one who came to the first meeting? She kicked him out for not showing up for the meetings after that. She only wants serious people."

"How did she know that? This is the first meeting I've ever seen her at," I ask.

"Oh, she knows."

I have to admit, Cody has grown on me, and I have him to thank for this opened door I am about to walk through. I always thought he was a shady, gossiping dude that thinks he knows it all, but in fact, he's just gay and does know it all.

"So, have you hooked up with Tiera yet?" he asks.

"Tiera? Who the hell is that?" I reply. He points to the HR lady.

"Oh, that's her name?"

"Chile, how do you not know that? Her name is everywhere. She said her name in the first meeting we were at."

I shrug. "I just know her as the HR lady, but I think you're right. I think she is feeling me."

"Well, duh. Have you talked to her yet?" he asks. I shake my head.

"Well, what are you waiting for?"

"She's a baddie but not really my type," I admit. We drop the conversation and we find our seats. When we walk in the main meeting room, there is nothing but classy, upscale black people. I didn't know our company had so many black managers. All our managers and supervisors at the office are white, and the owners whose pictures are up in the building are all white. But the big dogs of the company are mostly black, and I am honored to be a part of this meeting.

As the meeting goes on, there are some good speakers, and there are some speakers that are boring as fuck. An hour into the meeting, I am so over it and I start playing games on my phone.

-ding ding- Text From Twin

My phone goes off very loud, causing some people to look back at me as I shuffled trying to put it on vibrate.

8:01 p.m.

Twin: hey what time your meeting over

8:03 p.m.

Me: Not really sure, why what's up? Sean cool

8:05 p.m.

Twin: Yea, just pick him up after school tomorrow, I'm about to give him a bath and lay him down. It's getting late. He already got clothes here.

8:06 p.m.

Me: You sure?

8:08 p.m.

Twin: Yea

8:09 p.m.

Twin: stay as long as you need to so you can get a corporate job and can afford a nanny lol

8:11 p.m.

Me: I'm only gon hire you

8:15 p.m.

Twin: That's fine as long as all my bills get paid, plus I need extra spending money.

8:18 p.m.

Me: lol bet, I got u, thanks see you tomorrow

8:20 p.m.

Twin: NP

The crowd claps and the meeting planner announces the next speaker.

"Thank you, Mr. Potter. Our next guest has been with the company for 11 years. Please give a warm welcome to our newest human resources supervisor of the shipping and receiving department for our Philadelphia location, Ms. Tiera Anderson.

Cody hits my shoulder. I don't know why he thinks I'll be a good fit with this woman. She's fuckable for sure, but his constant insisting is getting on my nerves.

-buzz, buzz, buzz- Incoming Call From Makayla

What the hell does she want? I ignore the call because I'm still pissed at her.

-buzz, buzz, buzz- Incoming Call From Makayla

I ignore the call again.

-buzz, buzz, buzz- Incoming Call From Makayla

"Damn, who's hitting you up?" Cody asks.

"No one important." My head is telling me not to answer it, but my heart wants to. What if something is wrong? What if she needs me? Nah, I have to shake this feeling.

-ding ding- Text from Makayla

8:45 p.m.

Makayla: Can you pick up please??

-buzz, buzz, buzz- Incoming Call From Makayla

I leave the meeting and go outside to answer her call. As soon as I walk out, she calls again, and I pick up.

Me: Yeah, Makayla.

Makayla: Don't answer the phone like that.

Me: What's up.

Makayla: Ummm, I just wanna see how Sean is doing.

Me: After seven months? He's fine.

Makayla: Six but I'm still his mother and I can call and check in on him.

Me: He's fine. Can I help you with something?

Makayla: You don't have to be rude. Can I talk to him?

Me: I'm at work and he's with Twin.

Makayla: Work? It's almost 9 p.m. Don't try and play me. What, you at some bitch's house? Am I interrupting you?

Me: Nah, I said I'm at work and Lil Sean is at Twin's house. Call over there if you wanna talk to him.

Makayla: Nah, I'm good. So what, you got a new job or something now?"

Me: Nope. Same Job.

The line is quiet for about 20 seconds, but then she goes on asking me about my day and how I've been, despite me being cold with her and not giving her any real info. Honestly, I don't want the conversation to end. I want her to say she's coming home and that she's sorry, but I know that's not going to happen, so I play hard. She asks if she can pick Lil Sean up this weekend and take him out. I tell her I would have to think about it, and of course, she throws the fact that he's her son too in there and makes a big fuss about it. I don't want to cause any conflict or even upset myself before I head back in the meeting, so I just tell her we can talk about it later when I got home.

Makayla: Whatever, Sean.
Me: Is that it?

Makayla huffs. "Wow. Yeah, that's it. Well, I mis-" I hang up the phone before she can finish. I look through the glass doors and I can see that the meeting is over. Everyone is trickling out to eat and drink more, so I call Twin to ask her for advice. Of course, Twin is very cautious and doesn't want to hear me out. Everything I ask she disagrees with, but eventually she caves in.

As we hang up, Tiera, the HR lady, walks outside and posts up right in my way.

"So, do I bore you?" she asks with a half-smile.

Confused, I say, "Sorry, I don't understand."

"Well, the last two meetings I spoke in, you walked out when I started talking."

I laugh. "No, it's not like that. I have a son who I need to check on or pick up from school. He only has me, so don't take it personally," I tell her.

"Oh okay, I understand. Say no more." She steps back from blocking the door. I laugh, and just as I head inside, I stop. Something in my head says take the bait. If me and Makayla are going to get back together, then I will make her jealous first.

"Hey, would you like to go out some time? Get a drink, talk, have some fun?"

I think I shocked the hell out of her because she looks like she doesn't know what to say.

"Sorry to be so forward with you, but I would like to take you out. So what do you say? No pressure," I say, flashing my smile.

"Um, yeah… Yes, sure."

"Saturday night okay with you?"

"Um, yes that's fine."

"Good." I walk back in the center and leave her shocked and confused outside.

The Replay

Tiera

-ding ding- Text from Bestie

7:45 a.m.

Bestie: Good Morning boo

7:47 a.m.

Me: Hey boo

7:48 a.m.

Bestie: What time you coming in today

7:50 a.m.

Me: I'm here already, Tracey got me here early getting things ready for the meeting tonight

7:50 a.m.

Bestie: Damn, sidekick

7:55 a.m.

Me: lol, I know right, but it's not hard work, this is the easy part

7:58 a.m.

Bestie: Well alright girl I'll see you when I get there, I'll bring you a mocha latte.

8:00 a.m.

Me: My fav thanks babe

Around 8:45 a.m., my bestie walks in my office.

"Good Morning, doll face," Bestie greets. I can already taste the latte and am already feeling energized and ready to go. We hug and give side kisses as he hands me the drink. I met my best friend working at the Best Trucking New Jersey office. We both worked there for six years, but then Bestie got married, moved to Philadelphia, and started working at the Philadelphia location. I stayed in New Jersey for five more years, since I live there, and once I put in for the supervisor position, I came over here, and now we're back together again.

"What time do you have to take all this stuff over there?" Bestie asks.

"We're supposed to be setting everything up around 4 p.m. but knowing Tracey, she'll want us to arrive by three," I say.

"What the boss lady wants, she gets," says Bestie and I nod in agreement.

"Well, you will be the boss soon."

"Yeah, one day. You know they want me to get my master's degree before they can even consider me for manager? Like, how am I supposed to work, go to school, and pay for school for both me and Skylar? It's a lot to do and a lot to pay," I explain.

"Well, this is where a husband comes in handy!" Bestie says with a smirk.

"Husband? Ha! I can't find a good, real man to save my life," I reply and turn back to my computer.

"Well…."

"Well what?" I sit back in my chair, turn my chair back around and hear Bestie out. He looks over his shoulder and then closes my office door.

"Have you talked to him?"

"No," I say, shaking my head.

"Why not? You practically fell into his arms 3 months ago," he points out.

I correct him. "That was like four weeks ago."

"Well, honey, as slow as you're moving, it feels like a year ago."

We both laugh, but it's hard for me to see how this would work out.

"He's young and I'm probably not his type, anyway."

"He's 30 and you're 34."

"Right, I'm older than him, and I'm sure he has a flock of girls chasing after him," I add.

"You damn right he does, especially in here. The man is fine."

"He is, isn't he…" I bite my pen cap and daydream but then quickly bring myself back to reality. "Wait, what do you mean by especially in here?"

"Girl, first off, he looks good, second, he looks good, and third, he's fine as hell. Almost every girl I know has tried to get with the man and I'm sure some guys in here want him too. Shit, I want some," Bestie says, laughing.

"So why hasn't he talked to anyone yet? If he has, then cross him off. I don't want any drama. I just got here, and I don't have time for childish games," I say.

"Well, I don't know the man's personal life, but let's just say this, if he has, it wasn't public. He stays to himself, he does his work, and goes home. He gives a couple fake smiles, but I rarely ever see him talk with anyone, to be honest."

"So, what if something is wrong with him? Like he's crazy or something?" I ask.

"Girl, he's not. Now you're just being dramatic. I got to go clock in. Text me later," Bestie says before strolling out.

Around lunch time, I receive a text from my bestie.

-ding ding- Text from Bestie

1:00 p.m.

Bestie: Girl, he's coming down, now is your chance

As soon as I get the text, I jump up and run out into the hallway to bump into him again. I walk out and then make a quick U-turn back into the office. I can't just stand in the hallway looking crazy and like I'm waiting for him. I search my office to see what I can find to make me look busy.

I find my iPad, go back out in the hall, and start dawdling and staring down at my iPad as if I'm really into what I'm doing. I see him walking down the steps and now he's just down the hall.

"What are you working on, T?" I turn around and it's my boss, Tracey, behind me.

"Oh, nothing really. I was about to walk out to my car to grab something."

I watch as he walks closer, and any chance I have to talk to him is about to pass me by since my boss is here.

"So, how are we looking on the name tags for the meeting tonight?" she asks.

"Great, I just finished them up, and they are boxed and ready to go."

He's about 10 feet away and looking down at his phone. I wonder who he is talking to. Damn, he looks good in that suit; his jacket is open, he has the top two buttons undone on his crispy clean white shirt and he has one hand in his pocket.

"Great, you're always on top of things. That's what I love about you," she compliments me. She goes on and on and I can't shake her in time to talk to Sean before he walks right by us. I think the moment is gone, but then my boss calls out to him, and he turns around.

She never speaks to anyone, and by the look on his face, I'm guessing he is wondering how she knows him. My heart is racing, so I keep my head down on my iPad like I'm doing some very serious work.

If he were to say something to me, I wouldn't know what to say. He makes me nervous for some reason; I've honestly never felt this way about anyone, and especially someone at my job. Maybe it's his gentle eyes or his swag; he's always so cool like he lives his life to the fullest. The man is stunning; he has the most beautiful skin tone and his short, black wavy hair that fully connects to his beard is so attractive, and it surrounds his perfectly pink, plumped lips. The things I could do with those lips. The thought gets me wet. I'm 5'11", so any guy taller than me is a plus. When he walks in the room, he exudes so much confidence that it's no wonder women love him.

My palms are sweaty, and my boss continues to engage in her meet and greet, and I'm hoping I'm not pulled into their little conversation. They keep things short, and as he walks away, I look back at him. As soon as I look at him, someone calls his name and he turns around, catching me staring at him. Shit. I look back at my iPad.

"T, make sure Debbie gets candle stick holders," Tracey says as she leaves.

"Sure thing," I reply. By this time, Jaz, the girl who called him, is walking down the hall to him. I am in the perfect spot to listen in since he is only about six feet away from me. I stay in the hallway and use my iPad.

What does this chick want with him? Are they dating? Was he texting her as he was walking down here? I eavesdrop on their conversation. She asks him out to lunch, and he agrees. I watch him walk back down the hall with her and then out the door. What could he see in her?

"Damn," I think to myself as I saunter into my office and plop down in my chair. Best friend was right; girls are all over him. Well, he is fine. I text best friend because I can't even process what just happened by myself.

1:20 p.m.

Me: ugh

1:21 p.m.

Bestie: ugh what? What happen

1:21 p.m.

Me: so long story short, I went out to talk to him, got stopped in a conversation with Tracey about the meeting, Tracey ends up stopping him and talking to him. Tracey leaves and Jaz asks him out to lunch. So, it's not meant to be.

1:23 p.m.

Bestie: lol chile, 1st off Tracey don't talk to anyone

1:25 p.m.

Me: I know, I don't even think he knew she knew him

1:26 p.m.

Bestie: that's crazy, and how do you know Jaz asked him out for lunch

1:27 p.m.

Me: She called out to him in the hall, and after Tracey left, I eavesdropped on their convo, acted like I was busy on my iPad.

1:30 p.m.

Bestie: Im crying, so everyone got to him before you did, lol

1:33 p.m.

Me: Pretty much, I'm over it

1:35 p.m.

Bestie: Relax I know for a fact that he's not into Jaz, yes they do go to lunch sometimes when he bored but other than that he pays her no mind. Butttttttt….

1:36 p.m.

Me: but what

1:37 p.m.

Bestie: He has been single for some time now, that's why I been telling you to shoot your shot now. I been telling you since before you even transferred here that I thought he would be the perfect guy for you.

1:39 p.m.

Me: How long has he been single

1:40 p.m.

Bestie: Chile god works in mysterious ways, him and his girl broke up a week after you got here. Now tell me that isn't a sign.

1:42 p.m.

Me: I don't know, I'll see you tonight. Tracey is calling

Why do I have to go to him? Why can't he come to me? He's the guy. This is all too much. I haven't even been with or even thought about being with someone in almost two years. What's another two or ten years. I've been doing fine by myself, just me and my daughter.

I arrive in Delaware at three to set up for this event and everything is ready just in time for the people arriving at six. I am nervous about giving my speech tonight, but more nervous that he will be watching. My best friend walks in just in time to help me deal with all this.

"Hey babe, this looks nice! You hooked this place up. It's all shiny and thangs," Bestie said.

"Thanks love. Tracey had us in here working like slaves," I reply and we laugh.

"So, is lover boy here yet?"

"I don't know, I haven't check for him. We've been busy."

"Bish don't lie. I spotted you watching the door like a hawk when I walked in," Bestie says, and we laugh again.

"Fine, he's not here, but you know what is here?" I ask him with a smirk.

"What?"

"The wine."

"Say less. Chardonnay for two please," Bestie says as we laugh, lock arms, and head to the bar.

Around 6:30, Sean walks in, and no, I wasn't watching the door. Although I am anticipating his arrival, I am talking to the regional manager about a few job openings and we just so happen to be near the door. I want to talk to him, but everywhere I look, someone wants to talk to me. I am getting pulled left and right and the one second I think I have to say something to Sean, Tracey grabs me and takes me to meet more people and I'm not even able to get a pep talk from my bestie before the meeting starts.

Each person giving a speech tonight sits on stage and one by one, everyone does their spiel. The speeches are long, but informative, and I am very grateful to be where I am today versus where I was years ago. It was my dream to move up the career ladder, and I'm hoping to become the HR manager for the entire region soon. It's what I have been working so hard for.

After an hour and a half, it's finally my turn to speak. The announcer introduces me, and as I get up, everyone claps, but all I can notice is him. He looks right at me. He is in the back, but it's like everyone else in the room isn't there and that makes me even more nervous, but I start anyway. I look over to Tracey and the rest of the panel, thanking them for the opportunity for letting me speak today. As I turn back around, I immediately spot Sean getting up and walking out.

Wait, so he sits here for everyone's speech and then walks out when it's time for me to talk? I think to myself. I am disappointed but also relieved that I don't have to talk in front of him. While I speak, all I can think about is if I bore him. I then remember the last time I spoke to everyone when I first came aboard, and how he walked out and never came back. The thought of him not being into me or never being into me crosses my mind about 100 times.

After I finish, the announcer closes out the meeting and it's over. While everyone walks out, I meet up with my best friend.

"That was extraordinary, honey. You really did your thing up there. I told you – you're the next boss," Bestie says.

"Thanks love. I'm just glad it's over," I respond.

"Yes, let's go get you a glass of wine."

As we walk out the auditorium, I see that Sean is standing outside talking on the phone. I turn to my best friend and say, "Babe, go get us a glass, I'll be right back," and I head straight for the door. I can't stop thinking about this guy, and I wasn't going to let anything step in the way this time. I'm going to say something to him.

As I walk outside, he gets off the phone, and he is smiling. My first thought is to turn around because I know it had to be some girl that had him smiling like that, but I just had to know what the deal was with this guy. So, I clear my throat and speak as soon as I walk out.

I start off defensive and ready to accept rejection, but the conversation goes beyond better than expected. I can not only leave knowing I talked to him, but that I'll get another chance to see this man beyond the walls of our office.

Right after I agree to go out with him, he walks back inside, leaving me standing there for a while as I process what just happened. He was smooth with it and I like his flare. I am as happy as a teenager inside, but I pull myself together once I see someone watching me smile to myself like a fool. I say hi to the person watching me, take out my phone, and go back inside.

7

Feeling Her Feeling Me

Sean

It's Friday and I feel kind of good. I ask my son if he wants to hang out with his mother this weekend and he's excited, so my weekend is free. The crew is hanging out and I plan to invite Tiera to come along. When I get to my desk, I find her on IM and send her a message.

9:45 a.m.

Sean Johnson: Good Morning

9:46 a.m.

Tiera Anderson: Good Morning, how are you?

9:50 a.m.

Sean Johnson: I'm Fine and you?

9:51 a.m.

Tiera Anderson: Honestly still very tired from last night, we didn't get out of there until almost 12am

9:52 a.m.

Sean Johnson: Wow, well I never got your number and I don't feel comfortable speaking over IM you never know whose snooping, so my number is 2155585559

9:54 a.m.

Tiera Anderson: ok got it, texting you now

-ding ding- Text from Unknown

9:55 a.m.

215-555-9999: Tiera

9:57 a.m.

Me: Got it

9:59 a.m.

HR: Great

10:01 a.m.

Me: So are you still interested in going out tomorrow

10:02 a.m.

HR: Yes

10:03 a.m.

HR: What did you have in mind??

10:33 a.m.

Me: Sorry about that, had to send out some emails, but every 1st sat of the month me and my crew get together and go out bowling, is that something you're cool with

10:34 a.m.

HR: Its ok trust me I understand all the emails…Your crew?

10:35 a.m.

Me: Yea it's me, my sister, her husband and a few other friends from college, it's like our thing.

10:36 a.m.

HR: oh ok sounds interesting, I don't know how to bowl

10:38 a.m.

Me: Its nothing to it, I got you, you can be on my team

Me: ill show you how

10:39 a.m.

HR: sounds good, so is there a time you had in mind

10:40 a.m.

Me: Don't have a time at time moment, but I'll hit you up tonight if that's ok and let you know, but we bowl at West bowl which is not too far from here

10:42 a.m.

HR: Yea that's perfectly fine and I know where that is

10:43 a.m.

Me: Ard, well I'll talk to you then

10:44 a.m.

HR: sounds good

-ding ding- Text from Makayla

Here we go. Let the games began. I'm excited that she hit me up' but I'm even more excited about how this will play out this time. No more Mr. Nice Guy. She follows my lead now, no more following hers.

10:45 a.m.

Makayla: hey you

10:47 a.m.

Me: Kinda busy right now, what's up

10:49 a.m.

Makayla: oh ok just text me back when you can xoxo

I never text back. I figure I'll try something new. Makayla always has me in her pocket, and now it's time to turn the tables a little. Will I let her back? Probably. Hey, I still love the girl, but this time I'm going to play hard ball for a while and let Ms. HR occupy my time.

Later on that night, after I get my son packed to spend time with his mother, I ask him again if he's sure he wants to go with her, and he is thrilled that she wants to spend time with him and can't wait to go. It's not that I think she would harm him in any way, but she hasn't been around, so I need to make sure he is comfortable in this situation.

After I lay him down, I check my phone and see that I have three missed calls and five missed texts from Makayla. I look at my phone and laugh. I don't know why, but it feels so good to make her wait on me instead of the other way around. Her texts are so friendly and sweet, it makes me laugh even harder. What people don't understand is as much as I can't stay away from her, she can't stay away from me. She has walked out on me four times, once in college and three times since we had Sean. This time, if she wants to come back, she has to work hard for it, not only with me, but with my son. This time, I want to see tears in her eyes and her on her knees begging for this family.

Before I text Makayla back, I text HR.

9:15pm

Me: hey sorry I'm texting you so late, I had to get my son situated

9:20pm

HR: No need to be sorry, I know how it is

9:22pm

Me: So we all are going to meet up at 8 at west bowl, does that work for you

9:24pm

HR: Yea that's fine, I'll just text you when I get there

9:25pm

Me: Perfect

9:30pm

HR: Great, well Good night Mr. Johnson

Something about her calling me Mr. Johnson sends a chill down my back. I like it.

9:31pm

Sean Good Night Ms. HR

9:32pm

HR lol

I plan to text Makayla back, but I will make her sweat first. It feels good to be in the driver's seat for once, and I am not about to pull over and let her take the wheel. I'll see her when she gets here tomorrow.

The next morning, I wake up to the smell of bacon, and I'm confused because only me and my son should be here. Makayla has keys, but she doesn't just pop up like that. I get up and check my son's room, and he's not in there. Lil Sean is only three, so I know he's not cooking. I walk into the kitchen and low and behold, good ol' Twin is here cooking up some grub.

"You know it's a crime to break in people's houses and make breakfast," I say to Twin. She's at the stove making pancakes, wearing PJ's and drinking coffee, just like mom used to do. Big Man says good morning and I say it back as I rub his head and grab a piece of bacon off the plate.

"What are you doing here, anyway, cooking and shit," I ask as I kiss her on the cheek.

She says, "Well, my baby is going with his mother, and I need to make sure he eats…" Then she whispers, "…In case she doesn't feed him."

I laugh and tell Sean to go play. "I think she's gon' feed him," I respond.

"Well I'm not taking any chances. Here, look." She points to the table.

"I got him all the snacks he likes and I will put them in his little bag in case he gets hungry. Check this out…" She reaches in her pocketbook.

"I got him this little phone. He can only make calls to me, you, and Joe."

I laugh. "Woman, are you insane?" I ask, laughing as I pick up the flip phone.

"What does he need a phone for? He's only three."

"A very smart three, thanks to me. And he may need to call for help. You never know. You trust the bitch, but I don't," she says handing me a plate.

"I'm about to teach him how to work the phone," she says, finishing up her last batch of pancakes.

I yell for Sean to come eat, but Twin says he ate already.

"The early bird gets the worm. All this is yours," she adds.

"Well, damn. How early did y'all get up?" I ask Twin as she walks out the kitchen.

"Early enough," she yells back.

After breakfast, I clean up the kitchen and lay out over the sofa.

Feeling full and satisfied, I yell out to Twin, "Thanks! That was sent from heaven." She walks into the living room.

"Who taught you to cook like that?" I ask.

"Your mother. The same person who taught you," she says.

"True that, true that," I say as I rub my belly. Twin knocks my feet off the sofa and says, "The same mother that would kick your ass if she saw your feet on the furniture."

"First of all, this is my couch. I bought it." I prop my leg back up on my couch, which annoys Twin. She shakes her head, pushes my leg off again, and sits next to me.

"So you cool?" she asks.

"Cool with what?"

"Makayla coming here… seeing her again… I mean it was only seven months ago when you were about to off her."

I laugh. "Yes, Mom. I'm good. In fact, I'm great. I'm in control now," I say.

"Oh, is that right?"

"Yup, I'm riding this wave, darling. She's not riding me. I haven't even answered her phone calls or texted her back, and I'm bringing the HR lady bowling tonight. BOOM. Take that," I say, pretty proud of myself.

"You just don't listen, do you? She looks up to the ceiling, starch out her arms and yells out, "Mom, why you leave me here with him? He is more than I can bare." I laugh as she continues on. "Messing with this girl is messing with your money. Lord, how are you my twin?" She throws a pillow at me. "Ugh, I could really punch you in the face sometimes. You're so damn hard-headed and you take stubborn to a whole new level God didn't even attend for it to be." She shakes her fist at me, and I laugh.

"It's not that big of a deal," I tell her. "We will see how it plays out," I say.

"It is, though. Once you get off this wave, Makayla jumps back on the surfboard, and you will fuck her over like you did Brittany, your ass could end up fired and then what?" Twin questions. "You ain't moving in with me and Joe."

I laugh because she's being ridiculous. "But that's my momma's house."

"It was *our* momma's house, but she left it to me," she reminds me.

"I got this, and she's not my HR person. She's HR for another department."

"Well, all I'm saying is just think about what you're doing, and who your hurting. Don't be to other people what Makayla has been to you. You're better than that," she says, staring me in my eyes.

"I hear you, Mom." I laugh and she laughs too.

"You make me sick always thinking something is a joke. What is this girl's name, because all you keep saying is HR lady," she asks.

"Her name is Tiera."

"Okay Tiera, the HR lady." She stands up. "Well, I'll see you and Tiera tonight. Maybe this one can be your wife," she says. I laugh as Twin says goodbye to Lil Sean. When she comes back out, she goes over what she packed for Sean for the second time.

"All right, his snacks are packed, and his phone is in his bag under his clothes. He knows how to use it. I wrote his number down, and it's in the kitchen."

"Fo' sho'. Thanks so much," I say.

"Yup, well let me get out of here before this bitch comes and I have to put hands on her. See you tonight," she says.

I go in the room and check my phone, and just as I pick it up, Makayla calls.

Me: Yo.

Makayla: Hey, is it okay if I come around 12?

Me: That's cool and don't change your mind because he is really looking forward to it.

Makayla: I'm not, I am coming. I can't wait to see him… see y'all. I miss y'all, and I know you may not believe me, but I can show you better than I can tell you.

Me: All right.

Makayla: Okay, well I'll just see you later then…

Me: Cool.

Makayla shows up exactly at 12 o'clock to pick up Sean. She texts me and tells me that she's at the door. I open the door and there she is, the love of my life and the mother of my child looking hella good. Her hair has grown from the last time and pulled back in a ponytail. She looks like she is ready for a playdate. She doesn't have on any make-up and has on oversized sweat clothes and sneakers, but it looks very sexy. I keep playing it cool and show no interest.

She walks in and touches my face. "Hey," she says. I chuckle and pull my head back and I show no love. I'm melting like butter on the inside, but I will not let it show.

"What's up? How are you?" I reply.

"I'm good and you?"

"Same."

Lil Sean comes running out the room and dashes right to Makayla. "Mommy! Mommy!"

"My baby!" she says. "You're getting so big!" She picks him up and gives him a hug, and that shit just melts my heart. I know she loves him, she's just trying to find her way in the world. She puts him down.

"Go get your stuff so we can go," she tells him.

"Okay," he answers and runs back into his room. I sit on the sofa and she sits next to me.

"Well, you still looking fine as ever," she says, raising her eyebrow and give a smirk.

"I try," I reply.

She laughs. "Still cocky as ever."

"Well, it's hard to be me," I say.

"So, everything good, you good?" She asks, looking genuinely interested.

"Yeah, fine. You?"

She shrugs. "Same ol', same ol'." The room gets quiet.

"You know, I'm sorry how things ended. I was out of line. I was just lost." She looks at me.

"It's cool. No sweat." I'm trying to keep my cool even though all I really want to do is smack the shit out of her for her bullshit, then hug and kiss her, and tell her how much I love her, but she doesn't react to nice Sean, so I have to give her a taste of her own medicine. Less is more.

She grabs my hand as it rests on my lap and says, "Well, I-"

"I'm ready, mommy!" Lil Sean walks out with his bag on his back and cuts her off. She turns to him and gets excited.

"Well, let's go then!" she says to Lil Sean. She lets go of my hand, looks me up and down and says to me, "We best be going." She walks over to Sean and says, "Let's go, my baby. Go give daddy a kiss bye bye." Lil Sean runs over to me.

"Bye daddy!" I give him a big hug and kiss his forehead.

"Be good for mommy, okay?"

"Yes," he replies before he runs back over to her. She opens the door and gives me a smile before she locks and closes the door behind her. I can't help but to think about how much I miss her, but I can't tell her just yet. I have to keep it pushing.

I get ready for my little date around 6. I throw on some fitted jeans, my MazeTown U hoodie, some sneakers that match my shirt, and I spray on my Dior cologne. I arrive at the bowling alley around 7:45 because I don't want to be late and I don't want Tiera to wait on me.

I pull up the same time as Twin, Joe and Tiff, but I stay in the car and wait for Tiera's arrival. She pulls up around 8:05 and texts me she's outside. I see her park, so I get out my Jeep and walk over to her SUV. She shuts off the car and I can see that she's looking in her phone, waiting on me to reply. I knock on her window and she jumps as I wave. She opens the door and I give her my hand, helping her out of the car.

"Hello, and thank you," she says.

I check her out; she has on some fitted jeans that stop a little above the ankle, a white and black college T-shirt, a zip-up black cardigan, and black toms. It it's different from what I'm used to seeing her in, but it is cute and well put together. She is a classy lady.

"My pleasure. I didn't mean to frighten you." I closed the door for her.

"Thanks for coming!" I add.

"Thanks for inviting me, and its fine, I just wasn't expecting that." I can feel that she is nervous.

"I hope you don't mind hanging out with my crew tonight. I promise you, it will be fun. They are good people."

"I don't mind at all," she says.

We walk in, I pay for us, and get our shoes. I spot Twin, Tiff, and Joe at the alley they already claimed.

"We over here," I say to Tiera and she follows behind me.

"Hey hey, y'all!" I give Twin a kiss, Joe a handshake, and Tiff a hug and kiss.

"This is Tiera. Tiera, this is Twin, my baby sister," I say.

"His twin sister. Same age," Twin says as she rolls her eyes.

"But I'm older. I came out first," I add.

"You always come first from what I heard," Twin responds and laughs as she pushes me to the side. She gives Tiera a handshake and says, "Nice to meet you. You are gorgeous! What are you doing with him?"

"Likewise, and thank you," Tiera says with as she smile and blush. Damn, her smile is beautiful; I never saw her smile like this before. I introduce her to Joe and Tiff, and just as they finish exchanging more pleasantries and compliments, in walks James and Mally.

"MazeTown in the house!" Mally yells as he walks in. He runs over, hugs and daps up everyone, but then sees Tiera and says, "Damn, you fine! Who you?"

"Damn, don't be rude!" Twin interjects.

"This is Tiera," I introduce them. "Tiera, this is Mally."

"This you, Sean?" He asks.

"No, I'm me and he's him and we're just here together," Tiera says.

"Tell him, girl," cheers Twin.

Mally puts his hand over his heart and says, "I meant no disrespect, honey."

"None taken," she says, accepting his apology. He reaches his hand out to shake hers and I slap his hand back while putting on my shoes before he could touch her, which makes Tiera laugh.

"Cool. I'm gonna get my shoes. Yo, who taking shots?! I'm 'bout to go over to the bar," Mally says.

"Go get your shoes before the line gets long, then we can get drinks, nigga," Joe says.

"All right, all right, I'm going," Mally replies. James finally walks over after getting his shoes, and I introduce him to Tiera. They speak and shake hands.

"All right y'all, so we playing teams. Me and Twin, Tiff and Kels, Sean and Tiera, and Mally and James. Y'all good with that?" Joe asks. Everyone agrees.

"Yo, I'm going to the bar. Y'all want me to order for y'all?" I ask. I take everyone's drink orders and head to the bar.

Side Conversation with Twin

Tiera

His sister moves over closer to me as soon as Sean leaves for the bar.

"So how do you know my brother?" she asks me.

"We both work at Best Trucking."

"Okay, so what you do there, if you don't mind me asking?"

She's asking a lot of questions, but I don't mind. I think it's genuine and kind of sweet.

"Yea sure, that's no problem. I'm the human resource supervisor for shipping and receiving," I respond.

We continue to talk about my job and then she goes on telling me how good of a person Sean is, which is something I have to see for myself. I feel I can trust what she's telling me, but I like the interest that she is taking in what may come out of this. She tells me more about their crew, explaining how fun and laid back they are, and soon, their other friend, Tiff chimes in.

"Some of us are fun to be around," Tiff says.

"Okay, yes, some of us. We have one asshole friend, Kelly. She will throw hella shade all night, She's our friend, so we deal with it, but just be prepared for it. She's harmless, though, so please don't punch her in the mouth," Twin says, chuckling.

"One of us probably will want to punch her in the mouth by the end of the night, but we love her," Tiff adds.

"Yes, we do," Twin says

I laugh it off and just hope that things don't turn awkward.

Sean

While at the bar, I call Makayla to check up on Sean and once I'm finished, I hang up the phone, grab our drinks, and head back over to the group. As we sip, we hear both Mally and Kelly's loud asses walking back over. Kelly runs up and starts twerking to a song playing over the speakers, wearing these very tight jeans with holes everywhere and half of her ass is hanging out. Twin and Tiff hype her up, and she goes off. She looks up at the names on the screen, stops, and says, "Who the fuck is Tiera?"

Twin taps Tiera and says, "That's Kels." Kelly turns around.

I say, "This is Tiera. Tiera, this is Kelly." Kelly gives her a fake smile and they awkwardly exchange hellos.

Kelly says to me, "Okay Sean, you're on your DJ Khaled shit out here–another one," as she walks away. The crew laughs, and Twin tells Tiera to pay her no mind.

"Here we go," Tiff stands up and claps her hands. "All right, come on, let's get this game started!" Tiff says. When it's mine and Tiera's turns, I let her take the first turn. I get up with her, help her find the right size ball, then I stand behind her.

As I help her hold the ball, I can smell her natural scent and it is intoxicating. She doesn't smell sweet and girly, and she isn't wearing any of that strong perfume. It's just her and her scent mixed with a little coconut oil, but my pheromones are going crazy. I show her how to pull back and release, Kelly says, "You always liked it from the back, didn't you Sean?"

I shake my head and whisper in Tiera's ear, "Please ignore her." Tiera pulls back, throws the ball with a curve and hits a strike on her first try.

"Okay, sis!" Tiff yells out. "I guess she also likes it from the back!" Everyone but Kelly laughs, and I walk over to Tiera, and give her a high five. She smiles, covers her face with her hands and laughs.

I take her hands and say, "We about to kill them!" She laughs and hugs me, and it catches me off guard because when she does, she caresses the back of my head and neck. Something goes through my body–something I haven't felt in a long time. She pulls back, smiles again, and I look her in her eyes. Damn, she's really beautiful.

"I think we got this," she says.

"Feeling lucky, huh?" I respond with a smile. She nods with a smirk and I say, "Let's do this then."

The night is great; we laugh, we drink, and it feels like Tiera has always been a part of the group. Tiera and Twin talk like they have always been friends, and we kill it as a team. I mean, we don't win–Twin and Joe do–but we come in second. It doesn't even matter who won, because the vibe is just so right. Most women I bring to the group don't really fit in with us, but this time, it's different. She is different. When it is time to leave, Twin pulls me to the side.

"Bro, go to the bar with me." We walk over to the bar and Twin looks at me smiling.

"What?" I ask.

"I like her. I mean, I really like her, Sean."

"You want me to hook you up? I mean, I don't know how Joe is going to take it, but you know I'm on your side," I joke.

"Shut up, stupid. You know what I mean," she says laughing.

I say, "Yeah, she's cool."

"She really is, and the way y'all interact with one another is sweet."

"Yeah, whatever. She's cool. I'm sure I'll hit."

Twin shakes her head. "Well, if I ever get into females, I'll take her off your hands." She sticks her tongue out and wiggles it, making me to laugh.

"You fucking freak, I'm telling Joe," I say as we walk back to the group.

"Joe isn't my daddy," Twin says as Joe overhears her.

"What do you mean, I ain't your daddy?" Joe asks as he takes off his bowling shoes.

"You not my daddy, you my zaddy. There's a difference, Bae," Twin says as she sits on his lap and kisses him.

"Okay, it's getting way to freaky over here. I'm out."

I look at Tiera, "You ready?"

She cuts her conversation short with Tiff, looks up at me and says, "I'm ready when you are."

Damn, she fine as fuck, I think to myself.

"All right, we out then. Aye, y'all! Get with me tomorrow!" We all say our goodbyes and Twin even invites Tiera to come back out with us as she gives her a hug.

"Okay, sure!" Tiera says.

"As a matter of fact," Twin adds. "You should come out for our birthday party in two weeks. It's gonna be so much fun!"

"Yeah, you should! I look much different when I'm out on the town," Mally says as he winks at her and does a sexual dance.

"Nigga, she doesn't want you," Twin says as Tiera laughs.

"Damn, it's their first date and y'all already inviting her places," Kelly says as she grabs her shoes to take them back and walks away.

I playfully push Kelly as she walks by, and I tell Tiera, "Sorry that my friend is so rude," as I motion towards Kelly.

Tiera shrugs, "Its fine, it's been like this all night, so I'm used to it," she laughs. "I'll see if I can come."

"Okay, sounds like a plan." Twin says. Tiera and I say our final goodbyes as we walk out. It's May but it's late and a little chilly outside. I put my hood over my head and Tiera zips up her cardigan as we walk to our cars.

"So, it's almost your birthday?" Tiera asks.

"Yes, the big three one."

"You're a baby!" she turns to me and smiles.

"How old are you, if you don't mind me asking?"

"Thirty-four."

"Damn, grandma!" Her jaw drops, she punches my shoulder, and laughs. "I'm just joking," I say.

"You better be! I'm not that old." We continue walking to the car. "So how old is your son?" she asks.

"He's three going on 30," I respond.

She chuckles. "I know what you mean."

"Do you have any children?" I ask.

"Yes, I have a daughter named Skylar. She's my everything."

"Nice. How old is she?" I ask and she immediately looks at me funny.

"What?"

"Don't judge me… I had her at a very young age."

"Nah, never."

She pauses and acts hesitant to say. "Well…she's 18 and just started her first year in college."

"Wow," I say shocked. She hits me again in the same spot, this time causing me to wince.

"See, I knew you were going to judge me. I get the same reaction from everyone," she says.

"I'm in no space to judge anyone," I tell her.

"I had her when I was 16. It was unfortunate, but a blessing at the same time. She's the best thing in my life."

"I feel the same about my son. Honestly, if it wasn't for him, I'd probably be under a freeway cracked out somewhere."

"I can relate."

We are in front of her car and a gust of wind blows by, causing us both to shiver.

"It's getting real chilly out here. Do you want to sit in my car?" she asks.

"Sure."

We sit in her car until dawn, having deep, intellectual, and inspirational conversation. I haven't stayed up all night talking to a girl since I was in high school. I not only learn a lot about her, but also learn a few things about myself. If I can put into words how astounding our conversation was, I would say we are mentally having sex, and I never experienced that before. I am so intrigued by the way she speaks. She tells me things about her home life, like how her parents made her go live with her grandmother after she got pregnant and how she still doesn't really have a relationship with them now. I tell her about my father and how he left my mother, and how when she passed, she left Twin the house and left me and my son money. I tell her a lot of shit that no one knows besides Twin. So much is shared on this first date that it seems like we have been together for years. She seems comfortable and I feel safe. The heat is on, and some Jill Scott is playing real low on the radio. My seat is back and her back is to her window as she sits with one of her legs under her and rests her head on the head rest while we look at each other. The vibe is amazing.

We talk until six in the morning and I get home around seven. It was one of the best nights I had in a long time, and as soon as I walk in, I text T to make sure she got in safely.

7:02 a.m.

Me: You make it home safe

7:05 a.m.

HR: Yes thanks for asking and thank you for a great night

7:10 a.m.

Me: We must do it again sometime

7:12 a.m.

HR: Sure thing, Good Night

HR: Or should I say Good Morning lol

7:15 a.m.

Me: lol Good Morning, and thanks you were the best part of the night

7:16 a.m.

HR: :)

I crash right after and don't wake up until three that afternoon. I wake up to multiple texts from almost everyone.

Text from Twin

11:45am

Twin: She's a good look for you!

Text from Mally

12:12pm

Mally: Tell me you popped shawty?

Text from James

2:20pm

James: Nigga where you find her at, she got friends

Text from Makayla

2:45pm

Makayla: Hey you

Text from Kelly

2:50pm

Kelly: Me and Tiff coming over later stupid, so have your hoe gone by then

Text from Makayla

3:00 p.m.

Makayla: Im dropping Sean off around, 330 let me know if that's ok

3:15 p.m.

Me: Yea that's fine, im home

3:20 p.m.

Makayla: I know I see your car we just pulled up

I get up, throw some drawers on, and answer the door.

"Big Man!" I say as I open the door. I pick him up and he gives me the biggest hug ever. I swear he's the greatest gift of all.

"Were you good?" I ask and he nods.

"Did you have fun?"

"Yes, and I got you something."

"Oh word? For me?" I put him down, he goes in his bag, and pulls out my favorite candy bar.

"For me?"

"Yes, Mommy got it." I look over at Makayla, who is standing in the doorway, and she smiles. I look back down at Lil Sean and can't help but smile.

"Aww buddy, thank you. I will eat it right now. Go take your stuff in your room." He trots into the room and I return my attention back to Makayla.

"Thanks for the candy," I say.

"He picked it out, I just paid for it."

"Well, thanks. And thanks for spending time with him."

Just as I'm closing the door, she says, "Can we talk?" and I let her in.

"What's up?"

"I hope I'm not interrupting you," she says.

"Nah, you good. Tiff and Kelly are coming over, but nothing other than that." I go to sit on the sofa and she follows behind me.

"Okay cool. I'm sure they don't want to see me, so I'll make it fast. I was thinking, maybe I could start getting him every weekend or every other weekend and pick him up from school? I know I messed up before, but he's getting older now and I really want to be in his life more," she says.

"Sure."

She's in utter shock because we have never come to an agreement so quickly before.

"I'm sure we can work something out. Shit, he has a doctor's appointment coming up that you can take him to," I say jokingly.

"Sure, anything. Whatever, I just want to be around more," she claims.

"Sounds good to me."

"Good and umm…" she pauses.

"Yeah?" I'm waiting for her to ask to get back together because I'm ready to take her back, but there is a knock at the door. I get up to answer it and it's Kelly and Tiff.

"Hey boo," Tiff greets as she's the first to walk in.

"Smells like sex in here. You got freaky last night?" Kelly asks as she laughs and gives me a hug.

Makayla gets up and greets them both. "Hey."

Kelly and Tiff don't reply back, but they are shocked to see her and just stand there in the hallway.

"Well, I have to get going. We'll talk later, Sean," Makayla says as she rushes out.

"Umm…." Tiff says.

"Umm, what?" I reply.

"So, miss HR was a front. I knew that tired-looking bitch wasn't your type," Kelly says as she picks up my mail from the hall table and looks through it.

I snatch my mail out of her hand. "First off, you don't know my type, and second, nothing is going on between me and Makayla. She just brought Sean home."

"Whatever, nigga. So, what happened with you and ol' girl last night?" Tiff asks as she smacks her gum. She walks in the living room and sits on the chair.

"Nothing. We just talked all night. We didn't even leave the alley until six in the morning."

"Six in the morning? What the fuck did y'all have to talk about? Y'all just met," Kelly says twisting up her face.

"Real life shit," I respond back coldly. Damn, I love these girls but sometimes they are like mini versions of my sister, who already gives me an ear full and stays in my business.

"So, y'all didn't do nothing? Like nothing at all?" Tiff asks.

"We didn't even kiss. Shit, the conversation was satisfying enough."

"Okay baby boy, look at you, getting off on a convo. That's that king and queen, Malcom X and Betty type shit. Okay, brother," Tiff says.

I laugh. "Yes, something like that." Tiff asks where Lil Sean is, and I call him in to see them.

"There goes my baby! Come here, nephew!" Lil Sean runs to her and sits on her lap, while Kelly follows me into the kitchen.

"So, are you getting back with Makayla?" Kelly asks.

"I don't know, why?"

"Just asking. I just don't know why you keep going back to her."

"You don't have to know, so leave it alone," I tell her before leaving her alone in the kitchen.

8
Decisions

Sean

Over the next two weeks or so, T and I become very friendly, talking on the phone and going out to lunch almost every other day, if not every day. I end up officially inviting her to come out and spend my birthday with me since it would be rude to go back on Twin's invite, but I also genuinely want her to come. She's a good time and I really like hanging out with her.

I have also been seeing a lot of change in Makayla. We never finished the conversation she wanted to have before Tiff and Kelly came over, but I sort of guessed what she wanted. She's been picking Sean up every day from school and spending a lot of time with him, which he loves. We don't talk often, but when we do, it's never on some bad shit. If she wants to get back together, now is the perfect time because she has really proven herself.

Tonight is my party and I'm ready to set it off. I get my own suite since T is coming, just in case she wants to stay the night with me. It's been two weeks and I haven't even kissed the girl, so maybe tonight I'll get lucky. Since it's my birthday weekend, Makayla will crash at my place and watch Sean for the weekend. She said too many people were at her sister's house and she just wanted some alone time with him and it's fine with me. At least I know he's safe.

I ride my bike down to Atlantic City. Thankfully, Kelly is now riding with Tiff, and since it's going to be perfect weather all weekend, I have the perfect excuse to ride out. I don't get that much time on the bike since my boy is always with me. I get to Atlantic City around 6 p.m. Twin and Joe are already checking in when I walk into the hotel.

"Y'all ready to get lit?!" I ask as I walk in. They turn around.

Twin says, "The question is are you with the shits, because I am ready for whatever!"

"That's my Twin! Turning any age with you for the rest of my life is the greatest gift of all," I say to Twin and touch her face.

"Aww, you've been drinking, haven't you?" She tilts her head to the side and smiles while nodding.

"Nah, damn, that was from the heart."

"Where's your girl? I thought she was coming?" Joe asks.

"I don't have a girl, but T is on her way. She's bringing two of her friends."

As we get checked in, we make plans for the night, starting with a pre-game in my room at nine and then heading to dinner at 10. After we part ways, I immediately head to my suite and it's nice and big; it has a living room that is separated from the bedroom and a shower with seating inside, two flat screens, a little kitchen, a lot of seating, and I think I can hit it, here, here, and oh yes there, as I walk through the suite pointing out places to fuck. It's really sexy up in here.

-ding ding- Text from T

7:15 p.m.

T: Hey I just parked about to go in now, are you here yet?

7:17 p.m.

Me: Yes Ma'am Im here, I'll meet you in the lobby

7:18 p.m.

T: Ok

I head down to the lobby to meet her. I feel like a little kid running to go get ice cream from an ice cream truck. To tell you the truth, I can't wait until her cream touches my cone if you know what I mean. As I walk in the lobby, I see her and she smiles as soon as she sees me. I run over to help her with her bags.

"Here, I got those for you."

"Thank you. Sean, this is my friend, Lay. Lay, this is Sean." Lay is exactly what I thought one of T's friends would look like, uppity; hair in a ponytail, shades on, and a Gucci bag that matches her heels and fitted jeans.

"Nice to meet you," I say as I shake Lay's hand.

"Nice to meet you as well," Lay says with a smile.

"I thought you were bringing two of your friends?" I ask.

"Yeah, my other friend will arrive later on tonight."

"Okay, cool." We walk over to get them checked in.

"So, man of the hour, what's the plan for the night? I'm ready to get turnt!" Lay says.

"Oh yeah, you'll fit right in," I say with a chuckle and T laughs.

"Well, we're all going to meet up in my room at 9 to pre-game, we got reservations at 10 at the restaurant down the hall, and then to the club. We got a VIP section."

"Yes pregame! Y'all know how to party," Lay pulls a bottle from her bag. "I'm wit' it!"

I laugh and T shakes her head. "Okay, where is Tower two?" T asks. I point her in the right direction and let her know that she'll be near Twin.

"Well, what tower are you in?" T asks.

I move closer to her. "Why? Are you coming to see me or something?" she laughs and puts her hand on my chest.

"Yes, at nine when everyone else is coming."

I touch her hand and before I can say anything, all I hear is, "Birthday boy! We finna get lit!" Kelly screams in the lobby. Tiff starts dancing with two bottles in her hand. They get me hype, so I start dancing as well.

They chant, "It's your birthday! It's your birthday!" and I do the tootsie roll. James and Mally walk in right behind them and start chanting, "MazeTown!" and we say, "You know!" The whole lobby is looking at us like we're crazy, and we crack up. This is how my crew gets down and I love it. I even see Lay do a little dance move as T just stands there laughing. She's not the loud, ratchet type. It's kind of cute–not what I'm used to, but I like it. After we calm down, I introduce everyone to Lay and they all say hi. I let everyone know the plan and we agree to meet up on time.

After I escort T and Lay to their room, it's game time. It's my birthday night, so I have to look fly. After a nice, long hot shower, I put on my navy blue suit, pants tapered that stops just above the ankle, a black custom fit crewneck shirt, my black Gucci loafers with no socks, and top it off with my Tom Ford cologne. My beard is trimmed right, and my hair cut is fresh. I'm ready to party.

Around 8:50, I get a knock at the door. It can only be two people, and just like I thought, Twin and Joe are at the door. These two are never late. In fact, they are always early.

"Damn, baby boy, look at you! You are looking handsome!" Twin says.

"Yeah kid, them shoes are dope!" Joe compliments.

"Thank you. You know I do what it do. Baby sis, you looking fly yourself. I see you got the knees out and hair all did. Joe is tapping that ass tonight."

"You damn right," Joe says as they both laugh and he pulls Twin closer to him. Soon after, there's another knock at the door and it's Mally and James.

"Yo fly boy, look at you! Ol' girl 'bout to be looking at the ceiling tonight!" Mally says.

"Or the headboard," James adds.

"You already know," I say as we laugh and dap it up.

"Aye, you got some cologne I can borrow? I left mine at home." Mally asks.

"Nah, nigga. I don't want you smelling like me," I reply. Just as I go to close the door, Kelly busts in.

"Happy birthday, my beautiful babies!" she yells. Tiff walks in right after her, shaking the two bottles and dancing in the doorway, saying, "Shots! Shots! Shots!" They pull out the cups so we can take shots.

"Let's wait until Sean's boo gets here first," Twin says.

"Boo? Ha! More like a classy fuck," Kelly says.

"Don't start your shit," I tell Kelly. "And we have never had sex, thank you very much!"

"Dog, you haven't hit yet? What are you waiting for?!" Mally asks.

"Because he knows she's probably a weak fuck. Just look at her bougie ass. She looks like she fucks with her pinky up screaming out 'Cheerio darling, cheerio!'" Kelly says before the whole group falls out laughing. Even I laughed.

"Aye yo, fuck you Kels." I laugh again.

"No, I think he really likes her," Tiff says sitting on the arm of the sofa crossing her legs.

"We're just friends. Y'all need to cool it, all right?" I flag them off.

-ding ding- Text from T

9:20 p.m.

T: Hey sorry we won't be able to make the pre-game. This girl is taking forever to get dressed. Can we just meet you at the restaurant?

9:22 p.m.

Me: Yea sure no rush, we gone head down around 9:45-50, its Los DaeArae, to the left of the lobby.

9:25 p.m.

T: ok great see you then, and I'm sorry

"Let's take these shots. T is gon' meet us down there," I say.

"What? She's too good to have a drink with us regular folk? We don't have any tea or biscotti for her liking?" Kelly says, rolling her eyes.

"Bitch, I'm not regular," Tiff jumps in.

"That's right, Tiff, tell her. You ain't regular, you're below average," Mally says, making us laugh even more. After having a few shots back to back, we head down.

As soon as we get off the elevator, I see T and Lay waiting in the lobby. God damn, she looks good, and we must've been thinking alike because our outfit colors match perfectly. She has on a shoulder-less tight, black dress that hugs every part of her body and it comes down just above her knees. She's wearing navy blue heels, like my suit, and has a small bag to match. I notice that her hair is down, which I have never seen her with her hair down before.

As I walk over to her, she tucks her hair behind her left ear, showing off her diamond earring. Someone could talk to me now and I wouldn't even hear them because all I see is her.

I walk up to her and say, "Wow, you look phenomenal."

She runs her hand down the collar of my suit jacket and says, "You clean up very well yourself."

She introduces Lay to Twin and Joe, gives Tiff and Twin hugs, and tells Twin happy birthday. I can't stop looking at her. She's fine as fuck.

As we walk into the restaurant, I put my arm around her and she puts her arm around my lower back. Once we get to our table, I pull the chairs out for her and Lay. When we all get situated, the waiter comes and takes our orders.

"Should we do one bill or separate bills?" the waiter asks. James,

Tiff, and Twin scream out separate, and me and Joe laugh because we know Kelly and Mally will order everything and then try to split the bill knowing damn well most of the shit is theirs. Joe tells the waiter to put him and Twin together and I tell him he could put me and T's bill together, as it's only right that I pay.

When our drinks come we all hold our glasses up and Tiff says, "Cheers to 31 years!" We clink and throw back our shots or in T's case, sip back her wine. We laugh, we drink, we eat, and we talk. I can't stop thinking about how good T looks and smells. I keep my arm around her the whole time, and she loves it. I even let her taste food off my plate, and she feeds me things off hers.

Right before we get our checks, Tiff has the waiter bring out some fancy cheesecake slices for me and Twin. The crew stands up and gets the whole restaurant to sing "Happy Birthday" to us–the Stevie Wonder version, not the regular version.

When the checks come, I take the check, but T takes it from me and tells me she's paying, so I take it back.

"Nah, it's cool. I got it, don't worry. I got you."

She replies, "I know that the man in you feels like you have to pay every tab, but the woman in me wants to let that man know that today he can just be the birthday boy. I got this." She puts her hand out for the check, I hand it back to her and smile.

"Thank you."

"You're welcome," she says. I sit back in my chair and look over to Twin, she smiles and raises her glass to me and mouths, "That's a real woman."

After dinner, we walk to the club. As I walk side by side with T, out of nowhere, she takes my hand and holds it, like we are together. I'm not a hand holder, but with her, it feels right. I look over to her and smile; I feel like a power couple at that moment, like Jay and Bey. We both walked tall and with confidence. Maybe Twin is right; she is a good look for me. We arrive at the club and we skip past the line and go straight to our VIP section.

"Damn, Joe! You went all out!" I say. The section is extraordinary. We are right in the middle of the action, but it's still very private. We have suede chairs, a TV, champagne bottles on ice, and on the side of us is a mini waterfall which is dope.

"Bro, pop that shit! Let's get it started!" Twin says. I take the champagne out the ice bucket, pop it, fill our glasses, and we toast.

"To another one of many more birthdays to come!" I say.

"To Sean and Twin!" James says as we raise our glasses and cheer. It's already 11:15 p.m., and the girls are ready to get out on the floor and dance. James started talking to Lay in the restaurant, so I guess he wanted to keep talking, but the rest of us get out on the floor.

"Let's go birthday boy!" Kelly says.

"Come dance with me," I say to T as I grab her hand.

She smiles but shakes her head. "I don't dance. You go ahead and have fun. I'll be here when you get back."

"You sure?" I ask, really hoping she will change her mind.

"Yes, go!"

I go out with Kelly and we kill it on the floor like we always do. Sometimes Kelly gets a little sexual when we're partying, but I'm not into it tonight, so I try my hardest to keep it clean, even though she tries her hardest not to. I guess she wants to make T jealous.

Around about the 6th song, I take my jacket off because I am getting sweaty. I go back to our section and asked T if she wants to go to the bar and get something to drink and she agrees. So many guys are looking at her, and one guy even tries to talk to her as we walk by, and it kind of gets me uptight. I know the guy saw me standing there, but before I can say something, she grabs my hand and pushes past him. It was refreshing to know that she was interested in only me.

At the bar, I call the bartender over and ask T what she's drinking.

She replies, "No, what are you drinking?" and took out her credit card.

"So, you're just not going to let me pay for anything tonight?"

"It's your birthday, why would I?" she asks.

"I guess I've been hanging out with the wrong girls."

"I guess so. It's a good thing I'm all woman," she says, winking at me.

"That you are." I smile. I can't believe how amazing she is. I'm starting to really like her. I order Jack and she gets a mixed drink. We get our drinks and walk back over to our section and once we sit down, Kelly comes running over to me to get back on the dance floor. "Nice for What" by Drake is on and it's one of her favorite songs. T insists that I go back out there and dance, so I do, and Kelly and I fuck it up. When the break of the song comes, Kelly backs up on me, but suddenly, I feel a tap on my shoulder. I turn around, and there is T. She extends her hand, I take it, and then she turns around and bends over. She grinds her ass all on me. I'm impressed that she can even drop it like she does, and I'm not the only one; I hear Twin and Tiff screaming, "Fuck it up, T!" Kelly is pissed and walks back over to our section.

As soon as that song is over, my son's favorite song, "Slow Down" by Skip Marley and H.E.R., comes on. My son loves this song so much it has become mine and Twin's favorite song too, so Twin and I get hype.

She nudges me and says, "Looks like Lil Sean approves." We smile and she dances with Joe, and I with T. We two step and get it like an old couple that's been together for years, both of us smiling and having a good time. When H.E.R.'s part comes on, Twin asks to switch, so T dances with Joe and she dances with me. We've heard this song so many times, so we go hard on the verse as we dance. Once the chorus comes back around, we switch back. T's back is up against me, my arms around her, and we are stuck in this slow dance groove. I'm breathing in her neck and she lays her head back on my shoulder.

As the song ends, T turns around and looks at me. I lean in and she kisses me, and man, we kiss like there is no tomorrow. Her kiss is everything, and I swear fireworks go off. It feels like the whole club disappeared and it is just me and her. I hold her waist and she wraps her arms around my neck, her hands caressing the back of her head. When we finish, we stare at each other for a few moments until Mally calls us over for another toast since it's almost me and Twins birthday. Me and T walk hand in hand over towards the group. I rub my hands down my beard and take a deep breath because that kiss was intense and almost had me buckle at the knees. Mally has the drinks poured up and we all raise our glasses.

Twin begins. "I would like to thank all my wonderful friends and family for joining us tonight in celebration of me and my brother's birthday. Thank you to my husband, who got us in VIP tonight!" Everyone cheers. "And most importantly, I just wanna say, Sean, I love you and happy birthday."

Everyone cheers again and screams out, "Speech! Speech!" so I did our school shout, "MazeTown! You know!" and begin speaking.

"All right, I just wanna say thank you to all of you that made this happen tonight. Thanks for all your love and support, and to my sister, Seana, every year we share is the ultimate gift and blessing. To us!"

"Aww, happy birthday!" everyone shouts, and we toss back our shots.

I hug and kiss Twin. "I guess everyone's getting kisses tonight but me," Kelly says, but everyone ignores it. We sit around taking selfies and group photos.

After me and T take a photo together, Kelly jumps up and says, "Oh Twin, take a pic of me and my bestie," and she hands Twin her phone. Kelly jumps on my lap and turns to T.

"Don't worry, we friends."

T comes back with, "I'm not worried." It's the first time T ever replied to Kelly's smart-ass comments. Twin takes her glass and raises it to T.

"As you shouldn't be," Twin says.

"Shit, I ain't the one you need to be worried about anyway," Kelly laughs as she gets up and takes her phone back from Twin.

"Come on, Kelly. Not tonight," Joe says.

"What? It's not my fault he leaves everyone for his baby momma. So, yes baby girl, it's not me you should be worried about. It's Makayla, the one he's stuck on." I jump up, grab Kelly by her arm, making her drop and break her glass, and I drag her outside the club. Once outside, I swing her around by her arm to face me.

I ask, "What the fuck is wrong with you? Not only have you been throwing bullshit at T all night–well, giving her hell, since you met her–but you are disrespecting the fuck out of me on my birthday. You need to get your shit together, Kels. It's not cute."

I let go of her arm and walk back in the club, when Kelly yells, "Oh so and what you're doing is cute?"

I turn around. "What?"

"Year after year, I watch you cycle from Makayla to these other bitches, but what about me?"

"What about you, Kelly?" I ask confused as I walk back over to her.

"I've been here this whole time, the whole fucking time!" she screams right in my face. "When Makayla leaves you, I'm here to talk to you, I become your best friend and your partner in everything we do–game night, dancing, bowling, whatever and then you find someone else and I'm nothing again."

"Kelly, you're drunk." I put my hand up and proceed to walk away again, but I stop when she starts yelling again.

"I know what the fuck I'm saying, Sean! Why them? Why not me? I'll take the backseat to Makayla, fine. I know you really love her, but all these other bitches, Sean? How do you think I feel? I have to hear about all the hoes you sleep with, how you touch them and make them feel. The same way you used to touch me and make me feel. I'm the one that loves you. I'm the one that's always here. I fucking love you, can't you see that?"

Damn, I knew she still had feelings for me, but I didn't know they were still that deep. I feel bad in a way and it kind of upsets me.

"Kels, I love you like a sister, like how I love Tiff and Twin. What we had has been over since college." I try to break it down to her gently, but she doesn't say anything and starts to cry. I walk closer to her and try to wipe her tears, but she pushes my hand away. "Look Kelly, I'm sorry if I ever made you feel any type of way. I thought we were on the same page. That college stuff was behind us and all the little flirting we did was just play… I'm sorry, Kels, but I just don't see us being anything other than friends."

"Well, maybe we shouldn't be friends at all," she says.

I shake my head. "Yeah, maybe."

"Happy Birthday, Sean," she says before she walks away, leaving the club. I walk back in the club to our section.

As soon as I get over there, Twin asks, "Are you okay? And where's Kel?"

"Yeah, and I don't know. I think she went back to her room."

Tiff stands up and says, "I'll go find her. She's super drunk." I sit down and take two shots back to back.

"Sean, this is my best friend," I look up from my glass.

"Cody?" I say. I didn't even notice he was sitting here.

"Happy birthday," he says with a smile. I'm completely shocked, and a little confused. I can't believe he's her best friend. I reach over and give him a handshake.

"Thanks man! Wow… y'all are best friends," I laugh. "So, you're the middleman?"

"More like the wing man," he says and we laugh.

"Hey well let me introduce you to-"

"I already did that," T cuts in.

"Yes, we all met," Twin says. I call someone over to get Cody a drink and by the time we are all done taking shots, it's 2 a.m. and the club is closing down. We leave the club together and when we get into the lobby of the hotel, I see Tiff walking towards us.

"How's Kel?" Twin asks.

Tiff says, "She's fine, just drunk. I put her in bed. So what's the move? I know y'all ain't done already," Tiff says, still drunk herself as she pops her booty out.

"We gon' call it," Twin says as she hugs up on Joe.

"Well, all right ya nastys" Tiff says.

Lay strolls over and says, "It's a party! Where we at with it?"

"Oh, I like her," Tiff says.

"There's a bar across the street from here. Y'all tryna go?" Mally suggests. I look at T to see if she's interested.

"I'm down if you are," she says. We all agree to leave for the bar. The damn bar ended up being 10 blocks away. I've learned that you can never trust Mally. By the time we get there and get drinks, we don't even want to be there anymore. All of us are drunk already anyway and now we are tired from the walk there and tired just thinking about the walk back. When you're in your 30s, shit sounds fun until you end up doing it.

When we get back to the hotel, James and Mally go to the casino, and Tiff calls it a night. Holding T's hand, I ask her if she wants me to walk her back to her room. She tells me to hold on, and she walks over to Lay and Cody, they chat for a moment, and then she comes right back.

"No, they don't need us to walk them to the room," she says with a smirk.

"So, you're staying the night with me?" I smile.

"Yes. I mean, if that's okay with you. Is someone else staying in your room?"

"Nah, we good."

"Good, but no sex," she says in a drunken voice as she puts one finger on my lips.

I laugh. "That's fine with me," I say. As we walk back to my room, I notice she is walking really slow, and she is drunk as hell.

"You good?" I ask.

"Yeah, my feet just hurt. I've been dancing and walking all night." I stop and take my shoes off.

"Here, walk in my shoes and I'll carry yours."

"Aww, that's sweet, but I'm not about to let you walk on this nasty floor barefooted." I put my shoes back on and hold her hand as we walk into the elevator. Once it stops on my floor, she asks how far my room is, and when I tell her, she laughs and claims that it's far, so I pick her up and carry her the rest of the way.

"You don't have to do this," she says.

"I want too," I reply. Once we get in the room, she goes straight to the bed.

"Nice room."

"Thank you much."

"Were you planning on getting lucky tonight in here?" she asks.

I laugh. "Nah, I just knew people were gon' meet up in here."

"Oh okay. Do you have a shirt I can sleep in?" she asks. I go into my bag, get her a shirt, and hand it to her.

"Thanks, don't look," she says. I laugh. "I'm for real. Go in the bathroom or something." I go into the bathroom and take off all my clothes except for my drawers.

She yells, "You can come out now." I walk out with my hands over my eyes.

"You sure?" I ask.

"You play all the time, don't you?" she remarks as I remove my hands.

"Not all the time, just all the time." She laughs and gets under the covers.

"So, that's how you get all the girls, huh?"

"Nope. Have you seen me?" I say, causing her to laugh.

As I get in bed, she says, "You think you look good, huh?" I lean over to her and get inches away from her lips.

I say, "Yes," and then I kiss her. I pull back and she pulls me to her.

"Oh, you want some more, do you now?"

"I'm just giving you all you're going to get," she says. I laugh and we begin to kiss again. Our tongues become entangled as she rubs the back of my head. I feel her body movements in the bed and I swear I heard a little moan. I can tell she was getting hot and bothered, so I back off. She is drunk, and I want to respect her wishes. Once we have our moment, I turn the TV on.

"Oh no," she says.

"What?"

"Don't tell me you're the late-night TV person."

I laugh. "I don't watch it. It watches me, but if you want me to turn it off, I can," I reply and pick up the remote. She puts her hand over the remote.

"No, no, no. It's your birthday." She moves closer to me and puts her head on my chest.

"Goodnight," she says.

"Goodnight," I say back.

As she snuggles deep into my arms, she whispers, "Happy birthday, Sean."

*

Around 7 a.m. the next morning, Twin calls my phone and asks me to meet her downstairs in 10 minutes.

I look over at T, and she's out like a light, so I throw something on and meet Twin at the restaurant for breakfast.

"Happy birthday, baby!" Twin says.

"Happy birthday my cuddly pop." We laugh, hug and sit down. We order a big breakfast like we always do. She slides me a gift across the table and I slide hers back. We both laugh because we do this every year. I open my gift, and it's the newest Jordan's I couldn't get because they were all sold out.

I'm overjoyed. "You are the G.O.A.T.," I say and give her a kiss. She opens her gift and immediately begins to cry. She's so dramatic.

"Is this…?"

"Yeah."

"How did you… When did you get it out my house?"

"Joe got it for me. I know how much you love Mom's necklace and was so upset when the diamond came out, so I had it cleaned and put a new diamond in it."

"You are the best brother in the world, I swear. Can you?" She holds out the necklace, so I can put it on her. "Thank you so much, you don't understand how much this means to me," she says.

"I do, and you're welcome."

-ding ding- Incoming Call from Makayla

"Who is it?" Twin asks and when I tell her it's Makayla, she turns her face up.

"She's probably calling for Sean," I say, then I pick up. Lil Sean is on the other end of the line and I'm happy to hear my boy's voice. It's a quick call, him wishing me and Twin happy birthday before handing the phone over to Makayla for her to do the same, and I hang up with them just as our food comes.

"Makayla says happy birthday," I say, as I put down my phone and Twin rolls her eyes.

"On that note, I will say grace. Dear Lord, thank you for another year together. Without you, none of this would be possible. Continue to bless us, bless the food, and the hands that prepared it, in Jesus name we pray…" Twin prays.

"Yes, and tell Mommy we miss her so much and breakfast isn't the same without her," I add. Then we both say, "Amen."

"So, why is she at your apartment watching him again?" Twin asks.

"It was just easier. Anyway…" I say avoiding eye contact with her and trying to avoid this conversation.

"Yes, anyway, so what happen last night after I left?" Twin asks.

"Nothing much we went to a bar that Mally said was across the street and it ended up being 10 long ass blocks away."

She laughs and says, "Now y'all know never to trust Mally."

"Right. When we got there, it was crowded. It took us about a half an hour to get waited on and after the 1st round, we left. It was too much," I say.

"I bet y'all old asses got tired, thinking y'all still in y'all 20s. Those college days are gone… So, have you talked to Kelly since last night?" she asks.

"Nah."

"So, tell me what happened when you dragged her out the club?" she asked with a laugh. "I can't believe you did that."

"Yo, she was outta pocket for bringing Makayla up," I say.

"Damn right she was," Twin adds.

"She really crossed the line. Okay, you say your little shit here and there but when you become disrespectful… nah."

"She has never brought Makayla up before, which is crazy, so what happened, what did you say, and why didn't she come back?" Twin asks.

"I just told her to cut her shit, and that she was outta pocket.

Then she starts talking about how she takes the backseat to Makayla but not for these other chicks, and why not her and basically she's been waiting for me to be with her blah blah blah."

"Well, I could've told you that," Twin shares.

"I don't want to be with her."

"I could've told her that. That's why I told you to stop playing around with her, but you don't listen, once again," Twin says.

"Shit, I thought she knew we was playing."

"The girl has wanted to be with you since college, but you went back to Makayla and she sees the same cycle. She knows that you're not going to take another girl seriously, so she hopes when you're really done with Makayla, you will find love with her."

"Well that isn't happening, so…" I say.

"Well where is T, how long did y'all hang out last night?"

"She's back at the room."

"Ayyyye, so how was it?" she asks.

"What?"

"You took her back to your room, so I know you got in them skins."

"Nope."

"Nope? What you mean?" she asks, shocked.

"I didn't hit."

"Wait, so you're telling me you didn't hit after almost a month of spending time with this girl?"

"Yup, and I don't mind."

"Oh, nigga. Nigga, you in love," she says, and I laugh.

"In love? Nah, we just friends. Everything is cool."

"Friends don't make out on the dance floor like you two did," she adds.

"Well, it was my birthday," I say.

"And you don't ever drag Kels out a club because of something she said."

"Well, she was being disrespectful," I respond back.

"Yeah, okay," she says as she stuffs pancakes in her mouth.

"I'm just saying you're acting different with her; you take more time with her, and she's completely different from anyone you ever had. Plus, I peeped what she said to you when she paid the tab last night. You liked that," Twin says.

"Yeah, that was dope, but still. We just chilling, so leave it at that."

"Okay, lover boy." The waiter comes over and we order more food, plus some food for Joe and T. When we finish our food and pay our check, we grab the other food and go our separate ways, but not before agreeing to link up later.

I get back to the room and put the food on the table in the living room. I walk into the room and T is still sleeping, so I get ready to hop in the shower.

"Well, you're up early. Happy birthday," she says as she wakes up.

"Thank you. I just came back from breakfast with Twin."

"You could have woke me up."

"Nah, you needed your sleep, plus it's something we only do together," I say.

"You only eat breakfast with your sister?" she asks and I laugh.

"No not every day, just on our birthday." She looks at me confused. "See, when our father left, our mom didn't have a lot of money to throw birthday parties, so she always got up and made us this big breakfast and gave us each a gift. Even when we were in college, we always came home for breakfast no matter what." I sit on the bed next to her. "So when she died, we kept it going, just us and our one gift. We do it every year no matter what," I say.

She crawls over to me. "Wow that's thoughtful and sweet. I can respect that," she says.

"But I brought you some food back. It's on the table."

"Aww, thank you. You didn't have to do that."

"I wanted to. I got you a few things because I didn't know what you would like. You look like an eggs benedict type girl, but they didn't have that, so I got you a few other things," I say.

"An egg benedict type of girl?" she laughs. "What type of girl is that?"

"You know, the classy lady type." We laugh.

"Well, thank you for thinking of me as a classy lady." She leans over and kisses me. "But I'm not the eggs benedict type, and I'll eat anything that's not pork or beef," she explains.

"I did good then. I got turkey and pork bacon, so I'll just eat the pork. I'm about to get in the shower." I grab her hands and pull her off the bed.

"So, you go eat." I kiss her. "And I'll see you when I get out." I turn her around and slap her butt as if I was saying move it.

As soon as I get out the shower, there's a knock at the door. I wrap my towel around me and answer while T is texting and eating. I open the door and it's Kelly.

"Hey," she says very friendly.

"What's up?" I reply with suspicion.

"Umm, I just want to apologize for my behavior last night. I was just drunk. I didn't mean to start no shit." T is sitting right in the view of the door. Kelly sees her and walks in a little.

"I want to apologize to you too. I'm sorry if I made things uncomfortable for you in any way."

"Thank you," T says before Kelly steps back into the hallway.

"I never meant to disrespect you. I have the most respect for you, and you know that." Kelly half smiles and begins to walk away.

"Hey Kels…" She turns back towards me. "I really appreciate that. Thank you."

She nods and gives another half-smile. "Friends?" she asks.

"Always," I reply and she walks away. I feel bad because I know she's hurting inside. Her true feelings for me came out last night and now everything she felt is exposed.

I close the door and walk over to T, touch her face as she looks up and with a mouth full of food, I smile and then I walk into the room. Just as soon as I get my underwear on, she walks into the room and sits on the bed.

"That was good, thank you."

"No problem" I winked at her, and she smiles.

"So, what's the story behind this Makayla?"

I knew that this was going to come up at some point, but not this early. If Kelly didn't come by, I'm sure she would have forgotten. Oh well. Here we go.

"Makayla is the mother of my child. We dated on and off since 12th grade, went to college together, and had a baby," I tell her.

"Wow, that's a long time,"

"I know."

"So are y'all dating now?" she asks.

"No, not at all. She actually just came back around a few weeks ago. I guess she's just been trying to be a better mother."

"What do you mean by come back?"

"Well she leaves from time to time."

"For how long?" she asks, looking at me confused. I sit on the bed.

"Well, her longest time away was right after my son was born. She took off when he was three months and came back when he was around one and a half."

"Wow, I'm sorry," she says, rubbing my back.

"It's cool. I'm used to it now. Shit, we used to it now. It was hard back then, but we are okay."

"How is your son taking it?"

"Man, he's a strong little dude. He handles it better than me at times. He cried for her once, which really broke my heart."

"I bet."

"Other than that time, he just sees her when he sees her. I think because she really hasn't been around, he takes what he can get from her when she's around and when she's not, he's okay. He has me and Twin. Honestly, I think he looks at Twin as more like a mother figure then his own," I share.

I get up and grab my Bluetooth speaker, hoping that the conversation is over, but then she asks, "Do you still love her?" As my back is turned to her, I roll my eyes and mouth *Fuck*, and then turn around.

"She's the mother of my child. I'm going to always love her," I reply, avoiding eye contact with her.

"I can respect that," she adds. She's silent as I hook up my speaker to play some music to distract her from asking another question. She's not saying anything, but I wonder what she's thinking. Damn, I hope I didn't just mess things up. Even though I wasn't completely honest about my feelings for Makayla and haven't told her any of my history with her, I was still truthful on some level. I put on the Isley Brothers song, "For The Love of You", and start two stepping, snapping my fingers, and singing to her. She smiles and sings the hook.

I grab her hand, pull her up off the bed and start two stepping with her, she acts shy and laughs while shaking her head, but I pull her close and slow dance with her, still singing to her. After about 45 seconds, she fully gives in to it and we are holding each other and dancing. I spin her around and she comes back singing and smiling.

She asks, "Do you dance like this with all your girls?"

"Nope, just my favorite ones." She pushes back a little and looks at me with her face tuned up.

"My mother, my sister, and now you," I say. She smiles and looks deep in my eyes.

"I'm one of your favorites?"

"Yup."

She puts her arms on top of my shoulder and bends my head down so I can kiss her. We stop dancing, and at the moment, I don't even know if the song is still playing. Sparks are flying and if we keep kissing, something else will pop up. She takes her arms from around my neck, but she's still deeply in this kiss with me. She runs her hands down my chest and stops at my stomach. I'm trying to stay cool and stay down because I'm not sure if she wants to take it there, so I keep kissing her and rubbing on her back and waist. She must've thought about it for a second and just said fuck it because she puts her hands in my underwear. She plays around for about a minute and well, hello.

She smiles in the middle of our kiss and says, "Well that didn't take long," and she continues to kiss me. A few minutes later, she takes my hand and walks me over to the bed. She pushes me down and looks in her purse on the end table. I'm sitting there like a kid waiting to open gifts on Christmas. She pulls out a condom and walks over to me.

"It's going to be very hard to get this on if these are still on," she says, talking about my underwear. So, I take them off, and when I sit back up, she smiles. She rips opens the condom and puts it on me herself, and that is a first for me. How many dudes has she been fucking that she carries condoms around with her? The thought crosses my mind but quickly fades away as she slides her panties down and climbs on top of me. She sits, and the fit is so perfect; it's like her treasure was locked away waiting for me to find it. It isn't too tight, but just right, and I can tell she hasn't been fucking. Trust, I know when someone's getting hit on a regular. I learned it from Makayla.

She pushes my head back and kisses me as she rides. My God. It feels amazing, I could feel my toes curl up. She's rocking to a slow and steady beat. I don't know what song is playing, but I can feel the vibrations through my body. She moans, kisses, and only ever comes up for air to moan. It doesn't even occur to me that she still has my shirt on and I can't see her breasts. It's just that good, so fuck a titty.

About 10 minutes into it, she cums. I can feel the jerk in her body, but she keeps going. I try to hold out because I can let off at any minute too. Then, she does something I never had happen to me before–she stops holding me, pushes me back on the bed, and starts massaging my nut sack as she rides. I let go of her and start gripping the sheets like a little bitch. Oh, it feels so good. Every time she moans, I do the same thing. Man, I feel the Son, the Father, and the Holy Spirit. She comes again and the grip on my sack gets tighter. What is she doing to me? Shit, I'm about to start shaking. If I don't do something fast, I'm going to nut and cry all at the same time, but it feels so good, I didn't want to move. I understand the whip appeal that Babyface was talking about now.

I let her cum one more time before I have to get up. She isn't going to make no punk out of me. It's my birthday, damn it. I pick her up and put her back to the wall. Man, I give her all that I have. She isn't about to outdo me on our first round. I have to show her I can give it out too. I hold her legs and thrust my hips into hers. She is done kissing, and all she wants to do is moan now. I'm not rough with her; I'm very firm, but slow and steady. Her touch is graceful, and she doesn't scratch or bite like other females. She's very gentle, and her moans are very soft. Nah, man this isn't just having sex, we are making love. I feel it and I know she feels it too. I'm so deep inside her that I know for a fact that I touched her heart and her ovaries hugged me. Her insides embrace me so tight, it warms my soul.

After 20 minutes on the wall, I feel like I will die from trying not to let off, but I want to give her one last nut–seven in total that I know of–three on her own, and four from me. I'm competitive and I must have one up on her. She lets go of me and starts climbing up the wall as I hold her legs up higher and give her longer, deeper strokes. I bend my knees full squat and drop her down on me then bring her back up again and again. I am giving her one hell of a ride. She cums again and her head falls back against the wall then on my shoulder almost lifeless like.

She then brings her head up, looks me dead in my eyes, and says with the most beautiful straight face, "Cum," and instantly I came and I came hard. I bit her shirt just to muffle the moan I was letting out. If anyone were to come in this room right now, it would look like I was crying on her shoulder as she kisses my forehead like she is telling me it will be all right. Ah, man I was ugly. She breathes heavily into my neck as I get my shit together. We kiss again and look into each other's eyes with amazement, trying to process what just happened here. As we are kissing, there's a loud knock at the door.

"Tiera, I know you're in there, girl. Open up!" She laughs while we kiss, and it makes me laugh. They keep knocking on the door, so I put her down. As she stands up she loses her balance, which makes me laugh. I ask her if she's all right, and she catches herself on the wall and covers her face, as if she's embarrassed.

She quickly gets herself together and with a straight face, says, "Yes, I will be." I sneak into the bathroom as she opens the door.

"Um, what you doing up in here?" Cody asks and T laughs.

"Nothing, what y'all doing here?"

"Girl, we gotta check out soon. Why haven't you come back to the room yet?" Lay asks as they both walk in.

"Damn, this room is nice girl. He got some money," Cody says as they laugh.

"I was just about to come to the room."

"The lie is written all over your shirt. Where is Sean, by the way?" Cody asks, looking around.

"Is he handcuffed to the bed?" Lay whispers. I come out the bathroom with a towel on because that was all that was in there.

"What's up?" I say as they all stare.

"Hey chest." Cody bumps Lay. "I mean, Sean."

I laugh and T shakes her head and smiles. I walk into the room and close the door.

"God damn, that nigga fine. You see the print on that towel?" Lay asks Cody.

"Yup, I saw it, girl. Tiera lost all her walls last night."

"Oh my god, stop. I'm sure he can hear you," T says. She is right; they are talking loud enough for me and I'm sure the neighbors to hear. T walks in the room, and I'm laid out on the bed, tired as shit but feeling better than a motherfucker. She comes right in and jumps on top of me.

"So, I have to go now," she tells me as she pokes out her lips then lays her head on my chest. I rub her thighs as she sits on top of me.

"So soon?" I ask as I poke my lip out too.

"Yes." She sits up, gives me a kiss and then rocks side to side on my dick. "This is everything."

I sit up and pull her in close. "You're everything," I say. She smiles and lets out a groan as she gets up. I grab her by the bottom of my shirt and sit her back on the bed. I flip her hair to the other side, kiss her neck and touch her super soaked wet pussy. She lays back on me and rubs the back of my head. She opens her legs and quietly says "I have to go," as I rub my finger around her clit. As I get hard again, she quickly closes her legs while my hand is still in between them. She removes my hand, turns around to me kiss me on my cheek, and says again that she has to go. She gets up and takes the end of the towel I have wrapped around me and wipes herself off.

"Do you have any shorts or pants I can throw on to walk to my room? I really don't feel like putting back on my dress."

"Yeah, sure." I give her my ball shorts and my slides. She puts everything on and it's all baggy, but she looks so sexy in it.

"Thanks, I'll give them to you later. She gives me a kiss and collects her stuff. She opens the room door and looks back at me, licking her lips before she closes the door. I fall back on the bed and let out a deep breath. Damn, why did her friends have to show up?

"Bye, Sean!" They yell from the other side of the door.

"Bye!" I yell back.

Once I hear the door close, I look at the clock to see how long I can sneak in a nap. It's already 11:30, and we have to check out at 12, so I decide to just take a 20 minute nap. Just as I go to close my eyes, Twin calls and I reluctantly answer.

-ding ding- Incoming Call from Twin

Me: YES?

Twin: Oop. Did I interrupt something?

Me: A nap, what's up?

Twin: A nap? Nigga, it's our birthday. Get yo' ass up. Is T still there?

Me: Nah.

Twin: Oh all right, well let's go! We will see you at check out. Everyone wants to go to Dragon Hills Beach Front.

Me: All right, cool. I'll see you then.

I hang up and try to get these last 15min of shut eye.

Girl Talk

Tiera

"So, girl, how was that print?" Lay asks as she sits on the bed. I look back at Cody as he co-signs, I laugh, and start taking clothes out of my bag.

"What are you talking about? And stop talking about his print. That's my print." I smile, take off my shirt, and throw it at her.

"That good, huh," Lay says, and she laughs.

"Who said anything happened?" I ask.

"That shirt," Cody says.

"The evidence." Lay shakes the shirt and I laugh.

"Well, you're wrong," I say before jumping in the shower. About 20 minutes into my wash, I hear both Cody and Lay walk into the bathroom, asking me to tell them what happened. The pressure of them asking me brings up so many emotions inside of me. This man's sex just gave me life, and now I'm satisfied and scared at the same time. Before, he was just a fine guy that I was interested in, but now, I want him to be mine. All mine.

I start to cry and as soon as my friends hear me, they rip back the curtain and immediately jump to conclusions, threatening to fight Sean. It's so funny how hype they got that I laugh. I have to calm them down and let them know that he didn't do anything to me that I didn't want him to. I step out the shower and dry off. I go into the room as they follow me, anticipating a run-down of all the details. I lie down on the bed and both of them sit next to me.

"It was so good, y'all, like really *so* good."

"Must have been, bitch. You in here crying and shit, God damn," Lay says with a laugh.

"Right, I may have my husband call him to get some tips, shit. I wanna cry too," Cody says as he gives Lay a high five.

"I can't mess with him, I just can't. I've been hurt too many times, and you heard what his friend said last night," I remind them.

"No, what was said?" Cody asks.

"She said that he leaves everyone for his baby momma, and I don't want to be added to that list."

"Girl, fuck his baby momma, and fuck his friend. She's just mad he's not with her. I don't like that funky bitch," Lay says.

"Yes, she is. They dated back in college, and he left her to get back with his baby momma. I understand why she's mad. If he gave her what he gave me, I'd be snapping out at anyone he talks to, too," I say.

"How do you even know if he still loves his baby mom?" Cody asks.

"I asked him."

"What he say? Girl, I asked you for details about the night, spit it out!" Lay says as I sit up.

"Nothing happened last night. I told him no sex, and he respected my request."

"He didn't even try to rub the tip on your butt when y'all were in the bed?" Cody asks.

"Nope. He slept on his back and honestly, I wanted to jump on top of him every time I looked at him and smelled him, but we just slept. He went out and got me breakfast in the morning, and his friend, the one that brought up that baby momma stuff last night, came to the room and apologized to us."

"Oh, yeah. That nigga's dick good," says Lay.

"Exactly, so after she left, I asked him about his baby mom. He told me some stuff, but I don't think he was telling me everything. Anyway, I asked him if she still loved her and he said she's his child's mother and he's going to always love her."

"So, was this before or after you had sex with him?" Cody asks.

"After, why?"

"So, you still slept with him even though you knew he still loved his baby mom?" he asks.

"Yes, I know, I know, but he was looking so sexy in his black tight briefs when he started dancing,"

"Dancing?" Cody interjects.

"Briefs?" Lay adds.

"Girl, keep going. We'll come back to that last part. What happened next?" Cody asks.

I tell them every detail; how I couldn't resist, so I put my hands in his pants because I just had to know was it all dick or just big balls. It was all dick! I had to have it. I tell them how I sat on his lap, rode him like I never rode anyone before. I was so turned on by him, his lips, and his body that I wanted him deeper inside me, and I swear, when I pushed him back on the bed his penis went up in me an extra two inches. Even though it's been a long time since I've had sex, it didn't hurt at all and the fit was amazing.

"He fills me up," I sing in my Whitney Houston voice and they both fall over laughing. I tell them how he touched everything inside of me. It seemed like his penis knew exactly where my G-spot was and it made itself at home, moved in, and didn't leave. The climax was unreal and lasted for a long time. Just as I thought he was about to give out on me, he picked me up and put my back against the wall. Him using his strength to hold me up turned me on more. I came back to back like 8 times on that wall, but I didn't want him to know he was putting in that much work, so I tried my hardest to keep it in, but the man is a beast.

He kept going and wouldn't stop, pushing it in me deeper, and yet, was so gentle as he held me up. I wanted to have his babies, it was so good. I had to tell him to cum before he would have me crying in there. It was the best I ever had in my life. It must have been really good for him too, because when he came, he came hard. He made me feel like I was the best he ever had. He started biting my shirt and let out the sexiest strong manly moan that made me cum again.

"My panties got wet just listening to that," Lays says.

"Right, can we turn on the air, because I'm getting hot," Cody adds.

"I just don't know what to do, and that's why I was crying. He got me all in my feelings."

"Girl, fuck his baby mom and the college girl. Fuck them all! You made that tall, sexy, grown ass man moan and bite his own shirt. No worries. You got this," Lays says, comforting me.

"Yes, girl. Have fun. It's only been a month or so. Keep getting that cherry popped just in case you have to wait another few years," Cody says. They laugh and I throw pillows at them.

"We got to go, y'all." I get dressed, we pack up, and head downstairs to check out.

Let It Be

Sean

-ding ding- Incoming Call from Twin

Me: Hello?
Twin: Yo, where you at?
I jump up.
Me: Shit, what time is it?
Twin: 12:30. We all down here waiting for you.
Me: I fell asleep.
Twin: I told you not to take a nap! Now get up and come on!

I get up and grab my stuff, bird bath it real quick, get dressed, and head out. As I'm running to check out so I don't have to pay for an extra night, all I hear is clapping and smartass comments from my crew.

"Aye, there he go!"

"Old man needed a nap."

"Late night, early mornings?"

In mid-run, I spot T. I run over to her, kiss her, and then take off running again.

Everyone says "Aww," like children. I laugh and then trip as soon as I get to the counter.

Tiff yells, "I saw that." I make it just in time and won't be charged for another night. After I pay, I bend down to grab my bags and look up to see T walking over to me.

"Thanks for letting me borrow your clothes. I was tempted to keep the shirt," she says as she hands them over to me.

"Thanks, and here," I say, giving her back the shirt. "Think of me when you're alone," I reply as I take my other clothes and take her bag off her shoulder.

"Let me get that for you," I say to her before yelling at the rest of the group, "All right, let's go! Move it!"

"Now you wanna be in a hurry…" Tiff says as she walks behind me and jumps on my back.

"Happy birthday, boo!" she adds, kissing my cheek repeatedly. Then Kels comes over and hugs me, and then Mally, then Twin. James and Joe embrace me in a big bear hug, and we damn near fall over.

They all scream out, "Happy birthday!" The love and the comfort we get from our friends is always joyful, and I'm blessed to have all of them. After the group moment, we head out to the cars. I put T's bags in her car before heading off to my bike. As I pull off, T pulls up beside me and rolls down her window.

"You never told me you had a bike," she says.

"Well, now you know. You wanna ride, or are you done riding for the day?" I wink. I don't think any of them were expecting me to say that because they all opened their mouth wide in shock before they started laughing. T tells Lay to drive, and she hops out the car and jumps on the bike. I take off my helmet and give it to her.

Before she puts the helmet on, she says, "I can ride all night long, but the question is will you run out of gas?" I laugh. I like that answer. I can feel her comfort level with me and she's able to be her true self. She puts her arms around me and grabs my dick and I can't help but laugh.

"Well, that depends on how fast you wanna go." I pull off fast and she screams.

We all drive over to the beach bar, and after eating and drinking, we all go on the beach and sit around a fire pit that the bar has. It's the perfect day. One of the best birthdays that I had.

Me and T sit in the same lounger and talk, sleep, and watch the waves for about four hours. Everyone else would come and go, walking on the boardwalk, taking walks on the beach, or putting their feet in the water, but we just sat there holding each other, kissing each other. I watch the sunshine in her eyes and the wind blow through her hair. She kissed my face softly and even blew in my eye when sand went in it. I feel like a teenager again and I don't want to go home. When the sun sets, it was time to go. Before I walk T to her car, she walks the boardwalk with me to find some saltwater taffy for Lil Sean.

"You're such a good dad. I bet he thinks of you as his superhero," T says.

"He's my superhero. No matter what happens in my life, he's always there to brighten it up." She smiles and she dazes as she looks at me.

"What?"

"Nothing, I just love the love you have for your child. I wish all fathers were like that," she says. We walk in the store and grab Lil Sean's taffy and head back out.

"So, what's your baby daddy like?" I say as I take her hand and hold it. Feeling the breeze from the ocean water as we walk back down the boardwalk to our cars.

"Well, we were on and off for 10 years. He broke it off when I was about 25, Sky was 9 and a half. A few months before our wedding, he decided to be with someone else. He moved out our apartment, went to Delaware with the mother of his two other children that I didn't even know about, and married her a year later. He only talks to my daughter, maybe, once every two years," she shares.

"Whoa… before your wedding, though?"

"Yes. Crazy, right?"

"I never even got to planning my wedding. I asked Makayla to marry me the day our son was born, and she said yes, but three months later, she left, leaving the ring behind. I remember it so clearly because it was the day before my mother passed .

I can still feel the pain thinking about what that time of my life brought me. The day she left my heart was broken, but the day after she left, the day my mother passed, that day almost killed me. Man, that day was so cold that my soul was numb. The skies were dark, and it rained all day. The two most important ladies of my life were gone; one couldn't answer my calls ever again, and one just wouldn't. That day, I tried my hardest to be strong for Twin and since all of our friends and the family came over, I was able to keep my composure, but as soon as I got home, it was a different story.

Lil Sean cried nonstop. I swear, I tried everything to get him to stop, but he just wouldn't. I couldn't give him to his mother, and I didn't have my mother to help me through it like she had in the past. I was a new father; I didn't know what to do, and not knowing made me feel even worse. You would think something would let up but it didn't.

The lightning strikes were bright, and the thunder got louder. Lil Sean started screaming to the top of his lungs, turning red in the face while the rain hit the windows hard as if hail was coming down. I held him and rocked him, but he wouldn't stop. Alarms on my phone went off for weather alerts and my anxiety kicked in. I laid Lil Sean down and paced the floor as he screamed. I felt hopeless and became agitated, so I snapped. I yelled at him. My three-month-old. I told my baby to shut the fuck up. I blamed him, I cursed at him. I slammed the door and left him in the room by himself. I took my keys and walked out the front door.

The rain fell like buckets of water, the wind snapped tree branches, and the ground flooded. By the time I got to my car, I was soaked. I was so angry, and my heart was filled with so much pain and hurt. I jumped in the car and I threw the car into reverse and as I went to pull off, I looked back and saw my son's empty car seat. I immediately hit the brakes, making my tires skid. *What was I thinking?* I put the car into park right where it was. I jumped out the car and ran back in the house to my son. He was still screaming, so I ran in the room. I took off my soaked shirt and picked him up. I frantically kissed him and repeatedly told him I was sorry. I held him tight to my chest, dropped to my knees, and started singing the song that my mother always sang to me when I was upset–Lee Ann Womack's "I Hope You Dance."

As I sang, tears flowed from my eyes. I rocked him back and forth as I broke down. I didn't cry that whole day, but when I released the pain I had, I felt like a weight lifted off my chest. Maybe he felt it too, because he stopped crying. As I finished the song, the rain let up and, in that moment, his tiny hand wrapped around my finger. Tears continued to fall as I realized we both had all we needed. We had each other.

"Wow," T says, staring deeply in space.

"I know, but nine years of being in your child's life, and you leave her? That's messed up on a different level. I'm sure she had some many questions," I respond.

"Yeah, a lot of questions and tears. It's been rough, but she has become an amazing young woman and I'm so proud of her," she adds.

"Well, I'm sure you're an amazing mother and she's amazing because of you."

"Thank you, and I try," she says, giving a cocky hand gesture. By the time we make it back to the car, it is nightfall and Lay is asleep in the car. The hardest thing to do is say goodbye right now. The weekend has been great.

"Well, I guess we gotta go our separate ways now," I say.

"Ugh, already?" she says, chuckling. I move in close, tuck her hair behind her ear and look deep into her eyes.

"Thank you for coming out. I really appreciate it. I had fun," I say.

"Thank you for having me. I really had a great time too. I'll see you at work tomorrow?" she asks.

"Nah, I took off tomorrow in case I came back late tonight."

"Smart. I should have done the same."

"How far out are you? I ask her.

"About 20, 25-minute drive."

"Oh, so you're out here."

"Yeah. Here, give me your phone."

I give her my phone and she puts her address in the GPS.

"See? Twenty-four minutes. I'll be home in no time."

We kiss, hug, say goodbye, and then I close her car door and she pulls off.

Before I leave, I save T's address since it's obvious she wants me to have it. As I ride home I feel so good inside. I owned the road on my bike. Going fast, passing cars, I just feel so alive. I get back to my apartment around 9:30. I take my helmet off and text her while still sitting on my bike.

9:35pm

Me: Thank you again for a great weekend

9:38pm

T: Your welcome, hopefully we can do it again

T: All of it

9:39pm

Me: :) I would love that

9:40pm

T: lol Good night Mr. Johnson

9:40pm

Me: Good night Mrs. Anderson

When I walk in, there are balloons, banners, cards, and a cake. Makayla and Lil Sean planned a little surprise party for me, but unfortunately, my son couldn't hang and fell asleep. I go to his room, kiss him on his head, and leave his candy on his nightstand. As I walk back down the hall into the living room, I yell out to Makayla.

"Aye yo, thank you for all this. This is nice. I'm touched," I say to her.

"You're welcome and happy birthday," she replies. I thank her and admire the party decor. "How was Atlantic City?"

"It was cool. Same ol' same ol'. You know how the crew do."

"Yeah, I'm sure y'all got wasted."

"You damn right," I say, laughing.

"Well, it's not over yet. Wanna take a few shots, play cards, or eat cake? I don't know… just chill like we used to?" she asks.

"Yeah that would be fun," I agree before I can even think about what could happen. What would this lead to?

Hey, it's my birthday. What's meant to happen, will happen. We take a few to the head, smoke an L, eat cake, and play cards until we fall asleep on the sofa. This birthday is one of the best birthdays in a long time.

The next day, I wake up sick as a dog. I don't know if it was something I ate or if I was drunk, but I feel horrible and have the shits. Makayla offers to take Lil Sean to school and pick him up for me, so I go back to bed while she gets him ready.

-ding ding- Text from T

7:45am

T: Good Morning love

7:50pm

Sean: Not such a good morning

8:00am

T: Aww what's wrong

8:15am

Sean: Im hella sick right now

8:16am

T: Oh my, Im so sorry, what's the matter

8:17am

Sean: Not sure, but my stomach is doing something crazy

8:19am

T: Awwww poor baby I wish I could make you feel better

8:22am

Sean: I do too!

8:25am

T: Well get some rest and I'll call you and check on you later

8:30am

Sean: Ok thank you

8:35am

T: xoxo

I go to sleep and wake up around 11, and I talk to Twin on the phone. She tells me she will come over later to check on me and will bring Sean home. I go back to sleep and wake up again an hour later to a knock at the door. I drag myself out of bed to get up and answer it. It's Makayla.

"Hey. You feel any better?" she asks, walking in and touching my head.

"Not really."

"You're a little warm. Come on in the kitchen. I brought you some meds." I follow her into the kitchen and sit on the stool.

"Here," she says, feeding me two spoons as if I'm a baby. It feels good that she's caring for me like she is.

"Twin is coming over later. She said she would bring Sean home," I tell her. She says okay, kisses my face, and tells me to lay back down, so I do just that and go back to sleep. I don't know what's in that medicine, but I don't wake up until 3:30 p.m. and feel so much better. When I wake up, I notice that my phone isn't next to me. I walk in the living room and Makayla is laying on the sofa, watching TV.

"Hey," I say.

"Hey, you feel better?"

"Yeah, thank you."

"You're welcome." As I get closer, I see that my phone is on the floor. Confused on how my phone ended up out here, I say nothing about it. I pick it up and walk in the kitchen. As soon as I sit down and before I can unlock my phone, Makayla gets up and stands in the doorway.

"Who is she?" she asks me.

"Who is who?"

"T. The girl that's been calling you all day." She crosses her arms and stares at me.

"You went through my phone?"

"No. I didn't want the phone to wake you, so I took it out of the room."

"Oh." I look through my phone and notice that T called about three times and texted a few times, but none of the texts had been opened, so I know Makayla didn't read any.

"So, are you going to tell me?" she asks.

"She's a friend. Why does it matter?"

"Has she met my son?"

"Your son? I laugh. "No."

"Well, do you like her? Seems like she likes you a lot by the way she's been calling and texting, asking if you're okay. And no, again, I didn't go through your phone. I didn't fully read any of your texts. I just saw what popped up," she explains.

"We are friends. What's it to you? You the one fucking niggas in my Jeep." I look her up and down, walk out of the kitchen and sit on the sofa.

"Listen, I made some messed up decisions, but I'm trying to right my wrongs. I just want you to be honest with me."

"I am," I say. She walks over and sits next to me and touch my face.

"Sean, I want us to get back together."

"Why? Because some girl is texting me? Why do you do that?" I ask.

"Why do I do what?"

"Every time you think I'm talking to someone, you wanna pop back in my life, be here for a few months, and leave again. What's the point?"

"Sean, that's not true, and it's different this time. I really want to be with you. I miss you, I miss Lil Sean, and I miss us being a family. I'm so sorry for hurting you, but I'm trying to be better this time. For us," she says.

"You're always sorry, Makayla, and when your done being sorry, you run off again. You can't keep doing that. You're not only doing it to me, but you're doing it to your son, Kay! You're fucking son! You don't know how it feels to have him ask for you and I don't have anything to tell him," I respond.

"I know, I know, I swear I know. That's why I've been trying and working hard to do better."

"No, you don't know because you're not the one here to deal with it. Kay, you left me by myself when he was three months. Then, my mother died, and you didn't even show up, call, help me out, nothing!" I don't know why I was bringing up so much stuff, but all I know is that I was ready to let everything out.

"Baby, I know, and I regret that every day I live, I swear I do. I should have been there; I should have always been there. You just don't understand. I love you. It's hard to sleep, it's hard to eat. Shit, Sean, it's hard to even live without you!" she pleads.

"This is a lot right now." I get up to walk back into my room and she stops me, drops to her knees, and cries out to me.

"Babe, I'm so sorry! I'm a fuck up, but I love you and want to spend the rest of my life with you." She reaches into her pocket and pulls out the ring I proposed to her with.

"You keep this in your nightstand after all these years. I found it over the weekend. I know you love me, and I know you want what I want. Don't walk away from me, please," she begs.

"Kay, come on. Get up. You don't have to do all this."

"Yes, I do. I hurt you and I hurt my son, and I can never change what I did. but I can fix it now. Ask me, Sean. Ask me to marry you again, and I'll never take it off." She's still on her knees, now begging and crying even harder. I've never seen her like this before. She has never begged me to be with her before. Shit, she never had to, I just always took her back. I help her off the floor.

"You said we would always be a family. Remember, you told me that?" she says.

"Yes, I remember."

"I want to be that family, Sean. I want you. I want my son. I want everything we have worked so hard for. I promise I will never hurt you again, I swear on my mother." I pull her close to me and she cries on my chest. A few tears start rolling down my face because I can feel her pain.

"Shhh. Stop crying." I kiss her head and hold her face with both of my hands and wipe her tears with my thumbs.

"Kay, I love you with every bone in my body, and I've waited for this day for a long time–my whole adult life to be honest," I tell her. I take the ring from her and place it on her finger, and we both continue to let our tears free.

"You're right. I have been holding on to this ring hoping to get the chance to ask you again. I used to wake up in the middle of the night, take it out, and just look at it, missing you and wanting you to return home." She smiles and wipes my tears.

"So here, Kay. You keep it. You look at it and miss me. You miss what we had, because it's time that I let it go. It's time I let all of this go. I can't do this anymore, Kay." Her face drops and turns sickly.

"No. No. Baby. I'm sorry. Please!" She begins to shake.

"No. Kay, I'm sorry." She looks at me with shock and tears rolling down her face, then grabs her stuff off the sofa and walks out. I sit on the sofa and can't believe I just did that. Am I wrong? Did she really mean it this time? No more than two minutes later, Twin and Sean walk in right after.

"Daddy! Daddy! You feel better?" He runs and jumps on me.

"Yes, much better. How was school?"

"Fun. Can I have some taffy now?" I laugh and tell him he can have a few pieces since he already ate dinner at Twin's house and he runs to his room, giving me and Twin some time alone.

Twin standing in the hall and walks over to me.

"So, what just went on in here? I saw T driving out when I pulled in, and I saw Makayla getting in her car as I was parking.

"T? T wasn't here. She's never even been here," I say.

"You sure? I saw a girl that looks just like her drive out, Sean. It was her."

"Nah, it can't be. She don't know where I live."

"She was in a black car?" Twin asks. I shake my head and tell her T drives a white SUV.

"Oh okay, well someone in this complex looks just like her." She shrugs. "So, then why was Makayla here?"

"She took care of me all day," I say.

"I guess y'all will get back together soon." She shakes her head.

"No. that won't be happening," I say.

"Oh really?" she responds, looking like she doesn't believe me.

"Makayla just begged and cried for us to get back together, and I told her no. I gave her our old engagement ring back and all." Twin sits next to me, now shocked.

"Wait, you said no? No to Makayla?"

"Yeah." I smile at Twin.

"Are you lying to me right now? Are you serious? When–no–why… wait, what the hell?!"

"I know. I did it, Twin. I really did it. I put all the history aside and really thought about the now and what makes me happy. Twin, I'm free," I say.

Twin grabs my face and starts kissing my cheek.

"Ah!! I'm so proud of you! Thank you, God!" She points to the sky. "You're a real one." I laugh.

"Oh my God, Sean," she says with her eye narrowed. "You're in love, baby boy."

"No, I'm not. I just think it's time for a change."

"Nah, nigga. You're in love. You're straight up in love with T! I knew it!" She claps her hands and paces back and forth, smiling.

"I mean, I wouldn't say all that. I like her a lot, but that's it," I add

"You said no to the woman you've loved your entire life for her. That's love. Damn, boy she put that cougar on you – that 'had a baby at 16' snatch, the Harriet Tubman ran away love, I's free now kitty." I laugh, sit back, and smile.

Maybe I do love her. I don't know. I know I haven't felt this way about anyone for a long time. There's something about her I just can't put a finger on; it wasn't just her sex, it's something else. I mean, the sex is a major part, but not the only part.

The next day, I go to work, and I can't wait to see T and tell her everything that happened yesterday. I called her last night, but she never answered. I figured she was busy or something, I mean she is HR and all. As soon as I walk in, I head straight to her office and there she is, looking all good, classy and educated. I say hey to the other people in the office before I knock on her door.

"Hey, Sean," she says real dry as she keeps working. Not the kind of reaction I'm looking for, but I know she's busy. I walk over to her, grab her hands from off her keyboard and sit on her desk.

"Is it too early for me to tell you I missed you and want you to go to lunch with me today?" She lets go of my hands, quickly gets up, and closes her door.

"Well, I guess you missed me too. Where you want me at?" I ask jokingly as I lay back on her desk.

"You can't just come in here and sit on my desk or ask me out to lunch, Sean. No matter what happens between us, I'm still a human resource supervisor, and I take my job seriously." She grabs a file and sits back down. Maybe the job is stressing her out.

I get off her desk. "I know, I'm sorry. I wasn't thinking. That was very unprofessional," I say.

"Yeah, it was," she snaps back. Feeling confused, I stand there for a second, now afraid to ask her anything.

"So, lunch?"

"No, Sean."

"Dinner?"

"No. I just don't think this will work. We work together, and it's unprofessional. I don't think us talking is a good idea, and honestly, I'm just too busy right now to have my focus on other things."

"Um, yeah sure. I get it. Okay, yeah. Well, I'll see you around."

"Yeah."

I walk out her office with so many questions. Why is she so upset? Was it because I missed her phone calls? I feel my heart rip out of my chest, and it's hard to breathe. I wish I would have waited until lunch time to talk to her because now I have to go the whole day feeling fucked up. Damn, what happened? I thought we were good. Shit, I dismissed Makayla for her. What the hell was I thinking? I can't focus for the rest of the day. How did we go from a perfect weekend to this?

After work, I go to pick Sean up from Twin's house. When I walk in, Twin has a big smile on her face.

"So, did you tell her you love her?" she asks, as she blows kissy faces.

I plop down, feeling defeated. "No. She broke it off with me."

"What!? What you mean she broke it off with you?"

"She doesn't want to talk to me anymore because it's unprofessional."

"She didn't care about that before; did someone say something?"

"I don't know."

"Did you ask her why the sudden change? I mean, y'all were just talking yesterday."

"No, I didn't ask nothing. It is what it is. It's my fault. Karma, I guess. I broke so many hearts, including Makayla's..."

"Is your heart broken?"

I shrug. "I guess." Lil Sean is asleep, so I pick him up and grab his stuff. "I'll see you tomorrow," I say.

"Sean. Makayla has nothing to do with this. She broke your heart plenty of times before, so don't do nothing stupid."

"I'll see you later," I say and walk out.

The next day is even harder; she doesn't come to my floor, I don't see her in the hall, and as many times as I look on my phone, she hasn't said anything to me. The crazy part is, Makayla is texting me, and the whole time I'm wishing it was T and not her. Once again, I'm in my feelings. I tell myself to pull it together. T and I have no history and had only been talking for about a month. I don't have to take it as hard as I am.

-ding ding- Text from Makayla

11:20 a.m.

Makayla: Hey I know your done with me, but my car is not running right can I use your car to take Sean to the doctor's on Friday? If not ill just take him on the bus.

11:25 a.m.

Me: Yea

11:32 a.m.

Makayla: Thanks, I'll be there around 7am, if you need me to take you to work and pick you up for work I will, his appointment is not until 1030

11:34 a.m.

Me: Its cool I'll take the bike

11:35 a.m.

Makayla: Thanks, and again I'm sorry for all I put you through, I hope that we can still be friends and co-parent.

11:42 a.m.

Me: Ard

The rest of the week is rough. I start drinking every day after work, my sister and friends stop by and chill with me, but I'm just not in the mood. I don't tell them anything. When I'm alone, I walk around in my robe, lighting candles, incense, drinking wine, and singing sad songs. This one really stings.

When Friday comes, Makayla shows up just like she said she would. I take the bike to work and she takes the Jeep. As soon as I walk in this morning, I run into T in the hallway as she is talking to one of her bosses. I don't say hi, smile, or acknowledge that she's even there, and she does the same. So, I guess it's really over with us. Around 3 p.m., it starts to rain, so I call up Makayla and ask her to pick me up because I don't want to ride in the rain and my bike cover is in the back of my truck. When it's time to leave, it's raining so hard, so I run out and cover my bike, Makayla hops in the passenger seat, and I get in the driver's side and take off.

Traffic is hella crazy, and it takes us forever to get home. It's Friday, so I invite Makayla to hang with us. I order pizza and we watch movies and play games. While we are playing Candy Land, I get a call from Twin.

Me: Hello?
Twin: Hey, how you feel?
Me: I'm cool.
Twin: Did you see T today? Did you talk to her?
Me: Nah, I'm good. It's whatever.

Lil Sean and Makayla have a tickle fight in the background, and it gets loud, so I go into the kitchen.

Twin: Who is that?
Me: Who is who?
Twin: In the background playing with Sean?
Me: Damn, nosey. It's his mother.
Twin: Why is Makayla there?
Me: -whispers- She's here with her son, what you mean?
Twin: Is she there for her son or for you too? Sean, don't go backwards, that's all I'm saying.
Me: Drop it, Twin. It is what it is. I gotta go. I'm holding up the game.

I hang up.

After one more round of Candy Land and another movie, Lil Sean is rocked. I put him in his bed and sit back on the couch with Makayla.

"So, what time are y'all going to the water park tomorrow?" I ask.

"We supposed to be leaving around 12. My sister is supposed to pick us up from here, if you don't mind me staying the night." Now I'm thinking this whole day was a set up for her to get back next to me, but the way I'm feeling, I don't even care.

"Yeah, it's cool."

"I'll drop him off Sunday in the afternoon sometime."

"Great. He really loves spending time with you."

"Yeah, I really enjoy it too. I fucked up by not being around and watching him grow." She rubs the back of my head how T used to. She turns my head toward her, slides in my lap, and kisses me. All I can think of is my sister saying don't go backwards. But, fuck it, I'm all in, so I lay her back and climb on top of her.

"Daddy! Daddy!" Sean calls me from his room.

I get up to tend to him, but Makayla stops me and says, "Meet me in the bedroom. I got this," and I do just that. About five minutes go by and she walks in my room and close the door behind her. She drops her clothes before she even gets to the bed. She crawls on top of me, kissing down my chest. All that foreplay isn't happening tonight. Instead I get right too it.

I give it to her and I give it to her hard. I'm forceful and demanding. I'm rough and I want her to feel all the pain she put me through in her chest. For everything that I was trying to build with her, I knock down every wall she has inside of her. I go as hard as I can go and when I think about the past, I go harder. I choke her, I flip her, I spit on her, I pull her hair and I even fuck her in her ass. Everything about this is disrespectful. For everything that was and for everything that wasn't, I am Ali and every time her legs give out, all I can hear is "Down goes Frazier!" I pick her back up and beat it some more. This is for every girl I left behind for her. I keep going more and more, harder and harder until she cries and begs me to stop. I pull out and bust on her stomach. I turn into a monster and I didn't even know myself. I've disgusted myself, but I don't care. She hides her face with her hands and cries, saying she is sorry over and over. I feel nothing–no remorse, no love, no emotion, just an empty sack.

When she gets herself together, she takes her phone into the

Makayla

I walk into the bathroom feeling good but in pain. I check myself. Fuck, he made me bleed and I'm all swollen. I sit on the toilet and cry, not because I'm in pain but because I put him through so much pain. I have to stop my bullshit once and for all. He is my man and can't no one take him away from me. It's time for a change. I open my phone.

6:30 p.m.

Frank: Yo, where are you, I been hitting you all day

10:30 p.m.

Me: I'm sorry, I can't see you anymore, I'm back with my family and this is where I'm going to stay this time.

BLOCKED.

Twin Reacts

Twin

Me: Is she there for her son or for you too? Sean, don't go backwards, that's all I'm saying.

Sean: Drop it, Twin. It is what it is. I gotta go. I'm holding up the game.

Me: Hello? Hello? Sean!?

"Did he just hang up on me? That motha- Ooo!"

"Who hung up on you?" Joe asks.

"My dumb ass brother, that's who. He got Makayla at his apartment."

"Okay, what's wrong with that? Didn't that other girl cut ties with him?"

I roll my eyes because I know he's about to give his two cents where it's not needed.

"Yeah, Joe, but that don't mean go backwards and fall back into Makayla's trap… talking about she's over there to see Lil Sean. That's bullshit."

"Bae, you're stressing out for nothing. Sean is always going to do what he wants to do. He's a grown man, and he's not your problem."

I look at Joe, annoyed. "That's where you're wrong. He is my problem. He's my brother."

"Your brother, not your child. Pop your titty out his mouth, damn," he says, getting up and walking into the kitchen with me.

"Mind your damn business. I'm all he has, so leave me alone

before you piss me off, Joe."

"You're not all he has. He's a grown ass man, Seana. Back the fuck off."

I feel my body instantly become a hot tea pot. He's making the fire so hot right now that I'm about to steam, and when I'm ready to blow, I'm bound to say anything.

"Damn it, Joe! You're a grown ass man, yet you still got shit stains in your drawls. Now who's a grown ass man?" I slam my hands on the table.

"Fuck you. I'm not gon' fight with you over this bullshit. As your husband, I say leave it the fuck alone, Seana," he says as he walks upstairs.

"As your wife, I say wipe your fucking ass, Joe," I yell back at him.

I sit there just thinking about what to do. I'll be damned if he made it this far just to go backwards. What to do, what to do. And there it is, a sign. Lil Sean left his iPad. I grab the iPad off the table, search Sean's contacts, and low and behold, I find exactly what I'm looking for.

Tiera Anderson
562 Alben Lane
Sicklerville, NJ 38029

I grab my stuff and yell upstairs to Joe, "Bae, I'll be back!" then I run out the door. As I'm driving to her house, I try to convince myself that this isn't crazy, because deep down I know it is. I must get to the bottom of why she switched up all of a sudden. Something is not right; I feel it deep down and I must do this before my emotional ass brother does something stupid.

I pull up to T's place around 8:30 p.m.

"Okay, Ms. T. You got bank; two-story house, nice little front yard, a pull in driveway, and cut grass," I say, admiring her house. "See, this is who my brother needs to be with–someone with some goals in life. Here goes nothing," I say to myself. I get out the car and walk up her driveway. Sean was right–she does have a white SUV. Maybe it really wasn't her… shit, well, there's no turning back now. I walk up her steps and ring the doorbell. She opens the door and is shocked to see me.

"Hey Twin, what are you doing here?" she asks as she scans

outside and checks her surroundings.

"Hey girl. I'm so sorry to show up unannounced. I know this may seem a little crazy, me popping up out of nowhere, but I have to ask you a few questions, if you don't mind.

She laughs. "Just a little crazy, but sure. What's on your mind?"

"Okay. On Monday, were you driving a black car?"

"Yes, I had to go get an oil change, so I used my uncle's car while he did it."

"Yes! And did you go to Sean's apartment to see him?"

She hesitated and then said, "Yes. I'm so embarrassed. He told me he was sick, so I looked up his address at work and wanted to bring over some soup. I'm not a stalker."

"So, you're just as crazy as me." We laugh. "And why did you leave?"

"Well I overheard him-"

I cut her off. "That's all I needed to hear. Can we sit down and talk? Is now a good time?"

"Sure, I wasn't doing much," she opens the door wider and invites me in.

"Your house is very nice, T. Go 'head, girl."

"Thank you," she says with a giggle. "Here, we can sit in the kitchen. Would you like a glass of wine?"

"Don't mind if I do, thank you."

"Sure, no problem." She grabs two wine glasses and pops a nice bottle of something I had never tried before. "So, did Sean send you here?"

"Nope, and please don't tell him I was here. He will kill me. Now the reason that I am here–and let's be clear I've never ever done this for any girl Sean has ever liked or talked to– there's something I see in him when he's with you. It makes me so happy to finally see him so happy, and I want to clear a few things up because he is too stubborn to do it himself. He's not only stubborn; he's dealt with rejection for so long, so when it happens again, he just takes it instead of getting to the root of the real problem."

"I can see that," T says glaring at her wine glass.

"So, can you explain what happened on Monday?" I ask her.

"Well, I went to his apartment. His windows must have been open because as I walked closer to his place, I could hear him going back and forth with I guess his baby mom and she was begging him and crying, asking him to take her back. I just couldn't deal with it, so I left.

"Is that why you broke it off with him?"

"Well, not completely. I already knew something like this was going to happen when your friend said he leaves everyone for his ex. So then I hear it for myself, plus I understand how she feels from being in her same shoes years ago. I know what it feels like to beg for someone, hoping they will take you back. I just don't want to be that woman that takes another woman's man, you know?"

"I understand, and you have every right to feel the way you do, but her shoes are extra small, so it's not the same. Sean is not her man. He was her toy she picked up, played with, then put down when she was done. If I explain everything, I think you'll see things differently. Is that cool?"

"Sure. I'm open minded and I have a whole bottle of wine and nothing to do. Where do we start?"

"See, that's why I like you and why I can't let you walk away from this." We both laugh.

"He really has a big heart and can be very selfless. I know from experience that that man would give anyone he loves his last dollar just to make sure they can eat, make rent, or even go to prom." I take out my phone and show T a picture of me and him posing on prom night.

"Wow, you both look stunning," she says with a smile. She examines the picture closer and I can see the love she has for Sean in her eyes.

"He gave me the money for that dress. He worked tirelessly after school every day because my mom couldn't afford to buy us what we wanted. He wanted to make sure that the night was special for the both of us, so he did what he felt he needed to do just to make sure we could have one night of fun."

"That's really sweet," T responds, still smiling.

"I'm telling you this because one, my brother always has my back, so I'll always have his best interest at heart, which is why I'm here. I really want you to understand his and Makayla's history and what being a father means to him. When it all comes down to it, yes Makayla was the love of his life; anything she needed, anything she wanted, he did, he got, and he made it happen. No matter what she did to him, that was his girl, his love, his everything, and he wasn't leaving her. When they had Lil Sean, him never leaving her was now written in stone. Our dad left us, and Sean was never going to do that to them. He would never walk out on her, leaving a broken home for Lil Sean, even if that meant still having a toxic home together. Makayla takes total advantage of that because she knows my brother would give his life for her. I'm sure he has told you, but she has left him so many times. She keeps coming back, and he just takes her back, no matter what."

"So, what Kelly said was true," T says.

"All cards on the table, yes! Kelly blow up his spot. No matter who he's with, when she's ready to come back in his life, he drops everyone for her. He even does it to me sometimes, but I check him. It's like a cycle that never ends, and Lord knows how bad I want it to end."

"So, I was right. I'm glad I broke it off before I got myself hurt."

"No, you weren't. For the first time in 13 years, he told her no, and that he wasn't going to take her back. He did it for you."

T sits silently, trying to think of what to say. "Why me? And how do I know he won't do it later down the road?"

I don't know what else I can say to get it into her head, but I have all night. I sit with T and we just talk. It's obvious that she cares for Sean, so I'm not leaving until I help get them back on track. She mentions that she tried to reach out to him earlier that day through IM, but realized he left and when she went to catch up to him, she saw Makayla pick Sean up in his Jeep. Though that's a shock to me, I assure her that Sean doesn't want her. I can't lie though, in the back of my head, I'm wondering if I'm being honest with T and with myself. She wonders if she'll ever really be able to compete with Makayla, and I tell her that Makayla wishes she was in T's league. We laugh at that, but she still doesn't seem convinced and I'm all out of ideas.

"I don't know Twin, this is a lot," T says, finishing her second glass.

"I wouldn't be here if I didn't think it was worth it, trust me." We are silent for a while, just drinking our wine. I can see the wheels turning and all I can hope for is that she'll consider trying again with Sean.

"Well, I appreciate you coming. I understand a lot more, but I just have a lot to think about now."

"As you should. You have to do what's best for you, but love has no fear."

-ding ding- Incoming call from Tiffy Boo

I excuse myself from the table just as T offers more wine. I eagerly accept another glass and direct my attention to Tiff, who immediately begins telling me about some date she's going on. I let her rant for a few moments before realizing that she might be the key to making this drama go away quicker. I quietly get Tiera's attention and tell her to listen, and I put Tiff on speaker phone without her knowing.

Me: Guess what? You will never believe what happened!
Tiff: What?
Me: Sean told Makayla he didn't want to be with her anymore.
Tiff: Bitch, you are lying! Don't play with my heart like that!
Me: Nope! 100% truth.
Tiff: Whaaat?! Was it for that pretty bitch from Atlantic City?

I hit my head and shake it.

Me: That's the story that was told.
Tiff: Oh girl, he in love!
Me: That's what I been telling him.
Tiff: I can't believe this. He finally left "I'll leave my baby for some dick," Makayla. Hoe ass.

I laugh.

Me: Yes.
Tiff: Oh that pretty bitch must got some good cooch. that shit must be golden. First, he checks Kels, and then tells Makayla to beat it Michael Jackson style. Oh, she got the holy cooch. Sean gonna have to let me lick that. Shit, it may be the fountain of youth.

T shakes her head and we both try to muffle our laughter.

Tiff: Does Kels know? She finna be pissed.

Me: No one knows.
Tiff: Well, I'm about to tell her. I'll call you back.

Tiff laughs and hangs up.

"I'm sorry for the language. This went differently in my mind. She means bitch in a friendly way, but she may really mean the part about licking you," I say with a laugh.

T giggles and says, "It's fine and funny."

"I wanted you to see a real reaction. See, for him to say no to Makayla is rare. It never happens, so please, trust me when I say he really wants to be with you. I knew how Tiff would react, that's why I wanted you to hear it. As far as Kels is concerned, her and Sean are nothing more than friends. She is always going to be his friend, and he loves her like a sister, but he wants you.

"I want him too, and I don't have a problem with them being friends, as long as they keep things respectful, but I still need time to process some things."

"Take your time," I tell her.

-ding ding- Incoming Call from Teddy Bear

"Shit, that's my husband. What time is it?" I look at my phone and see that it's 11:30. "Damn, I have to go. Thank you for speaking with me so late.

"No, thank you for reaching out." T walks me out and we share a few more words.

"Just don't tell him I was here. Also, I think you will make a bomb ass sister-in-law." She laughs and we hug.

"I won't tell him and maybe..."

The Let Down

Sean

The next day when I open my eyes, Makayla is sitting up in the bed, looking at me.

"Um, good morning," I say.

"Good for who? I don't know about you, but my pussy has been pushed up to my throat," she says. I laugh and check my phone on the side of the bed. I have nothing from T, so I throw it back down.

"What? You didn't like it?" I ask as I walk around the bed.

"I didn't not like it, I mean I'm not begging for a round two right now. I just guess I understood it more than anything." I walk out the room and check on Lil Sean. He's still asleep, so I leave him alone and walk back into my room.

"What you mean you understood it?"

"Everything we've been through… all your hurt."

"You got all that just from last night?"

"Shit, I got no walls from last night." She stands up and touches my chest. "But yes, and I'm sorry."

"Okay," I say dryly.

She stands on her tippy toes and kisses me. "I love you."

"Yeah. Love you too." We order breakfast and sit around in our pjs until it's time for Makayla and Sean to get ready for the water park. I honestly can't wait for them to leave so I can be in my feelings. There is so much that I'm feeling, from telling Kay I don't want to be with her, to getting cut off by T, to even the senseless sex I had with Kay last night. When they finally leave, I turn into my mother on a Saturday morning. I put on Anita Baker, light my incense, and clean. I clean the entire apartment from top to bottom. I open up the windows and change all the sheets. I mop, sweep, dust, and vacuum. I light my sage and walk around the apartment from the kitchen to the bedrooms, getting rid of all negative energy in my path. I even pray. I just want to be alone and take time out to forget, forgive, and focus on the next step in my life. Was I really going to get back with Makayla?

As I'm thinking, Mally calls and lets me know he's outside, so I open the door for him.

"Damn, it smells good in here. You got a jawn in here or something?" Mally asks as he walks in with a big case of beer.

"This nigga got the incense burning and shit. You got some bitches coming through for us?" James says, bringing in a tray of hoagies.

"Nah, I just did a little cleaning. What are y'all doing here?" I ask.

"Well, we heard from Tiff that you got rid of Makayla, so we came to celebrate and hear how good that thang is on T." I shake my head, knowing Twin is the one who told it.

"Right. Tiff says she had good good," James says.

"Y'all need to stop listening to Tiff," I reply.

"Well, that's what we heard. Yo, where's my god son? He here?" Mally asks.

"Nah, he just left with Makayla."

"Makayla? Wait.... What, nigga? I thought that was done? Let me find out you smashing both chicks. Mally, you hearing this?" James asks.

"My man's a chiropractor. He stay cracking them backs," Mally jokes.

"Man, me and T are just friends, and yeah, I smashed Kay last night."

"Dilly, dilly, dilly. My nigga dick all over Philly," Mally says, laughing.

"So, did you ever hit in Atlantic City?" James asks.

"Yup, and it was nice too."

"Yo, it looked nice," James adds.

"Word, she looks like a classy freak nasty jawn. She on some Martha Stewart meets Cardi B type shit," Mally says, making me laugh.

"Man, what kind of combo is that?" I say.

"I don't know. That's the vibe I get from her, but if I'm wrong, fill us in on what went down."

"Nah, I'm good."

"Oh, yeah. She was a freak. You don't wanna give out no details. It's cool, it's cool," says Mally. Usually I would go into detail, telling them about jawns I knock off, but T is different. It is strictly confidential, plus, I don't want to get into her cutting me off, so I just move on to something else. I'm glad they came over, though. I know I said I wanted to be alone, but when my guys are around, it's such good vibes. We smoke, eat, knock off the whole case of beer, and enjoy just being. They both leave around 11 p.m., after the beer is gone. I am full, tipsy, high, and ready for bed. I get in bed and am rocked.

-Knock Knock-

I wake up and look at the clock. It's 1 a.m. Who the hell is at my door at this time?

-Knock Knock-

I slowly make my way towards the door. "Who is it?" I yell from the end of the hall. I can hear someone say something, but it's faint, so I open the door, and it's T. I'm shocked as all fuck.

She says, "Is it too early to say I missed you?" using the same words I said to her on Tuesday.

"Nah," I laugh. "Not at all." She comes in and kisses me, and I'm still shocked.

"Wh- what are you doing here?" I stutter.

"Um, I guess you can say I was in the neighborhood."

"Oh uh, well… come in." As she steps over the threshold, I stop her. "Wait… How do you even know where I live?"

"I have my ways."

"Well, shit. I don't even know what to say," I say. She walks over to me and kisses me again, but this time, it's long, soft, and passionate.

"I'm sorry. I was just scared, and I overheard-"

I cut her off. "It don't matter," I grab her and kiss her again and again. When I see that these kisses are about to turn into something else, I stop her.

"Wait."

"What's wrong?"

I pace the hall. "I-I just wanna be honest with you before this goes any further."

"Okay."

"I had sex with my ex on Friday. It didn't mean anything, it just happened." She nods, and I can see the disappointment on her face. She backs up towards the door.

"Do you still want to be with her?"

"No! No, not at all. Not if I could have you." She turns and walks to the door.

"Did you wear a condom?" she asks with her back towards me.

"Yes. Hell, yes. I did every time since my son was born." Her hand is on the doorknob and I just know she's about to leave. Shit, that's what I get for trying to be honest. That honesty shit doesn't work. She locks the door and turns back around to me.

"Well, that's your last time," she says, not asking but demanding in her boss lady, HR voice.

"Yes, my last time."

"Is your son asleep?"

"Nah, he's not here."

She holds out her hand. "Show me to your room."

I take her hand and do just that. As soon as we get to my room, it's a go. Clothes come off and we fall into bed.

We roll around in the sheets for hours. Kissing, touching, and licking every inch of each other's bodies. Places that I never let anyone touch before, she touches them. She tastes me and I taste her. We both bring the sun up with the thunder of ecstasy. The explosions of passion that we experience are like thunder crashing in a tropical rainstorm. The physique of this pleasure is strong and masculine, yet calm and feminine. Our formation is an art piece, a pottery class where we shape our love. Yes, we are making love. We use our hands and mold each other until we both take form into one another. It's on another level. We levitate into another galaxy once her volcano irrupts over and over again and my shooting star breaks into her atmosphere. I crash into her ocean, causing a tsunami that washes up on her shore, cooling off her lava. The steam of her love turns my past into ashes and dust, and it all fades away. Once the smoke clears, we stay, and we lay as the light shines on us from the sun. The sweat on her skin simmers like diamonds in the sand.

Even though we are up all night, neither one of us falls asleep. Instead, we stay up talking, laughing, and enjoy being in each other's company. I play with her hair, and she plays with my hands. We touch and notice everything about one another.

"You hungry?" I ask her.

"Yeah, I could eat. I guess it is breakfast time already, huh?"

"Shit, I don't know what time it is. It's probably lunch time." We both laugh, still holding each other like nothing else matters.

"I'm surprised you're still hungry," she says with a smirk.

"What you mean?" She grabs my chin and brings me in for a kiss.

"Because you ate a lot," she says before licking my top lip and then sucking on my bottom lip.

"Don't start nothing you can't finish."

"Oh, I can finish whatever I start."

"Oh, is that so?"

"Very much so."

I kiss her, and as I lay on top of her, I hear my front door open, and I stop.

"Did someone just come in?" she asks.

"Sounds like it, right?" I stay still and listen to the footsteps get a little louder. "Twin?" I yell out.

"Yea fool, it's me. Who else would it be," Twin yells back.

I get up out of bed quickly, throw on my shorts, walk out the room, and close the door behind me before Twin has the chance to bust into my room. I walk into the kitchen and see Twin bent over stocking my fridge with food she had brought from the market. She really is the best sister. I walk in and kiss her on the cheek and ask her what she is doing here so early. She stops what she is doing, looks at the oven clock and then back at me and asks me if I knew what time it was. I peek over to the clock. Damn, it's almost noon. I can't believe how long me and T have been up. I'm honestly still not even tired. As she sticks her head back in the fridge, she asks me what hoe had me up all night. I sit at the table, smile and wait for her to finish. If I wasn't so tall I would swing my feet because I'm so excited to tell her.

As soon as she closes the door she asks, "Who, and you better not say Makayla…"

"Nope."

"Then who?" she asks and I smile. "T?" she asks and I nod my head.

The way her mouth drops, I can tell that she is in shock. We both do a little quiet, excited dance in the kitchen like I just scored a touchdown in a football game and we both laugh. After our victory celebration, Twin grips me up by my shirt and brings me down to her level and tells me that I better not hurt her. I reassure her that I won't before she lets go. Twin tells me she is leaving and tells me to hurry back to T, since she has been in the room by herself. Knowing that Twin hates for me to order out so much, I ask her if she could make us breakfast before she goes. She confirms that she has in fact just brought and stocked my fridge so that I could cook my own food, so I poke out my lip and make a sad face. She rolls her eyes and agrees. I kiss her and say thank you before I head back to my room.

Once in the room T asks, "Did you tell Twin I was here?"

"Yeah."

"What did she say?"

"That she's going to make us breakfast."

"Aww that's sweet, well let me go help her" She get's out of bed and begins putting on her clothes.

"Bae, she's cool. She got it."

She looks back at me and smiles. "Bae? I'm Bae now?"

"Yeah, or you can be something more…"

"More," she says as she crawls back on the bed.

I pucker my lips for a kiss and she mushes my face. She reaches in her purse and grabs a wash cloth and a toothbrush.

"I see you came ready," I mention, impressed that she came prepared.

"If you stay ready, you don't have to get ready." She winks and walks out. When she comes back, she kisses me and leaves out again. After about five minutes of laying in the bed, smiling like a fool, I also get up, wash my face and brush my teeth, and walk into the kitchen. The girls are talking it up and drinking coffee. T offers to make me a cup before I let them know that I don't smell any food cooking and they both brush me off. I don't mind though; I just enjoy seeing my two girls get along. It's very stressful when the person you're in a relationship with doesn't get along with the other important people in your life, especially your twin sister.

Since I know that Twin isn't really going to let T help anyway, I put some Whitney on the record player and pull T out of the kitchen to dance with me. She tries to deny me and gets all shy, I guess because Twin is there, but I eventually get her to dance with me.

After a few songs, Twin brings us our plates and we all sit down, eat, and enjoy each other's company while Nina Simone softly plays in the background. After we eat, we sit there for a least another hour talking about different things that's happening in the world and Twin tells T that I can cook and to not be fooled or manipulated into accepting takeout all the time. As we laugh, there is a knock at the door, and I instantly get nervous. It slipped my mind that Makayla is dropping Lil Sean off.

When I open the door, Lil Sean comes flying in with Makayla right behind him. I grab him by his shirt before he can get past me and I pick him up and demand hugs and kisses as I tickle him and he screams. Makayla, looking down at her phone, tells me she has brought me food and walks into the living room and immediately stops.

She nods and says, "Seana."

Twin coldly replies back, "Makayla."

"Um… Makayla, this is Tiera. Tiera, this is Makayla, my sons' mother," I say as I sweat a little.

"Nice to see you again," Makayla says. I'm instantly confused about when they met. Am I missing something?

"Likewise," T replies and the room is silent for a few seconds.

Twin breaks the ice by calling Lil Sean over to her and introduces him and T to each other. The air is very thick.

Makayla turns to me. "So, what's good? This your girlfriend now or something?" she asks with an attitude. I look at T because I really don't know what to say. We haven't confirmed anything yet.

"So you need confirmation now? Is she your girl or not?" Makayla snaps at me.

"Yes, I'm his girl," T interjects as she takes a sip of her coffee.

Makayla laughs. "She talks for you now too, huh? Well that's funny because how are you his girl when he just fucked me Friday night?"

Twin scoffs and shakes her head.

"Makayla, let's go outside," I suggest.

"Nah, does your girlfriend know we had sex just a day ago? Does she know you told me you loved me, and that we are forever a family?"

"I know," T says boldly. "But we weren't together then, so it is and will be irrelevant to me." Her comeback is nice, and it even turns me on. I walk to the door and open it, motioning for Makayla to follow me.

"Makayla, come on." We walk out, and I close the door behind me.

"So, you gon' sit up here and tell me that this bitch is your girlfriend?"

"Watch your mouth. All that is uncalled for, and yeah, she is."

"Watch my mouth? Nigga, you just fucked me like you was insane on Friday and I took that shit for you! Now you gon' tell me to watch my mouth when I'm speaking about another bitch?"

"Look, I'm not gon' tell you again."

"And what the fuck you gon' do Sean? Hit me? Yo, I cried to you. I got on my knees. I left niggas for you and this is how you gon' do me?" she screams, clapping her hands together as she talks.

"Makayla, I told you I was done with this shit. This cycle has gone on for years and I'm over it."

"So, you're giving up on your family?"

"Don't you dare fucking say that. I was the only one trying to keep this family together while you were out fucking every nigga from west to northeast Philly." I can feel the pinned up hurt come out as I express myself. The audacity of her to even try to use that against me.

"I fucking love you, yo! She don't! We got history–years! Why her and why now? What the fuck she got on me? I had your son and you're just going to throw it away for some bitch you just started fucking? You pussy whipped now, Sean? Is that what it is?"

"No."

"Then what the fuck is it?" I stay quiet and shake my head. I want to tell her but I can't bring myself to hurt her by letting her know.

"Oh, now you don't have nothing to say, huh. You stuck on her fucking left titty. What the fuck is it?!"

"I fucking love her, Makayla! Damn!" Her face drops even harder than it did when I told her we were over last week, but this time she doesn't walk away.

"You love her?" She walks to me, pushes and punches me in my chest. "Fuck you mean you love her?" She tries to hit me again but I grab her hands and push her back but she continues to walk up on me and get in my face. "You love her, Sean? You don't even know her! How the fuck you love her and you just fucked me? You sound stupid! I should pick up one of these rocks and bust you in the fucking head."

"Listen, my days of explaining shit to you is over. It is what it is, so deal with it. Go home or wherever you end up going when you leave. This should be easy for you." I turn my back and head in, and I feel on top of the world.

"No, you deal with it. I'll see your ass in court. I'm taking custody of my son, pussy." I turn back to her, breaking my emotional high and laugh.

"Oh, that's how you gon' try to hurt me? By fighting me for my son? That's funny. Try to take my son if you want to. I'd like to see it. Be my guest."

I begin to walk off again and she says, "Who said he was yours?"

I stop dead in my tracks and walk back over to her because my mind can't process what she just said. I'm not sure if I heard her correctly.

"So, you trying to tell me my son isn't mine?" I ask, my voice cracking in the middle of me asking.

"That's what I said."

I guess Twin's been listening through the window because she comes running outside with fire in her eyes.

"Bitch, what you mean he's not his? You had my brother taking care of a kid who's not even his while your dusty ass is in the streets?" Twin screams as she dashes towards Makayla, while putting her hair up in a bun.

I grab her so she doesn't do anything crazy. "Twin go in the house."

"No, because I'm about to really kick this bitch's teeth down her throat. Three years, Sean! You've been that boy's father and now she's saying you may not be!" Twin says while trying to fight to get past me.

"Twin, relax!" By this time, Makayla has walked to her car and is getting ready to hop in without explaining herself.

I yell over to Makayla, "So, if he's not mine, who else could he belong to?" She smirks and walks back around the car.

"It don't matter now, Sean. He already has his father's name as a middle name." When I think of my son's middle name, I feel like I'm having a heart attack. It literally feels like my heart has stopped beating.

"Mike!" Twin yells. "Bitch, you fucked his best friend?! Nah, let me go! I'm really about to fuck her up!" Twin yells as I hold her back.

"Go in the fucking house, Twin!" I say and I push her back hard. I have no more energy to keep holding her.

I walk up to Makayla, who is trying to take off, and I grab the door just in time, snatch the keys out her hand, and throw them across the parking lot.

"You fucked Mike, huh? My best fucking friend?"

"Yup. A few times and Lil Sean, or should I say Lil Mike, just may be his," she says with a smile and sassy tone. It takes everything in me not to punch her in her face, body slam her on the hood of her car, and choke her out, but where will that lead me? In jail, losing my son to her, or even losing T because she thinks I beat on women.

"You wild," I laugh. All I can do is laugh because I'm pissed right now. "You ain't shit. My friends told me you wasn't shit."

"I told you she wasn't shit," Twin yells!

"Twin!" I yell back at her.

"My own mother told me you wasn't shit. In fact, she told me to get a blood test the day Lil Sean was born, and I didn't. I couldn't believe that you would ever do something like that to me."

"Well, maybe you should have listened to her. She was a smart woman," Makayla says coldly.

"But when you left, I didn't know what to believe anymore, so I had Sean tested at four months, and he is 99.98% mine. That's my boy." I bend down to her eye level and say, "Even though I would like to take your head and bust it through your car window, I won't. I have everything I need, and I know everything I need to know, so get the fuck out of my parking lot, you dusty bitch."

"Fuck you!" she screams before she spits in my face. In one swift motion, I wipe off the spit, snatch her whole body out of the car by her shirt, and grip her up on the car. At this point, I don't care about shit.

Twin runs up and says, "Stop, Sean! She's not worth it! I'll beat her ass for you. Let her go!"

"Twin, go in the damn house!"

"Okay, okay. Listen, I swear I'll go in the house, just let her go, please! Don't hurt her!" Twin says.

"Go 'head, Sean. Do it. Hit me. You mad, right? I fucked up your life, right? Do it. I know that's what you wanna do," Makayla says, sounding defeated. As much as I want to fuck her up, I just let her go, pushing her back and she falls back into the car. Twin grabs me.

"Bitch, you come back around here, and ain't no holding me back. I'm beating you the fuck up!" she says as she walks me back to the house. Kay gets out to get her keys and quickly pulls off. Once we get back inside the house, I see that Sean is sitting with T and they are drawing something together. When T sees me, she rushes over to me.

"Are you okay?" she asks. I tell her I'm good and I try to walk past her, but she grabs my hand and pulls me back towards her. She touches my face, looks directly into my eyes, and tells me she loves me too. I hug her, holding her tight as I tear up, not because I'm sad, but because I finally feel the release I needed. Maybe that's what I've been longing for–to finally be set free. I'm at ease now as T holds me and we share this moment. She rubs the back of my head and doesn't move or let go until I'm ready.

"Hey, I'm going to take Sean, so you can have some time to process some stuff," Twin says.

"No, leave him," I say, brushing her off.

"You sure? You good?"

"Yeah. I wanna spend time with my boy." I look down at Lil Sean, who looks up at me, and I smile.

"All right, then. Call me if you need me."

"Sure thing. Thank you for having my back."

"Always," Twin says as she leaves. Me, T, and Sean spend the rest of the day together. T and I officially confirm our relationship and we tell Lil Sean, together. After T leaves, I let Lil Sean sleep with me for the night. Just knowing that he could have been someone else's child makes me hold him a little tighter tonight. I wouldn't be who I am today without him.

9

A Different Vibe

Sean

T and I have been together for two months now. I must say, everything is way better than I could imagine. I enjoy seeing her every day at work.

Last week, she surprised me. I was on the phone with her all night and after we hung up, she texts me, asking if Lil Sean was asleep. I told her he was, and she told me to open the door. When I did, she was standing there with whipped cream in one hand, strawberries in the other hand, and she was wearing a long coat, looking amazing in her heels. She walked in, handed me the whipped cream and strawberries and asked me if I missed her.

I said, "Hell yeah," and she opened her coat. Underneath, she had on this sexy silk black bra and panty set. Without hesitation, I dropped the stuff on the table in the hall, and pinned her up against the door and kissed her. After remembering that Sean was in my bed, I quickly tucked him in his bed. When I walked back out to get T, she wasn't there. I went into the kitchen, and she was sitting on the countertop, legs crossed, and licking whipped cream off a strawberry. Instant hard on. I took her down right there on the counter, then we moved to the sofa, then finished off in my bed. I had never done so many positions in one night–it was crazy–and every position worked for both of us. I swear, she is made for me; my fit is just too perfect to believe anything else.

I woke up around 5 a.m., and I saw that she wasn't there. My initial thought was that she just treated me like a whore, but then when I went to check on Lil Sean, there she was, rocking him back to sleep in my robe. Honest to God, I haven't seen anything sexier in my life. My son had woken up in the middle of the night and tried to climb up in my bed like he usually does, but he woke T up and when he saw her, he went back in his room. She said she felt bad that she was in his spot, so she put my robe on and went in his room to go get him but ended up rocking him back to sleep. She is everything, you hear me? Everything. She's the total package.

Today is the day I meet her daughter for the first time, and I'm hoping everything goes well. I never really let Lil Sean meet anyone, let alone meet anyone else's child, but tonight, T is cooking dinner for all of us. This is not the first time I've been to T's house, just the first time we are all going to be in the same house together.

When we pull up to T's house, we are instantly greeted with a hug for Lil Sean and a kiss for me. T tells us to make ourselves at home in the living room while she prepares dinner, so we watch some TV to keep busy.

"Bae, you want a beer?" T yells from the kitchen.

"You got beer?" I ask, a little shocked.

"Yeah, for you," she says, opening the fridge, grabbing one and taking off the top for me.

"Sure," I say, walking into the kitchen. "I could have opened it," I say.

"It's fine, baby. I got you." I pull her close, kiss her, and thank her for the beer. As I'm kissing her, her daughter walks in the front door. I lean over the counter and T goes back to cooking.

"Hi." She waves to me. "Hey, Mom."

"Sky, this is Sean. Sean, this is Sky, my college girl." I walk over to her and shake her hand.

"Nice to meet you, Skylar."

"Likewise," she says dryly, sounding just like her mother.

"Big Man, come here," I call, prompting Lil Sean to run into the kitchen. I pick him up and introduce him to Skylar.

"This is Ms. T's daughter, Skylar."

"Hi, Skylar."

"Hey cutie! He's so adorable," Skylar says as she gushes over Sean.

"Thank you," Lil Sean and I say at the say time. I look at him adoring his manners and we all laugh.

"Skylar is studying child education at West Chester, babe," T explains while taking out food from the oven

"Dope. My sister studied the same thing."

"Cool… Well I'll be back. I'm going to put my stuff up."

"Okay, hurry up. Dinner is done." T says. As Skylar goes to leave, Lil Sean speaks up.

"Can I go with her?" he asks.

I laugh. "You don't even know her." He shrugs his shoulders, causing us to laugh.

"Yes, you can come with me," Skylar says, and reaches her hand out to him. He jumps down and runs over to her.

I throw my hands up. "You just going to leave daddy?" I ask him, pretending to pout.

"Yes," he states. I should be used to his matter-of-fact nature, but that stings a little.

"Wow, okay, fine. Go ahead," I say. Skylar takes his hand and they go upstairs. When T adds her finishing touches, she lays everything on her large dining room table for everyone to help themselves, and I feel like I'm a part of a family TV show. Smothered pork, turkey chops, mashed potatoes, and asparagus sit in the middle of the table and everything tastes amazing. Even Lil Sean eats all his food. I'm surprised that he preferred the turkey chop over the pork chop and he actually ate all his asparagus despite never having it before. I guess my son is on the uppity side, because he never eats the basic broccoli or string beans I make him. After dinner, T serves us warm apple pie and ice cream. You couldn't tell me we weren't the Huxtables or something, and I, for one, can get used to this.

Throughout the entire dinner, I try to connect with Skylar when Lil Sean isn't stealing the show.

"Three of my closest friends and my sister are teachers. What kind of teaching do you want to do?" I ask Skylar.

"Teach kids," she replies dryly.

"Oh… okay… is there a certain grade you want to teach?"

"None in mind," she responds quickly. She continues to answer me with one or two-word responses, and she barely even looks at me. It's clear that she doesn't like me or doesn't want me around. After dessert, Sean goes back upstairs with Skylar. Apparently, her hobby is painting and drawing, and she and Lil Sean paint and draw on her canvas together, which is great, because I get to spend time with T and not chase after him.

T pours us a couple glasses of wine, lights her candles, and turns on her electric fireplace to set the mood. This is the most romantic shit I've ever experienced.

As she hands me my glass and takes a seat next to me, I blurt out, "I don't think Skylar likes me."

She laughs and says, "She doesn't like anyone I date. She's overprotective. You have to give her a chance to warm up to you." She sits her glass on the table. "She just met you."

"Yeah, I guess you're right."

"Not everyone you meet is going to fall in love with you," she says with a smirk as she slides onto my lap.

"You're something special, you know that?" I say as she smiles.

"You already had me in bed, so what could you possibly want by telling me that?"

"You. Just you," I tell her, tucking her hair behind her ears. She puts her arm around me and kisses me. We talk and cuddle for hours. I put some old school tunes on her speaker and have her slow dance with me. After two bottles of wine, I decide it's time for us to go. It's already midnight, and I don't want to keep Sean out any later. T goes to get Sean while I get our stuff together, but she comes right back without him.

"Sean come here," she waves me over. She leads me to Skylar's room, and when we peek in, we see that both are knocked out, and the Disney Channel is on in the background.

"Looks like he had a good time," she says.

"Right. I'd hate to wake him." I whisper.

"Then don't. Stay the night," T says, wrapping her arms around me.

"You sure? Will your daughter be okay with that?"

She cocks her head back. "Does she pay bills?"

"Well, I didn't pack an overnight bag, and I have to put a pull-up on Sean, in case he pees."

"I got toothbrushes, wash cloths, and we can put a pull-up on him. Any other excuses?" she puts her hand on her hip.

"Well, my grandma-" I begin.

She jokingly hits me. "Shut up and go get the pull-up," she says. I go out to my car and grab Sean's bag. Luckily he has PJs and extra clothes in his bag, so he is all set. I head back into Skylar's room to get Sean dressed for bed, but Skylar is up and she is helping T undress Lil Sean.

"Hey, do you mind if he sleeps in here with you?" I ask Skylar.

"Yeah, he's fine," she replies.

"Okay, cool." We all work together to get Sean ready for bed without waking him. I tell Skylar that she can bring Lil Sean to me if he wakes up in the middle of the night and she agrees. Once they're settled, T and I head to T's room, where we also get dressed for bed. She turns on the TV, which is shocking.

"I thought you didn't watch TV before bed?" I ask her.

"I don't. You do, but don't get used to it," she says with a smile as she hands me the remote and cuddles up on me. Man, she is perfect, I swear. I push her hair back off her face and kiss her forehead. We don't do anything, and honestly I don't even mind. She lays in my arms and I hold her until morning.

When morning comes, there's a knock on the door and in comes Lil Sean, holding Skylar's hand. He runs over to me with a smile on his face.

"Hey Big Man, did you sleep good?" I ask, picking him up.

"Yes."

"Did you thank Skylar for letting you sleep in her bed?" He thanks her and I check his pull up to see if he peed and it's dry.

"Big Man, you didn't pee! Aye, that's my big boy! Give me five!" He gives me a high five and smiles. I take him to the bathroom because I'm sure his bladder is full.

"Remember what I told you?" I ask him.

"Put the seat up," he says.

"Right." I'm having a proud dad moment. Even though he's only three, he has learned a lot. When he's done and flushes, he goes to walk away. "Hey, what I say? When girls are around…"

"Put the seat down," he finishes. After putting the seat down, he washes his hands and says, "Good highteens keeps the Earth clean, Daddy."

I laugh. "That's my man. It's hygiene though, but you got it right. I'm proud of you." I pick him up, give him a kiss and tickle him. We walk back in the room, where T and Skylar are sitting on the bed, smiling.

"Lil Sean, you want to help me make breakfast?" Skylar asks.

"Yeah!" Lil Sean yells happily.

"You gon' leave Daddy again?" I ask.

"I sorry daddy," he says, hugging my head.

"That's okay, go 'head." I put him down and he runs to Skylar. She picks him up and walks out as they both scream, "Breakfast!" walking down the hall.

"When girls are around, put the seat down?" she says, laughing.

"Yes, I'm trying to teach him to be a gentleman."

"You two are so adorable."

"We try." She pulls the covers back and pats the space next to her. I jump back in bed and she climbs on top of me.

"It's kind of turning me on," she says, kissing me softly.

"What about the kids?" I ask. She gets up, locks the door, and holds her hands out for me to follow her.

"They are cooking, and they won't hear anything if we are in the shower."

"Shower?" I raise my eyebrows up and down

"Yes," she says as she licks her top lip. I rip my clothes off before we even hit the bathroom. With the steam coming from the hot shower, the water falling on us from her rainfall shower head, and the sweat from our bodies, we make love, and it's better than the last time. After our shower, we make our way back in her room and she lies on top of me, and as I caress her beautiful body, we enjoy just being. She kisses my chest, my nipples, my neck, my forehead, my cheek, my ear, and my nose. Where has she been all my life? How can this perfect woman make me feel the way I do? As we cuddle, there's a knock on the door. Lil Sean tries to open the door, but it's still locked so he just says that breakfast is ready.

"Thank you, I'll be down in a min. I'm getting dressed now, so go eat." T and I get dressed, but I quickly realize that I don't have any clean drawers to put on.

"Damn, I guess I gotta free ball in my jeans," I mention. She laughs and kisses me.

"Go look in my top drawer," she tells me.

"Why? I'm not wearing none of your ex's clothes."

"Just go look in the drawer, please." I get up and look in her drawer, and there is a brand new pack of underwear, new t-shirts, and a few pairs of lounge pants, all my size, and all my favorite brands.

"Who's stuff is this? You seeing someone on the side?" I joke.

"No, crazy. It's yours. I brought it for you in case you ever needed it whenever you slept over."

"If you stay ready, you never have to get ready, huh?" I say to her and she laughs. I walk back over and push her back on the bed. I touch her face, count her fingers, and put my ear up to her knees.

"What are you doing?" she asks, still laughing.

"I'm checking to see if you're real. This is so new to me, so I have to check." She takes my hand and puts it between her legs.

"Is that real?" she asks.

"Oh yeah, that's real. Wait, I'm not sure… I have to taste it to make sure." I go down on her and lick it. "Oh yeah, that's real good," I say before going back down. She moans, fighting to keep quiet, and pushes my head back.

"Stop, Bae. We have to go eat."

"I was about to eat." I go back down again, but this time she just laughs and pushes my head away again.

"Get dressed," she demands.

"Fine, fine." We get dressed and just as she walks past me, I grab her hand and pull her close. I look deep into her eyes and then kiss her hand.

"Go away with me," I tell her.

"Sure."

I look at her, shocked. I wasn't expecting a straight answer.

"What? Why are you looking at me like that? You didn't think I would say yes?" she asks.

"I thought you would ask a few questions, at least."

"I shouldn't have to. It's with you," she says, kissing my cheek.

"You really are something else."

"I am." She smiles as she walks out the room.

"So you got your passport?"

She stops right before she walks down the steps, turns around, and smiles. "No. We're going out the country?" she asks.

"I don't have one either, but of course. Why, what were you thinking?"

"I don't know; Maryland, Florida, something in the states. I've never been out of the country before." As we walk down the hall, I grab her hand.

"Me either, but I want my first time to be with you," I tell her. She smiles and seems just as excited as I am.

We don't end up going away until the middle of September, since we both had to wait on our passports, and because the summer wasn't over and T could spend it with Skylar before she went back to school.

I used half of the money I was saving for a house to pay for our entire trip, but T is worth every cent I had. We arrive at Jamaica on a Friday and stay until Monday. It's a quick getaway, but we enjoy it to the fullest.

The heat is on a different level in Jamaica; I swear, they got a whole different sun than the one we have back home, but it's beautiful.

We stay at a beautiful resort called Sand Castle Dreams, which is all-inclusive. We have an enormous suite that leads to a private mini infinity pool and just a quick walk down is a beach. It's a little expensive, but it's perfect. We are so impressed with our room that we spend a lot of time there. Anything we wanted, drinks or food, we call our butler. For the first two days, all we did was wake up, drink, make love, eat, drink, make love, get in the pool, drink, make love, eat, drink, make love again, walk the beach, drink, make more love, eat, drink and sleep. Oh, and I had little Ms. Human Resource take back an L with me; it was only right since we're here. At this moment in our relationship, we've done away with condoms, and T is on the pill, so the feeling of making love is 50 times better than anything I ever had before and it was just something we couldn't go without.

On Sunday, our last full day there, we do it all. We start out with a 5 a.m. boat ride to watch the sunrise and eat breakfast. Next, we go hang gliding, climb the Dunn's Waterfall, go parasailing, fall off jet skis, ride ATVs, kiss under a different water fall, have dinner at sunset on the beach, and then end the night with a boat ride out to the Luminous Lagoon to watch the ocean glow from the microorganisms in the water.

After that action-packed day, making love isn't even a thought; we go straight to bed. Our flight isn't until 5 p.m. Monday night, so the next day, we go shopping for souvenirs, spend some time on the beach and then in our pool until it's time to leave. Overall, I've had the best time of my life, and I think she did too. I'd say I spent close to $7000 on this trip, and if you ask me if I would do it again, I would in a heartbeat.

10
Accepting Responsibility

Sean

Tonight, we officially go public about our relationship. The boss, Ms. Tracey, is hosting the annual winter ball and you have to be someone, know someone, or be friends with someone at the top to get invited, and T is my ticket in. Yup, my lady is a boss herself.

It's been eight months so far with me and T and I can't be thankful enough. She has shown and given me more in these past eight months than my ex did in the past 13 years, or anyone else for that matter. She spends most of the time at my apartment when Skylar is away at school, and we go to her house any time Skylar comes home. My son loves to be around her, and he even calls Skylar his big sister. Skylar still hasn't fully come around to me yet–she is still keeping her distance, but I have made her laugh in front of her friends a few times with my foolish dancing, so I guess that's a start.

-ding ding- Incoming Call from Bae

Me: Yes, love?

T: Bae, what time are you getting here?

Me: I'm on my way now.

T: But how long, Bae? We're already late and it's 45 mins away.

Me: Stop it. We are not late. You're just always early. I'm pulling up now.

T: Okay, I'm unlocking the door. Got to go put my shoes on.

Skylar offered to watch Lil Sean tonight, and when we walk in, she and her friend are in the kitchen.

"Okay Mr. J, I see you," Lizzy says.

"You see me?" I say, spinning around and strutting into the living room like a model. I have on all-black with a maroon velvet dinner jacket, a maroon velvet bow tie, and a clean, semi-shiny prestige oxford shoe.

"Stank, come give me my hug!" Skylar says reaching out for Lil Sean. He runs over to her and she picks him up.

"I know my dad's number! Wanna hear it?" Lil Sean asks Skylar.

"Oh, wow! That's so good! Yes, tell me."

"215-555-1431," Sean recites. I smile knowing that my son is light years ahead of other kids his age.

"That's so good, Stanks," Skylar says.

"He will tell you about 100 more times before the night is over," I tell her. I walk to the bottom of the steps and yell for T to hurry up. She was just rushing me and now I'm waiting on her. She yells back that she's coming, and I check my watch because now I'm worried we're going to be late.

"Wait until you see Mom," Skylar says to me. She didn't give me a compliment, but it's cool. We're not there yet.

"Oh, before I forget," I reach in my pocket and pull out $50 and give it to Skylar. "I know you said you didn't want any money for watching him, but the least I can do is buy y'all some take out."

"Thanks," she says with a little smile as she takes the money.

"No, thank you," I say back.

Skylar asks Lil Sean and Lizzy what they want to eat, and they come to a consensus–pizza, wings, and milkshakes.

As Sky calls in the order, T walks down the steps. Damn, she looks good as hell. We've never been to a suit and tie event, so this is the time I'm seeing her all glammed out like this. She has on a long-sleeve, long maroon velvet dress, with a deep V cut down her chest, and a slit up the front that comes up to her knees, black closed-toe high heels with the back open that matches her purse perfectly, and a diamond necklace. Her hair is down and curled, just like I like it with some hair tucked behind her right ear to show her diamond earrings. She's my Mona Lisa. I bow at her feet when I see her, and she laughs.

"Why do you always have to play? Get up, you're going to get your pants dirty."

"Wow, Bae. You look captivating. Damn!" I say as I bite my fist.

"Thanks, love. Let me check you out though," T says as I spin around.

"You are one good looking man. Got your hair all cut, beard all trimmed up and, wait… She sniffs me. "Is that the new Dior I smell?"

"You know it." I put my hands in my pocket and pose.

"Oh, you been shopping, huh? Out here looking and smelling like a snack," T flirts as she steps closer for a kiss.

"Oh my–just get together. Let me get a picture of y'all," Skylar says. After our photo shoot, we head out. The Jeep is washed, cleaned, and waxed, I'm looking good, my lady is looking incredible, and we are ready.

We arrive at the hall exactly at 8:30. I can tell this will be fancy because there is valet parking only. From the time we get out the car, all eyes are on us. There are a lot of people I don't know, but a few faces I recognize, including my hating ass manager, Sarah. She's the reason I joined the leadership program–so I could get out from under her and have a real opportunity to advance.

"Bae, over there. Let's see what table we are sitting at," T says to me. We walk over to the table where everyone is picking out their name cards and table numbers. As we try to find our names, Sarah walks over to me.

"Sean?"

"Hey, Sarah."

"What are you doing here?" she asks with a little nervous chuckle.

"Same as you. We're here for the Winter Ball, right?"

"Right. So, who are you here with?" T turns around.

"He's here with me. Hello, Sarah," T greets her somewhat coldly.

"Tiera, hi! Don't you look dandy."

"Thank you, Sarah. Likewise."

"I see the leadership program was invited this year. That's so amazing!" Sarah says with this fake enthusiasm. T and I look at each other, knowing good and well that Sarah is agitated that I'm there.

"You know, Sean here…" She pats me on the back. "He is one of my top preforming employees," Sarah admits.

"Oh, is he now?" T asks, pretending to be interested.

"Yes. He's a very talented young man, I must say." Right at that moment, Tracey walks over.

"Oh my God, look at this fabulous couple! You guys look stunning," Tracey says.

"Oh, I didn't know you two were a couple," Sarah says, pointing at us, taken aback.

"We really don't broadcast our love, but yes, we are," I tell her.

"Hey, Tracey. Sarah was just telling me how Sean is one of her of her top employees," T says.

"Is that so?" Tracey asks interested.

"Yes, one of the best," Sarah says through her teeth.

"Well, I guess we are going to have to look into the reason why he didn't get the position he applied for. It was for a lead, right Sean?" Tracey asks in an upbeat and cheerful voice.

"Yes ma'am," I reply.

"Well-" Sarah starts to defend herself, but Tracey cuts her off.

"Excuse me, Sarah. I need to borrow these two." She takes me and T by the arms and we walk off. What a boss ass move. I guess that's why she's the boss.

"How did you know about the position?" I ask Tracey.

"I know everything, honey." Tracey explains. A smile spreads across my face and it feels great knowing I have the head honcho in my corner. "You have to watch out for that one. Trust me, they don't like when one of us is in charge, and they get even more pissed when they can't do a damn thing about it. Am I that right, T?"

"Definitely," T says

"If you have any more problems with your advancement, come talk to me," Tracey says.

"Yes ma'am." I nod.

"Now you two go enjoy yourself. Tiera, I'll grab you when John comes in. I want you to meet him." T agrees and Tracey walks off to greet the rest of the guests. I look at T, who has a sly smile on her face and I know it was her.

"So y'all are in cahoots, huh," I ask her.

"Something like that," T says and walks away. Damn, she's so sexy when she's being professional, and I love watching her walk in this dress. Oh yeah, she's getting all of it tonight.

"Bae, come on! Let me introduce you to someone." I walk over to our table. My heart drops to my shoes. How…wait…what? "This is Brittany, one of our newest supervisors. Brittany, this is my boyfriend, Sean. He's one of our marketers." Brittany stands up and holds out her hand for a handshake, and I'm stuck. T bumps me.

"Yeah, hi. Hello, Brittany," I say, stammering. She shakes my hand and I can tell there's just as much confusion going on in her head as there is in mine.

"Hello, Sean. Please excuse me, I need a drink," Brit says before walking away.

"Well, okay! That sounds like a good idea. Bae, what do you want? I can go get it," T says.

"Vodka straight."

"Oh okay, you feeling cute. Do you want it on the rocks, Mr. Johnson?" I laugh and she leaves to get our drinks. About five mins after T leaves, Tam shows up.

"Sean?"

"Hey Tam." I get up and give her a hug, "What you doing here?" I ask.

"Brit invited me," she responds.

"Oh, right. Obviously," I say. The night is just full of surprises, and I can't take another. "Well, Brit went to the bar."

"Yes, I already know her whereabouts, thank you, but Brit did not mention that you two were acquainted again! How wonderful is that?" Tam mentions, genuinely excited.

"Yeah, how wonderful is it, Sean?" T asks as she stands behind me holding our drinks.

Fuck. "Bae, umm this is Tam, Tiff's sister. Tam, this is Tiera, my girlfriend."

"Oh- oooooh! Well, hello, Tiera. It's very nice to meet you."

"Likewise. Sean, can I speak with you for a minute?" I agree, but I know I'm about to walk into a storm. T doesn't make it obvious, but she's mad as hell and she's about to let me have it. She excuses us from the table and leads me out of the party.

"Are you serious right now?" she hisses.

What?" I ask, pretending to be innocent.

"You dated one of my employees?!"

"Bae, that was before you…" I do my best to ease the situation, because it's as messy as it sounds, but T doesn't bite.

"So, you couldn't give me a heads up about who you dated at the company?" she asks me.

"I didn't even know the girl still worked here! After I called it off,

I never saw her again. Even when I tried to reach out, she didn't respond."

"When did you try to reach out to her?"

"A long time ago, Bae. That's done and over with. There's no need to worry."

"I'm not worried. Should I be since you're reaching out to people?"

"Yo, T, you gotta chill. Relax, baby," I say, grabbing her arms and pulling her close to me. "That's been over, and it was nothing. Can we just go back in there and enjoy the night?" I kiss her on the cheek.

"Is there anyone else at the job you dated?"

"No, I promise, and the only person I would want to be here with tonight is you," I say. She stares into my eyes and I know she can tell I'm sincere. Finally, she gives me a quick peck and fixes my bow tie.

"Fine," she says, "But we will finish this conversation later." Though I'd rather leave it in the past, I agree, and we go back to the table which is now full. We eat, drink, and mingle and between Brit being on her phone and T leaving the table to make introductions, me and Tam bust it up.

After the meal, the DJ plays all the classics, but no one dances until he plays my jam, Al. B Sure's "Off On Your Own." I sing to T at the table and she smiles. As aggravated as she was earlier, she is loving the attention I'm giving her now. Tam starts dancing in her chair, and Brit gets up and walks away. When the second round of the chorus drops, I stand up and reach for T's hands, and she laughs, shaking her head.

"No, there is no one out there," she says.

"So? Are you here with them or are you here with me?" I challenge her. She shakes her head.

"Get out there!" the white guy at our table tells us. He and his wife pipe me up, and now I'm more confident than I was before.

"Get out there wit'cho man, chile," Tam says. She's been drinking, so she's less proper. I sing louder and threaten to get louder if she doesn't come with me. Eventually she agrees to join me, but still fights it as we make our way to the center of the dance floor.

"Why do we have to go all the way out here?" she complains. She looks around, feeling embarrassed and self-conscious, but I pull her close and stare into her eyes.

I tell her, "Because I want everyone to see how beautiful my lady is," and she is sold with that line. By the time, the DJ has changed the song to Zapp's "Computer Love", so we slow dance and I sing to her. She nestles her head in my neck, so I spin her. She smiles but is still being very shy. I look around the room and all eyes are on us as they watch and adore us from their seats.

Tracey shouts, "Yes! Get the party started!" as she grabs her husband and brings him out to the floor. Soon, everyone is making their way to the floor.

"See, Bae. We made this happen," I say.

"No, Bae," she laughs. "This is all you, and this is one of the reasons why I love you." I smile and keep singing and grooving with my love.

Five songs in, and T has to go to the bathroom, so we leave the floor. As T walks to the bathroom, I notice Brit walks out, so I follow her. When I get outside, B is smoking.

"Can I get one of those?" I ask.

She takes one look at me and scoffs. "You don't smoke… not this, anyway…"

"True, true…" We remain silent for a few moments, but I have to get what I'm thinking off my chest. "Listen B, if I hurt you in any way, I truly apologize. For the record, I really did get back with my baby mother, but it just didn't work out."

"So, now you're fucking my boss," she says as she blows out smoke.

"Well, yeah. I guess you can say that. I'm sorry if this whole thing is weird. Honestly, I didn't even know you still worked here."

"Yeah. The day you broke it off, I got accepted to become the overnight supervisor. I thought it was pointless to tell you."

"Congrats. You deserve it."

"Thanks." She glances at me and smiles a little. "We had some good times, huh?"

I laugh and chuckle. "Hella fun."

"And I must say… y'all are kinda cute together."

"Yeah, we are," I say tooting my own horn.

"Don't push it," she says, stubbing out her cigarette. When she looks at me, we both laugh. It feels good to see her smile, and even better knowing that we're all good.

"I really am sorry though. For real. If I knew you still worked here, I would of never-"

"You would have never found happiness, and it seems like you have," she says with a smile. I smile back and give her a hug. She still smells as good as she did before. After I hug her, I turn to leave and I see T standing at the door, watching us. I know this can't be good. I walk in the door and she doesn't say anything, she just looks at me and walks away. I hurry to catch her, but I'm not trying to make a scene, so I speed walk. As we get back inside of the event, I grab her arm.

"Bae, stop it's not what you think."

"Then what is it, Sean? Because it looks like the first chance I walk off, I catch you hugged up with her, so what the f-" T stops when she sees Tracey and greets her.

"Tiera, this is Gordon, the Human Resource Manager for Dallas," Tracey says.

"Nice to meet you," T says with a fake smile plastered on her face.

"And this is her boyfriend, Sean. He works in our marketing department." I put my hand out and shake his.

"The party starter," he says and I laugh.

"I guess you can say that," I reply.

"That means you take initiative. That's a good thing," he says.

"Thank you," I say.

"Well, I have to walk him out. Sean, save me a dance. I want to see what you got!" Tracey says as she walks out.

"I got you," I yell back.

"You got everyone, don't you… Who else you got?" T says, rolling her eyes before she walks back toward the table. I must say, she switches up very easily. It's almost natural for her. As we sit down, I get a FaceTime. It's Lil Sean calling from Skylar's phone. I ask if he's okay because he rarely ever calls me when he's with Skylar, but he only called to ask if he could have some candy. I agree and tell him to only call me if something is wrong. As we are talking, Tam asks to say hi since she hasn't seen him in a while. While she is talking to him, she lets Lil Sean say hi to Brittany. You can hear the excitement in his voice when he sees her; after all, for a short time, she was a part of his life. I think to myself, *Damn, my son is going to grow up with woman issues stemming from all the disappearing women from his childhood. I have to do better.* Brit calls him Big Man and asks him how he is doing, and I know that will cause a problem because no one calls him that but me.

I try not to turn T's way as they talk on the phone; I don't want to catch her eye, but I can already feel the heat coming off her on the side of my face. Then Lil Sean asks Brittany if she was with me, so I quickly take my phone back before he can ask any more questions. I turn the phone to face T and tell him that I'm with her. They say hi to each other and smile before I end the phone call.

"Sean, he has a great vocabulary for three," Tam compliments.

"All because of Twin. She teaches him new things every day." T gets up, and I grab her hand before she walks off.

"Where are you going?" I look up to her as she stands.

"To the bar," she says coldly. I stand up to go with her, but she tells me to stay.

"Is she all right?" Tam asks.

"Yeah, she's good," I say as I follow her over to the bar.

I call her name to get her attention as and she immediately snaps at me quietly. "I thought you said you didn't let Lil Sean meet any of your…" She comes closer and whispers, "… little fucks."

"He met B, but that was all," I say.

"So, she was more than just nothing then."

"Tiera, why are you freaking out about something that happened so long ago?" I ask.

"Because you're telling me it was nothing, yet she met your son. He knows her by name, and it's clear she's spent time with him. She even calls him what you call him, so it seems like you're lying or hiding something," T snaps as she grabs her drink and walks back to the table. As she walks away, the DJ calls for requests, so I do something I have never done before. Since I know T is feeling some type of way, and this is supposed to be a night that we both enjoy, I go up to the DJ and request a song but I tell him I'm going to sing it. I can actually sing, but I never use my real voice while singing around people because it was something I always did with my mother. Besides Twin, no one knows I can sing. Well, everyone I work with is about to find out.

I tap the mic. "Good evening, everyone."

Everyone turns around and the spotlight is on me. I want to run, but I have to finish what I started.

"I want to dedicate this song to the most beautiful girl in this room, tonight. I think everyone already knows who she is." The DJ plays "Good Night" by John Legend. The music starts and I snap my fingers and find my groove. I get chills down my back as I bring the mic closer to my lips. Here goes nothing. The entire room is in shock that I can sing, but T is surprised the most. I look dead at her and sing every word to her like no one else is in the room. When I catch her smiling, I get another boost of confidence and I hop off the stage and walk up to her.

People pull out their phones and record, T and Tam included. Everyone claps and dances, but I never take my eyes off of T. I dance to the song and pull out my best vocals for her. It isn't my song, but the way I'm singing it and by the way everyone is into it, you would have thought it was my concert. By the end of the song, everyone is singing along to the chorus with me. I head back to the stage just before the song was over. I replace the mic back on the stand, say thank you and take a bow. I hop off the stage again and rush back over to T. People pat me on the back and tell me how good I was as I make my way through the crowd, but I don't care about any of that. I want to know what she thought.

She has a big smile on her face and I see she's impressed. "I guess you've been hiding something after all. You never told me you can sing!" T says. "You never sing like that when we are in the house. Where did that come from?" she asks.

"I was saving it for the perfect time," I reply. As she kisses me, some lady walks by and gets T's attention.

"You're a lucky lady. I wish my husband could sing like that," she said with a chuckle. "You sound great, young man."

"Thank you," I say.

Tracey walks over saying, "Okay, see, now you have to come to all the parties, even the ones not work-related." We all laugh.

She turns to T. "I like him," she says and winks.

"Yeah, I kind of like him too," T responds, staring at me.

"Well, keep him," Tracey says, giving me a high five before walking off.

Tam asks us to pose for a pic, and then we head back out to the dance floor. We dance for the rest of the night and I even get that dance with Tracey. The night started out rocky, but end the end, it was a success. We leave around one in the morning. When we get in the car, I check my phone and I can tell Tam sent the video she took of me singing because my group chat is blowing up. I have 78 missed messages. As I look up from my phone, I notice that T is staring at me.

I laugh. "What? It's my group chat."

"I don't care about your phone," she says.

"Then what?"

"Oh, nothing." She says turns her head to look out the window. I grab her hand and kiss it.

"What are you thinking about, love?" I ask.

"If I ask, will you answer me honestly?" She turns to look at me and I nod.

"Was she good?"

"Oh my God, Tiera. Are you kidding me?"

"Bae, I just want to know. You asked me what I was thinking. That's what I was thinking."

"Out of all the things you could have been thinking about, that's what's on your mind?" I question.

"Was she?"

I look at her, start the car and pull off. "Yes, she was, if we're being honest."

"Oh, okay." She stares out the window.

"See, now you're upset. Why would you even ask a question like that if you didn't want to know the answer?"

"No, I'm not upset, honestly…" she asks me a few more questions, probing me about my relationship with Brit, and I am honest, but I assure her that no one holds a candle to her.

"Bae, yes. She was a good fuck, okay? But making love to you is something more, something special. I crave your body, your touch, and you as a whole. So yes, I fucked her, yes it was good, yes she met my son, and he even liked her, but no, she hasn't had my love the way I give it to you mentally, emotionally or physically."

"You mean that?"

"We are being honest, right?" I remind her.

"Right… you ever sing to her?"

I groan. "No, T… I never even sang to Makayla, only my mother and sister, and now you. It's only you."

"You really love me, huh?"

"No… I'm in love with you, Tiera." Her face lights up and she puts her hand on top of mine.

"You're definitely getting some tonight," she says with a smile.

*

A few weeks go by and everything is still good. Makayla even came back around, but for Lil Sean, not me this time. She's being reasonable and we are working on this co-parenting thing. We have agreed that she will get Sean every other weekend and so far, so good.

-ding ding- Incoming Call from Unknown

Me:… Hello?
You have a collect call from inmate Skylar Robinson. Do you accept the charges?
Me: Yes.
Skylar: Sean?
Me: Yeah, Skylar, what's wrong?! What's going on?!
Skylar: Can you come get me, please? I was arrested for public intoxication…
Me: Where are you?
Skylar: West Chester Police Department.
Me: All right, I'm on my way.
Skylar: Please, don't call Mom.
Me: Okay. I'm coming.

It's three in the morning on a Saturday, but I quickly get up and head out. Thank God Makayla has Sean this weekend. I take about 45 minutes to get to the station, and when I get there, they tell me her bail is set at $5,000. I only have to pay 10% of that for them to release her, but I don't have $500 on me, so I have to run to the nearest ATM and take it out. When I get back, I have to wait two hours for them to release her. When she sees me, she runs straight to me and hugs me.

"Are you okay?" I ask.

"Yeah, I just wanna go home," she says.

"Jersey home or your dorm?"

"Dorm…" She holds me tight and we walk out the door together.

Once we get in the car, she asks, "Did you tell Mom?"

"No. I wasn't with her and I didn't call her."

"Thank you… I'm sorry I woke you, but I didn't have anyone else to call. I didn't want to call Mom because I knew she would freak out and I tried calling my dad, but he didn't answer. I remembered your number thanks to Lil Sean repeating it 40 times." We both chuckle, but I can't keep the moment light. This could have ended up worse than it was, and I hope she learned her lesson.

"It's no problem… so what happened?"

"Well, me and a few friends went to a party, and yeah, we were all drinking, but I wasn't messed up like them. I was trying to get two of them back to the dorm, but security caught us. They made us take a breathalyzer test, and they said mine was over the limit, so I got booked too."

"Well, Sky," I begin. "I'm not gon' sit up here and act like I didn't party when I was in college because I did and I partied hard, but the bottom line is you shouldn't be drinking at all. You're only 18, and if something was to happen to you, your mom would be devastated. We all would be. Someone could have put something into your drink, you could have gotten hurt or even kicked out of school. So please, and I ask you this from the bottom of my heart, slow down, baby girl. You have three more years. Twenty-one is coming, so don't rush your time. Rushing time only destroys your future… you get me?"

"Yes. I won't, and I promise I will pay you back for bailing me out."

"No, don't worry about that. I got you, and as long as I'm with your mother, I will always have you. Know that."

"Thanks… you really love my mom, huh?" she asks.

I laugh. "You know, you sound just like her... but yes, I really do."

"Thanks again," Sky says as we pull up to her dorm.

"You're welcome, and hey, if you're going to drink, do it responsibly… and get some friends who can hold their liquor," I tell her.

She laughs, agrees to be better, and closes the door.

I roll down the window and shout, "Aye," to which she turns around. "Don't let it happen again, or I'm telling your momma."

"I won't!" she yells back. I wait until she gets in, and then I pull off.

11

The End of the Road

Sean

Two years have passed now. Lil Sean and I moved into Tiera's house after she asked me if I wanted to take our relationship to another level. That was a big step for me, but I was happy to do it, plus Lil Sean still got his own room, so everything worked out perfectly.

We are officially a family. The kids already call each other brother and sister, Tiera treats Sean like he's her own son–they even go out on mommy-son dates, and ever since I bailed Sky out, we have been the best of friends. I brought her a four-wheeler like mine and Lil Sean's for her birthday and we ride out together. She really enjoys it, and she is fearless.

She texts me just to tell me about the problems she's having and always asks for advice. I really feel like a father figure in her life and I love every bit of it. Everything is perfect on the home front. However, not so much with Makayla. She flipped out when I told her me and Sean moved. She started begging for us to be together again, but I'm happy where I'm at. T began feeling uneasy when Makayla started texting often and calling wanting to speak to me, so I remind her daily that I'm in this relationship until the wheels fall off.

I've been secretly taking driving classes after work to get my CDL to drive for Best Trucking since they make more money than I currently do. I want to be able to provide more for my family so T doesn't have to work so hard. I want to surprise her by doing it on my own rather than getting her help as the HR supervisor who is close with Tracey. I'm my own man.

*

-Beep Beep Beep-

I get up to turn off the alarm. It's Saturday, but I'm going into work today to do some overtime. I've been saving up money to buy T an engagement ring. I found the perfect one and now I just have to find the perfect time to ask her.

"Bae, you're working another weekend?" she sadly asks.

"Yeah," I whisper, trying not to make too much commotion.

"You want me to make you some coffee or something?"

"No Bae, go back to sleep." I get up and get dressed, go into Lil Sean's room, kiss him on the head, and leave out. It's five in the morning, and the air is crisp and clean. Damn, I love living out here. I pull out the driveway and head off to work.

Mommy's Here

Tiera

I wake up around 7:30 in the morning to a very low, soft crying noise, so I get out of bed, and trudge into the hallway. As I walk out of my room, my daughter comes walking out of hers too.

"You hear that?" I ask her.

"Yeah, I was just about to come get you and ask you the same." While standing in the hall, we wait quietly until we hear it again.

"It sounds like it's coming from Lil Sean's room," I say. We both rush in there to see what is going on and it looks like he is having a bad dream. We run to his bed and we can see tears coming from his little eyes. I pick him up and lightly nudge him to wake him.

He screams out, "No mom!" before he wakes up. Me and Sky both look at each other. He grabs me tight after he opens his eyes, and he's breathing heavily. I lean him back so he can look at me.

"I got you. Shhh, I got you. It's okay." Sky bends down and rubs his leg.

"Stank, are you okay? You had a bad dream?" Sky asks, and he nods.

"Aww my stank, it's okay." She rubs his head and kisses him on the cheek. She tries to pick him up and usually Skylar is his go-to person in the house, but when she reaches for him, he grabs me tighter.

"It's Sky, Big Man. You don't want your Sky?" I ask. He shakes his head no. I'm really concerned because he is not talking. I lift him up so he can look directly at me, and he just wraps his arms around my neck and lays his head on my shoulder. I put my arm under his butt, and I can feel that he is wet.

I mouth to Sky, "He peed." Skylar pulls back his covers and we see a big wet spot. We both know something is wrong. Lil Sean has never peed on himself, not since I met him at three and he's five now. I feel his head just to check to see if he is running a fever, and he isn't.

"Do you feel sick?" I ask him before kissing his cheek. He shakes his head no. Skylar tears up, so I tell her to go get some new pjs and underwear for him and that I'll wash him up. While I'm washing him up, Skylar washes his sheets and sprays down his bed. After we get him washed and dressed, we all get in my bed and lay down. I turn on the TV, hoping it would keep him calm and distract him, but he just lays in my arms.

Before he goes back to sleep, he snuggles up closer to me and says, "Can you be my mommy now?" My heart melts and a tear rolls down my cheek. I look at Sky and she's emotional.

"I'll be anything you want me to be, my sweet boy," I tell him, kissing him. Sky snuggles closer on his other side and we both lie there and watch him sleep. Sean comes in before lunch and walks into the room.

"Bae, where is–oh, there he is!" he says. "Look at y'all, all cuddled up. He's going to be more spoiled than he already is." He kisses me and seems to be in good spirits.

"Morning Bae. Morning, Sky," he officially greets us.

"Bae, we need to talk." He looks at me funny and then looks at Sky. Sky's eyes shift to Lil Sean.

"Yeah, what's up?"

"I think something is going on when Lil Sean is with Makayla…"

Sean is confused. "What you mean?"

"Well, he was crying in his sleep, having a bad dream and when I woke him up, he screamed out, 'No mommy!'" I explain.

"Yeah, and he peed on himself. We all know he don't do that. I read up on children peeing in their sleep, and it's not normal if that's not what they usually do. It's a sign that something is wrong, or he has a fear," Skylar adds. Sean sits on the bed and crawls up next to him.

"Did he call out for me?" Sean asks as he stares at Lil Sean, who is now sleeping peacefully.

"No, in fact, he only wanted Mom. He wouldn't even come to me," Sky says.

"And he asked if I could be his mommy now. Something is not right, Sean." Sean immediately wakes Lil Sean.

"Hey, buddy, it's daddy," he says.

Lil Sean takes a second to fully wake up, but when he does, he's happy to see Sean. "Hi daddy," he says before giving his dad a hug. Sean picks him up.

"You had a bad dream?" he asks him. Lil Sean nods. "And you peed?"

He sheepishly nods again and hides his face. "Yes, sorry daddy."

"No, it's okay, don't worry about that. What did you dream about?" Lil Sean doesn't say anything. Instead, he just lays his head on big Sean.

"Big Man, you can tell daddy anything, okay?"

Lil Sean nods, and then says, "Mommy was being mean to me."

"You had a dream about mommy being mean to you?" Lil Sean nods. "Was mommy mean to you when you went over her house?" He nods again. I can see Sean getting heated. His breathing becomes heavy, and he clenches his jaw to keep from screaming.

"What happened?"

"She told me not to tell, or she would be mean again." Sean looks at me and I can see his eyes fill up. He sucks it up and turns Lil Sean around to face him.

"Remember, you can tell me anything. I promise she will never be mean to you, again. You don't even have to go back over there if you don't want to, okay?" Lil Sean nods that he understands and my heart hurts for him. "Daddy will protect you and keep you safe, okay?"

"Yes," Lil Sean answers.

"So, what happened?"

"She pushed me down," Lil Sean says as he points to a scar on his knee.

"So, you didn't fall off your bike?" Lil Sean shakes his head no. Sean continues to probe Lil Sean, and all the while, I can't take it.

"She yells at me and won't let me call you, because she said this not my home, and she called me a bad word because I was crying." The anger and tension continue to build up in Sean's face.

"Is that all?"

"Yes."

"You sure?"

"Yes."

"Don't be afraid to tell me anything. You tell me everything that's wrong, even if they tell you not to tell me, you still can tell me, okay?"

Lil Sean says okay, and they both hug. Sean immediately puts Lil Sean back on the bed, stands up and paces the floor. He then grabs his phone and makes a call. I can tell he is furious. I signal Sky to take Sean out of the room. She asks him if he wants to help make breakfast and he agrees, leaving Sean and I alone.

"Bitch, if you ever put your hands on my son again, I will fucking kill you. You told him not to tell me you pushed him and scarred up his knee? Are you dumb? You thought I wouldn't find out, bitch, I'm his fucking parent, not you!"

He gets loud, and I try to get him to calm down, but he is too heated and he is going off. He continues, "You so mad that I won't be with you, so you take it out on my son? No, bitch, he's not your son, he's my son!"

Sean walks out the room, stomps down the stairs, and slams the front door. As I'm looking for shoes to go follow him, Twin calls my phone.

Me: Hey Twin, what's up?

Twin: Hey, I've been trying to call Sean, but it seems like he keeps sending me to voicemail.

Me: Yeah, he's on the phone cussing Makayla out.

Twin: Why? What she do now?

Me: Well, apparently, she pushed Sean down. He scraped his knee, and she told him to tell Sean that he fell off his bike, but today he told Sean that she has been mistreating him, and Sean went off.

Twin: Where is he?! Whatever you do, don't let him leave!

I run downstairs and race outside. As I open the door, Sean pulls off.

Me: Oh no, Twin. He just pulled off…

Twin: Fuck! He's going to kill her! I know where he's going…

Me: Kill her?! What?! Where is he going? Twin? Hello?

She hung up on me. I dash back in the house and try to call Sean's phone, but get no answer.

"Mom, what's going on? Did Sean leave?"

"Yeah," I say as I keep trying to call him.

"Good. Bust that bitch's head to the white meat," Sky says. I stop and glare at her.

"Who are you? And watch your mouth!"

"Sorry Mom, but she deserves what she gets," Sky says as she walks back in the kitchen with Lil Sean.

The Free Fall

Sean

It usually takes me at least 30 minutes to get to Makayla's house from Jersey, but today it only takes me 20 because I do about 90 the whole way there. I pull up and double parked across from Makayla's house, where she's sitting on the steps. She jumps up when she sees me and starts walking up her steps. I hop out and as I'm walking across the street ready to choke the hell out of this bitch, Joe steps in front of me, and stops me.

"What the–Joe?!" Where did he come from and why is he here? Once Makayla sees Joe in front of me, she jumps bad and starts walking back down the steps.

"Yeah, you better have someone hold you back, pussy! You little bitc-" and before she can get the word out, Twin runs up on her and socks the shit out of her, dropping her where she stood, and she rolls down the last step.

Wait a minute now… what is happening? I ask myself.

Twin wraps her hair up and says, "Get up, bitch! Come on! I've been waiting for this day for so long!" Makayla gets up and Twin swings on her again but misses. Makayla runs back up the steps and her sister, Tasha, comes running out the house. Makayla jumps bad now that she has back up and they both charge at Twin but then Tasha is met by Tiff and Kelly, who grab her and drag her down the steps, punching her while Tasha tries to kick them. Twin catches Makayla off guard and lands a two piece right to her face before grabbing Makayla by the shirt and dragging her back down the steps. Makayla grabs Twin's hair, but the whole time, Twin is using her right jab, going hard on Makayla's ribs while the girls stomp out Tasha.

"Yo, what the fuck is going on? Move, Joe!" I yell, trying to get around Joe.

Joe pushes me all the way back to my car and says, "You're the only one who has a child to go home to. We got this. Get in your car and go."

"Nah, fuck that! This bitch got my son scared to even tell me what's going on!"

"Twin got it!" He pushes me backwards. "What you gon' do, hit her and lose him to her? Go home, Sean. Now!"

I see out the corner of my eye, Makayla's nephew running up the street. He's only 19, but he's a big nigga. I push Joe back as hard as I can, just enough to get past him, and I run over to get him before he gets to the girls. Out of nowhere, James comes full speed and tackles him down to the sidewalk, and it's like the bar fight we got into back in college all over again.

What the hell is going on?! I think to myself. As James pins the nephew on the ground, Mally hops out the car and tells me to leave. As I hear the cop sirens, I go back to my car and hop in. Joe taps the car signaling me to pull off and I go. I drive straight to Twin and Joe's house and wait on the steps. I know that, if anything, this would be the place everyone will come back to. After waiting for a half an hour, everyone pulls up. They all jump out, and I walk over to Tiff and Kelly.

"Y'all cool? What happened? Is everyone good? And where the fuck did y'all all come from?!"

"Yeah, we good. They not though," Kels says and laughs.

"Twin called us when T told her what happened and we all rode out," Tiff explains.

"All for one, and one for all," James says as he walks up. I don't see Joe or Twin.

"Yo, where's my sister?" I panic, but then I see Joe's car. Joe hops out, but Twin isn't with him.

"Yo, where's my sister?"

"She got booked," Joe says.

"What the fuck? Y'all let her get booked?!"

"Sean, she wanted to take the fall for everyone, so she stayed and had us bounce," Joe says.

"Fuck you mean!? And y'all let her?"

"Nigga, she been planned this shit. She already knew that there was going to come a day, she just waited for you to jump first. She already had money aside for bail and everything. She will call and let us know when to come get her."

"What the–she's crazy. Now she's gon' have a record," I say, still pissed.

"Better her than you getting Lil Sean taken for killing his mother. Plus, she knows someone at the police station. Trust me, my wife, your sister, is good."

"I keep telling you, Twin is the bid for real," Mally says. I sit back on the steps and Kelly sits next to me, puts her head on my shoulder, and holds my hand.

"You know, we all got your back. Someone messing with your son is like someone messing with all of our sons. We all love Lil Sean and we all love you, so us risking that L for you to keep winning goes without saying," Kelly says.

"I appreciate you all, real shit, and that's from the heart. Y'all some fucking riders, coming out like the Power Rangers morphing and shit." I yell to them and we laugh.

"It was the college bar fight all over again," Tiff interjects and everyone nods in agreement.

"We got you, nigga," Mally says.

"Nigga, you was the look out. Shit, I'm the one that got my knees all scraped up," James says with a laugh.

"I helped you up though," Mally responds. "Nigga thought he was a quarter back again." We all laugh. Man, I love my crew. I rest my head on Kelly's head and two minutes later, T pulls up, though I didn't even notice her at first until I saw her glaring at me and Kelly. I jump up and run over to her car.

"Bae, what you doing here? Where is Lil Sean?" I ask.

"He's with Sky. You weren't answering your phone, I was worried. I didn't know where to go, so I came here. I thought you may be hurt or locked up, but you all hugged up on the steps. What is really going on?" She takes her hands off the wheel, sits back in her seat, and twists up her face, so I know she has a problem.

"T, don't start. It's not what you think. A lot of shit just went down and she was just making sure I was okay."

"So y'all have to be cuddled up for that to happen?"

"Bae, we wasn't cuddled up-"

"Aye Sean! Twin is ready," Joe yells.

"Look, I'll tell you all about it later when I get home, but right now, we gotta go bail Twin outta jail." I tell T to go home, but she insists on coming along, so Joe, T and I hop in my Jeep, and we hurry to the station. Just 20 minutes after we arrive, Twin comes out smiling and laughing with some lady officer.

I ran up to her. "You good? You okay?" I pick her up and kiss her repeatedly and tell her never to do that again.

"Yeah, I'm fine." I scan her body to make sure she isn't hurt and thankfully, besides a scratch above her eye, she is good. She walks over and hugs and kisses Joe.

"That was fast. How you make bail so quick?" Joe asks her.

"They let me off with a warning. Supposedly, the police been watching Tasha's house, anyway. They suspect drugs have been going in and out," Twin says nonchalantly. She looks over at the officer she is with and smiles. "This is my friend, Melanie. She's a DEA agent and the mother of one of my students. She pulled some strings once I told her what happened."

"Thank you so much," I say, shaking her hand.

"No problem, Sean."

"You know who I am?"

"Of course. Our sons go to the same school. You're the only father there that's really involved, and I must say, its impressive," she says, which causes me to smile.

"Anything for my son," I proudly say.

"She has agreed to report what happened to Lil Sean and back you in court," Twin explains. I thank her and she suggests that we start off with getting an official report. She asks if Lil Sean is around and if she can speak with him, but since he isn't, I suggest she speak with me and T, since he told both of us.

"Tell me what he told you and then let's make an appointment to have you bring him in so we can talk with him. When you get home, check his body for any marks and take pictures if you see any." We tell her what we know, she makes a report, and we agree on a date and time to bring Lil Sean back in.

On the way back to Twin and Joe's, Twin tells T everything that happened. When we pull up to the house, the crew is outside with party hats on, and when Twin gets out the car, they pop some champaign like she's been in jail for 30-plus years and just got out. James has the grill going and it's an all-out celebration.

Twin screams, "MazeTown!" so we say, "You know!"

I ask T if I can use her phone since mine is dead and I call Sky to check in on them and make sure they are good. As I'm talking to Lil Sean, Twin dashes over to talk to him.

"Hey man, I just want you to know Auntie loves you so much. You have so many people that love you and will always keep you safe, okay?" I stare at Twin with a smile, knowing that I'm not the only one who would go to jail for my boy. I talk with him and Sky for a little while longer and send Sky some money on BucksApp so she can order some food if they get hungry.

What a day. We sit around, laughing and joking about everything that happened today. We take shots, eat, and toast to a successful ass beating.

"Yo, this is the bar fight all over again," Twin says with a chuckle.

"Everyone keeps saying that," I say, laughing.

"What happened at the bar fight?" T asks.

Kelly stands up and says, "I'll take this one. So, it was our Junior year of college, and we all went to this bar outside of town…" she begins.

She explains that while her and Twin were getting their drinks, this white guy tried to hit on her, but he was being way too aggressive, so Twin jumped in and cursed the guy out. The guy got mad and called Twin a black bitch as they walked away. Of course, Twin took offense to that, so Twin doubled back, got in his face, and asked him to say it one more time.

Kelly claps her hands together, and she says, "Before I knew it, Sean popped up and punched the guy out, knocking him between the bar and stools." Kelly stands up from the table and starts running in place as she acts out how Mally and James ran right over to help me as the guy's friends jumped in. She pushes the chairs out of the way to recreate how Joe ran through the crowd knocking people out the way after seeing Twin get gripped up by her neck after hitting one of the guys with a bottle.

"Did y'all get locked up?" T asks.

"Nope," Kelly responds with a smirk.

"How did y'all get away?" Everyone's smile fades. We all look around, waiting for someone to say it, so I speak up.

"Makayla…" Now all eyes are on me and the air is thick. "She pulled the car to the back right before the cops came and got us out just in time."

I can tell everyone has mixed emotions. Makayla was once a good friend to them, a best friend to Twin, and a girlfriend to me. I guess the saying is right; you can't take everyone with you.

*

Over the next few months, I've gone back and forth to court for full custody of my son. I was finally awarded full custody of him and child support, but I refused the child support. We were good before, and we are even better now. Lil Sean started calling T Mom and he barely even mentions Makayla anymore. Sky doesn't call me Dad, but my name is saved in her phone as "Pops" and her name is saved in mine as "Lil Baby."

I thought we were all good; I was still taking driving lessons after work for my CDL and still working overtime on weekends to get T a ring, but T started acting differently ever since she saw me on the steps with Kelly. Her mood has been off; one day, she's hot and the next, she's cold. All I can come up with is that she is coming up on 40, but that's in three more years. I try to stay out her way and support whatever mood she is in.

On Thursday, I get home around 7 p.m., earlier than most days. Twin had taken Lil Sean with her, so I don't have to worry about getting him. When I get home, T is in the kitchen cooking and I can tell she is in one of her moods. She's moving around quickly, closing the cabinets hard, and is pushing things out the way. I simply say hi, kiss her, and make myself comfortable on the sofa because I don't want any parts of that drama. The house has an open floor plan, so she can see me from the kitchen. I reply back to Sky's text, asking me how my last day of classes went. I tell her it went well, that I am happy it's over, and that my exam is tomorrow.

Then out of nowhere, T slams a pot down and yells, "Are you cheating on me?!" I admit it scared me a little because it was so loud.

I turn around, confused, and ask, "What?"

"Are you seeing someone else, Sean?" She breathes heavily as she drums her fingers on the table.

I walk into the kitchen, sit my phone on the island. "No, T. Why would you even think something like that?"

"Because I know you are," she claims with her head leaned back and eyes narrowed, looking at me as if I'm lying to her.

"Well, you're wrong because I have never cheated on you." I stare at her and I can see her eyes are watery. I walk over to her and try to reassure her I'm not cheating but then she pulls out a paper and slams it on the island and points to it.

"So, what's this?" I look at it.

"This is my time sheet. How–why do you even have this?" I ask.

"You're doing overtime every day, right? So why doesn't your time sheet say so? Where are your hours? What are you doing every day after work?" she asks, tapping the paper hard with her finger and yelling.

"Why are you going through my shit? You checking up on me now? You don't trust me?" At this point, I am very annoyed with her.

"I just want to know how the hell you're working three and four extra hours a day all week and work on Saturdays, but only got 45 hours? How? Explain!" She demands as she stands in my face and yell.

I shake my head and walk around to the other side of the table. "You really should respect my privacy." I pick up my time sheet. "This right here is called abusing your power," I say, waving the sheet in her face.

"Who is she? Does she work with us? Did you meet her somewhere? Is it Kelly? Brittany?" she asks, looking crazy and deranged. She has worked herself up so much that she starts to sweat.

"Brittany?! Really? I thought we already talked about that? And Kelly, after all this time? Come on, man. You trying to put something together that's not even there, so drop it." I feel myself losing control and I become louder.

"Then explain the damn hours then!" My phone goes off and T grabs my phone.

"Who the hell is Lil Baby?!"

"That's Sky."

"Why is she saved in your phone as Lil Baby?!"

"What the hell do you mean why? That's the nickname I gave her.

You really bugging out. Your moods have been all over the place." While we continue going back and forth, Sky walks in, hears us, and walks into the kitchen.

"Hey, hey! What's going on?"

"Your mom thinks I'm cheating on her because I've been staying at work late." Sky knows all about what I've been trying to do, so she understands.

"Don't bring her into this," T says.

"Mom, relax. He's not cheating on you," Sky explains.

"Thank you," I say as I plop back down on the sofa. I feel relieved because I think T will take Sky's word, but I thought wrong.

"Oh, because you would know, huh? Because you two are so buddy, buddy now?" T turns off the stove. "When did you two even get so close? Now y'all using nicknames and texting all the time? Shit, are you fucking him?"

"Mom!" Sky yells. She is probably more confused than I am.

"Aye, yo! You need to chill the fuck out!" I jump up. Now I'm on fire from the level of disrespect.

"Why? You like them young, don't you? Isn't that why you were sleeping with Brittany? She was only what, 24 when y'all were having sex? I'm someone's grandmother compared to all your other hoes! Am I too old for you now, huh? Is that it?" T goes off.

"First off, say whatever you want to say to me, but don't you dare disrespect Sky like that. That's where I draw the line. Tiera, I don't know what brand of cocaine you're on, but you need to bring it down and get your shit together," I tell her.

"Get my shit together? Y'all the ones sneaking around here sniffing each other's asses. Maybe y'all had a few bumps of whatever brand of coke you think I'm on."

I shake my head and turn to Sky. "Can you excuse us?"

"No Sky, you don't have to go anywhere. Don't tell my daughter what to do!" T yells.

"Mom, stop it!" Sky interjects.

"Your daughter?" I ask.

"Yes, my daughter. Did you give birth to her? Better yet, did you bust in me to have her? I don't think so, so yes, my daughter!"

I rub my head. "Wow, see I thought we were doing this whole parenting thing together, but I guess I was wrong," I say. I keep my composure but that shit really stings.

"I guess so," she adds.

"So, you got my son walking around here calling you Mom when in reality, he's just my son, and Sky is just your daughter?" I ask her. T shrugs.

"Mom, you don't mean that!" Sky says, staring at T confused.

"Wow, okay." I laugh and shake my head. "I don't even know who you are anymore. I guess this is not my home either, so I'll go."

"Go ahead. Go be with your little young hoes!"

I grab my phone and keys and head out. My anger quickly turned to heartbreak. For her to act like this makes me question a lot. Is she showing her true colors right now?

Sky comes running after me.

"No, please. Don't go. Please…" I walk out the door and before the screen door closes behind me, she calls out, "Dad!"

I stop on the top step, my heart melting. Over these past two years, we have really connected, but T is right. Sky isn't my daughter. I keep walking, jump in my truck, and ride off.

Settle the Smoke

Tiera

He leaves, and all I can think is, *What did I just do? Did Sky really just call him dad? What is wrong with me?* I walk out the kitchen and see Sky at the door, watching him pull off.

She looks back at me and snaps, "What's wrong with you?" and runs upstairs. I saunter to the door and once I see he is really gone, my heart breaks. I stand at the door for 10 minutes, hoping he would come back and all the while, I try to process all that happened. The fight got out of hand, but I never wanted him to leave. I notice a car pulling up in the driveway, but it isn't Sean. Sky comes running down the steps with a bag. I can tell that she was crying.

"That's my ZuberDash. I'm going back to school," she tells me.

"Wait, Sky!" I try to reach out to her and she pulls away.

"No, Mom, did you hear yourself in there? No guy you have ever been with has ever cared about you or me the way Sean does, and you just let him walk out of our lives!"

"I know, Sky. I'm-"

"No, you don't know!" she yells as she pulls out her phone, showing me her texts with Sean. His name is "Pops" in her phone and it breaks my heart even more.

"Here, look!" she says, trying to shove the phone in my face.

"No, Sky. I trust you. I don't know what I was saying. I don't need to–"

"No, look! All we talk about is you all the time; things he can do for you to make you happy, things that he can do to make you feel better when work is killing you. He gives me advice about boys and makes sure I'm okay when I'm at school." She scrolls down. "You see this? This is us talking about him training for his CDL, which is why he stays after work. He didn't tell you because he wanted to surprise you when he passed the exam that he is taking tomorrow." She scrolls back up. "See here where he says he hates driving?"

"Yeah," I say.

"Do you know why he's still going to do it?" she asks.

"No."

"Because it makes more money. He's willing to do whatever it takes to provide more for you and all of us." She scrolls again, points to a conversation and demands I read it.

10:32 p.m.

Pops: Hey lil baby, I know you up cramming tonight for your midterms, check your BucksApp I sent you some cash for snacks to keep the night going while you're up, it's not for liquor tho ya old drunk lol! Good Luck baby girl you got this!

10:35 p.m.

Me: Ayyyyye you're the goat, shots, shots, shots!! No im just jk thanks a lot Sean at least one of you wished me good luck.

10:38 p.m.

Pops: Come on kid, you gotta give your mom a break, she's under a lot of stress right now from work, so how about you be the bigger person and just text her and say hey mom I love you.

10:42 p.m.

Me: Fine

After I read it, I look at her and cry as I see tears fall from her eyes.

"So, yes mom. I am your daughter, but he is my dad, even if you don't feel the same way," Sky says before walking out the door. I am at a loss for words.

Before the door closes, she looks back and says, "A year and a half ago, I got arrested for public intoxication on campus. I didn't want to call you because I was scared. I called my birth father and of course he didn't answer, so I called Sean. He got up at 3 a.m., bailed me out, and drove me back to campus. He never once asked me for the money back."

"I never knew that," I say.

"I know. I asked him to promise to keep this between us, and he said only if I promised not to let it happen again. Dads keeps their promises. Thanks for taking the only dad I had away," and she closes the door. I drop to the floor. It feels like all the wind in my body has been knocked out. I am heartbroken and crushed. I sit on the floor and cry for hours. What is wrong with me? I let the best man in my life walk out. I have pushed away the only man that truly loved me and my daughter. My daughter thinks of him as her own father. What did I do?

I don't get off the floor until night falls. When I do, I run straight to my phone and called Sean. I call and I call, and it keeps going to voicemail. He is very upset with me, and I don't blame him. I try to call Sky and she sends me to voicemail too. I've just torn my family apart with one argument. I take a shower and I cry, I look in the mirror and I cry; I cry so much that I end up crying myself to sleep.

The next day, I'm so drained that I have to pile my face with make up so I can walk into work. I get there late, and any other time, I would care but, today I don't. I look for Sean's car in the parking lot, but I don't see it. I head right in my office and check IM messenger to see if he is online, but he isn't. I must have left him a million voicemails and texts last night, but I haven't gotten anything in return. I wait an hour and sit at my desk, doing nothing before I go upstairs to see if he is here. When I get upstairs, I see his desk is empty. I ask Rachel and Oliver, who Sean sits between, if he is here today. They say he called out sick, but they're also giving me a look of confusing because everyone knows we live together, so I have to pull it off like I knew.

"Yeah, he said he was still going to try and make it. I guess it must be really bad. I may have to take an early day and go check on him," I say to them.

"Aww man. Tell him to get well soon," Rachel tells me.

"I will," I say with a fake smile. I walk back down stairs and I can't even think about doing work. I'm about to call up Tracey and tell her I need to take a personal day. As I'm walking down the steps, I run right into Cody, which is surprising because he now works at the location in Delaware.

"Hey, boo. I was just in your office," he says. I instantly break down and start crying. He brings me in close and walks me to my office, helping me hide my face from the rest of the world.

"What's wrong honey?" he asks as he closes and locks my office door. I break down again and he hands me a tissue.

"Baby, look at me. What's wrong? You never cry at work."

"I had a fight with Sean last night. He left, he won't answer my calls, and he's not here," I say in tears. "Oh, I messed up, Cody. I really did and now he's gone, and I don't think he's coming back," I say blowing my nose.

"Sit down and tell me what happened," Cody says, so I tell him everything. "Damn, girl. Wait, Sky was there when you accused him of sleeping with her?"

"Yeah, she came in and started taking up from him. I felt some type of way and I snapped."

"Whew, chile, not in front of the baby girl," Cody says, sighing.

"I know. When he walked out, she begged him not to go. She even called him dad." I cry again. He comforts me with his hugs and lets me cry in his shoulder. I feel awful.

"You're definitely going to have to make it up to him," Cody says to me. "Maybe you're just PMSing. Are you on your period, boo?"

"No…" I look at him and then quickly pull out my planner and check it.

"Oh no…" I say.

"What's wrong?" Cody asks.

"Shit. I haven't had a period for the past three months…" He looks at me and I look at him.

"Girl you're…"

"Don't say it… I can't be… I'm almost 40!" I say.

"I bet you didn't feel 40 when you had them legs up," Cody say, laughing. I quickly IM Tracey and tell her I have to take a personal day and that I will be back tomorrow. I grab Cody's hand.

"Come on!" I dial my doctor while walking down the hall and ask to make an appointment today and she says I can come right in. When we get in the car, I freeze.

I look at Cody. "What if I am pregnant? What if he doesn't want me or the baby?"

"Girl, Sean loves you. Just give him some time to cool down. You used some heavy words in that argument, so it may take him some time, but right now, we need to go see if I'm about to be an uncle again. Shit, the best way to get your man back is to tell him you're pregnant." We both laugh and we drive as fast as we can to the doctor's office.

"Thank you for being here. As a matter of fact, what are you doing here?" I ask him.

"I had off and needed some time away from the husband and kids, so I came to see my best friend. It seems like you really need me," he says, holding my hand.

"I'm so glad you came," I reply,

"Me too, doll face."

As we sit in the room waiting for the doctor to give me an ultrasound, Cody holds my hand but I wish it was Sean with me right now. I call him about five times in the waiting room, but he still won't answer. Tears start flowing again, but Cody gives me the pep talk I need, and just in time, because the doctor calls us in.

"At least we know if it's a bun in that oven he or she is going to be a cutie," he whispers to me just before the doctor greets us.

"Hello, Ms. Anderson. How are you feeling today?"

"I'm fine. A little stressed, but fine nonetheless."

"And hello, you must be the boyfriend?"

"No ma'am!" Cody says shaking his head. "I like links not patties, if you know what I mean," Cody says, making me laugh.

"No, Doctor Paul, this is just my best friend, Cody," I say. She apologizes with a chuckle and gets on with the visit. As she puts the gel on my stomach, she asks me the standard questions–whether I was trying to get pregnant, if I had gotten off birth control, etc. After a few moments of silence, she turns the screen around.

"Well my dear, it looks like you're going to be a mother. You are 10 weeks to be exact." Me and Cody smile at each other.

"So, you haven't had morning sickness or cravings?" she asks me. I shake my head. "Well, it's still early, but you're getting really close to the second trimester, so that may change. See right here? That's your baby," she says pointing to a small dot on the screen. I am in complete awe. "… and right here is your other baby."

My eyes get wide. "Other baby?!" Cody and I say at the same time.

"Yes. You're a mother of two. You're having twins! Congratulations." Dr. Paul says as she cleans off my stomach.

"Thank you," I say, practically speechless.

"You're so welcome. I will leave information about what to do, what not to do, all that stuff you already know. We will start you on prenatal care today and you can set up your next appointment at the front desk. Do you have any questions?" she asks.

"No, thank you very much, Dr. Paul."

"You're welcome. Enjoy your day."

She walks out and I look at Cody. "Oh my god, I'm pregnant!" I say.

"And with twins," Cody says, still in shock himself.

"Wow… what am I going to do?" I ask.

"Tell Daddy to come home. Y'all got two more children to raise," Cody replies.

The next day when I go to work, I sit at my desk just staring at my IM, waiting for it to say he's online. Last night, I could barely sleep. My house was cold, the kids weren't there, and neither was Sean. The only thing that kept me sane was knowing that I have two lives inside of me that belong to the man that I love.

When 9 a.m. comes, my heart skips a beat when I see his name pop up in the list of people online. The unknown is heartbreaking, and knowing he is here put me at peace. I write him right away and tell him we need to talk. I wait and wait, and he doesn't respond, so I text him. I know he is getting my messages, and it's really stressing me out and making me sick. I can't eat, it's hard to sleep, and I can't stop crying. If he is trying to get me back for what I said, he is doing one hell of a job.

I wait until lunch time and I stand by the steps, waiting for him to come down. He takes his time, but when I see him, my world feels whole again. He strolls down the steps, looks at me, and walks right past me. I run and grab his arm and he snatches it away.

"Sean, stop! I don't want to do this anymore!" I say.

"Do what? Accuse me of sleeping around?" he asks.

"Bae, can you talk to me please?"

"Talk about what Tiera?!" he asks with his voice raised. A few co-workers walk by and stare at him. He smiles and quickly changes his tone.

"Talk about what, huh? How you basically said I was fucking my daughter? Oh, wait sorry. Your daughter…"

"Bae, I'm so sorry. I didn't mean any of that, I just– I don't know I'm going through a lot of things right now, and we need to talk."

"I'm good," he says as he begins to walk away.

"So, you're not going to come home? You're going to just walk out and leave like Makayla did to you? You're going to treat me the same way?"

He stops and turns around.

I take a breath. "Look, just meet me at Del Caslo Restaurant tomorrow night at seven. I told Sky, and please bring Lil Sean. It's important, all right?"

He nods and walk away. My heart is racing as I walk back to my office. When I settle back at my desk, I rub my stomach.

"Guys, girls or both, I hope this works. I miss your daddy so much."

Love Unseen

Sean

Makayla, huh? I'm nothing like her. After my run in with T, I leave work to take my exam. So many things are going through my head that it's hard to focus. I've been staying at Mally's apartment for the past two nights and to tell you the truth, I haven't been sleeping. How could she think I would do something like that? But shit, maybe I should have just told her instead of trying to surprise her. I would think I was cheating too. Man, fuck that. She shouldn't have been looking up my shit, with her sneaky ass. I should tell her boss.

Damn, I miss her though. She looked good today, and is it me or did she get a little thicker? I laugh as I think to myself, *I really be putting in that work.* I don't know, maybe I'm tripping.

After the test, I pick Lil Sean up from school early and take him to get some water ice. We take a quick trip over to Jersey to grab some things before T gets home. When we get there, I notice there are tissues everywhere, so I can tell she has been crying or she got a real bad cold. I feel bad, and I wish I would have just told her so things wouldn't have gotten so out of hand.

As I'm in Lil Sean's room getting him a few things, he asks "Daddy, are we moving?"

"We going to stay at uncle Mally's house for a while."

"Where we used to live?" I nod my head. Mally moved into my apartment when we moved out.

"Are we going back to my real mommy?" he asks.

I laugh and shake my head. "No, Big Man."

"Good, because I like it here."

I sigh. "Me too, Big Man. Me too."

The next day, me and Lil Sean get up early and go to the mall to do a little shopping. That whole day, all I can think about is this meet up tonight and my stomach stays knotted up. I've been a complete asshole–not answering her calls, not coming home, running away from my problems instead of facing them. I just want this to be all over. I want to go home. I miss my family.

*

We get to the restaurant about 15 minutes late that night. When we walk in, I see T, and Sky is sitting across from her; T is waiting, and Sky is on her phone. Lil Sean dashes over to hug T and then Sky. Sky hugs him a few seconds longer and sits him next to her. I sit on the other side of him, and now it looks like it's us against T, so I move a little closer to T.

"Thank you for coming," she says.

"You're welcome" Lil Sean replies. Everyone smiles and opens out his arms. He's the definition of an icebreaker.

"I asked you all here today, one because no one would answer my calls." She laughs, but then tears start rolling down her face. "And two, I wanted to apologize to everyone for my behavior the other day. I am truly sorry from the bottom of my heart. Sky, you are everything to me, my life line, my baby girl and I'm so sorry for the way that I treated you. I didn't understand how much of a strong bond you have with Sean, and honestly, I was jealous of the bond you two formed. For the first time in a very long time, my baby girl, who only came to me for everything, was going to someone else for help, advice, and fun. I felt like I was losing my baby."

Sky tears up, "You can't lose me, mom. I'll always be your baby."

"I know, I was just going through some changes that I didn't know about at the time, but again, I'm sorry. Lil Sean, baby boy, I know you probably don't understand why I'm saying all this, but I want you to know, you are also a big part of my life, and I love you very, very much. You are my son, and you asking me to be your mom was one of the best days of my life. I will always be here for you and I will always be your mommy. I will love, protect you, and keep you safe, okay?" T says, her tears now freely flowing.

"Yes. Don't cry," Lil Sean says in a comforting tone.

"Okay, I'll try" not to," T says as she pats her tears with her napkin. The waiter comes over to get us started with our order, but T asks for a few more minutes to look over the menu.

"Sean you are everything I ever wanted and everything I ever dreamed of. Not only do you love me unconditionally, but you have accepted my child as yours and that is very rare. I know at first you were afraid of her not liking you, but now she adores you and so do I. Bae, I'm sorry. I can only explain my actions by saying I felt left out of your life as well. It's hard for me to trust, and things were so good that I got scared and felt like it couldn't be right. I should have never looked at your information and jumped to any conclusions without talking to you and telling you how I feel. I want this relationship to be based on trust, honesty, and of course, love. I love you more than you could ever know. I'm sorry for accusing you of sleeping around. I love you so much and the thought of you leaving, breaks my heart, and I would never recover from that. So, please forgive me. Please come home, our home. I want all of you to come home. It's not one without you." I clear my throat and wipe the corners of my eyes.

She looks down and tries to find the right words to say. "Lately I've been going through unknown changes and many moods that I couldn't understand until yesterday and well…" She looks around the table and takes a deep breath.

"Well, what Mom?" Sky asks.

T looks at me and says, "I'm pregnant." As I sip my water, I begin to choke.

"Oh my God, Mom! That's amazing!" Skylar says as her face lights up.

"What's pregnant?" Lil Sean asks.

"Mommy is having a baby!" Sky says, tickling him.

"Wow! I'm going to be another brother!" They laugh, knowing what Lil Sean meant to say.

"Yes, you are," T says, giggling but also still in tears. She then looks back at me. "Sean, how do you feel?" she asks me.

"Wow, I'm um… I'm shocked. This is so unexpected…" I say.

"Yeah, I felt the same way, but now I'm very happy and kind of excited," T says with a beaming smile. I scoot over and touch her stomach.

"You really having my baby?" I ask, now staring into her eyes.

"No, Bae…" she says. I sit back, confused, but then she laughs and grabs my face, pulling me close. "I'm having your babies. It's twins!" she announces.

I gasp. "We're having twins like me and Twin?!" I can't help but smile.

She laughs and tears of joy run down her face. "Yes, my love." I move closer and feel all over her stomach, whispering, "My babies." She laughs and cries at the same time.

"Can you forgive me, so we all can be a family again?" T asks.

"On one condition," I say.

"Whatever you want," she says without hesitation.

I push my chair back and I get on one knee as I pull a ring box out of my pocket and grab her hand.

"Tiera Anderson, mother of my now four children. I never knew real love until I found you. You stick by my side through the ups and the downs. You never leave and you never stop fighting for our love, our family and for that I want to love you every day for the rest of my life. T, will you marry me?"

"Yes, Sean! Oh my God, yes!" The whole restaurant claps. I stand up and help her up, hold her in my arms and kiss her. It's the happiest moment of my life aside from the birth of my son. She is overjoyed and the kids are ecstatic. The rest of the night goes great; we eat and toast with water to our new lives and the new lives coming.

After dinner, Sky says with a smile, "Hey Pops, you should ride with mom and let me drive your Jeep home." She's been dying to drive my car since she started driving last year.

"Drive my Jeep? That's a big boy. You think you can handle it?" I ask her.

"Duh! Were only 10 minutes from the house and y'all will be right behind me if anything happens."

"Should I?" I ask T.

"Hey, you're the one who taught her how to drive. It's your call daddy," T says with a smile. With her calling me pops, the baby announcement, and getting engaged, I am feeling so good inside, so I give her my key.

"Don't make me pull you over," I say, and she laughs.

"I won't. Thanks, Pops."

"Can I go with Sky, Daddy?" Lil Sean asks.

"Yeah son. Sky, make sure his butt is in that booster seat," I tell her.

"Got it," she replies. We all head out and I let the kids take off first so I can follow them, and I drive T's car. While we are waiting at the light, she looks at me and laughs.

"What now? Don't tell me you're having triplets." She laughs.

"No. I really love you, Mr. Johnson. So, so much." She looks over to me in a daze.

"I really love you too, soon-to-be Mrs. Johnson."

"Ooooh, I like that. Say it again,"

"Mrs. Johnson."

"Ooooh, say it again!"

"Mrs. Johnson." We both crack up laughing. The light turns green, but before taking off, I kiss her. I can't believe I'm kissing not only my future wife but also the soon to be mother of my twins. We get so lost in each other, but at that moment, in the blink of an eye, a car speeds right though the red light and smacks into my Jeep like a freight train just as the kids pull out. T screams and we both jump out the car. The car was going so fast, that it T-boned my truck, pushing it about 500 feet away and pinned it between a tree. Without thinking, I take off running, leaving T behind. I immediately look in the windows to see if the kids are fine and thankfully, I can see them moving, so they are alive, but then my car starts smoking.

I can't get them out because all the doors are jammed. The kids start screaming, and T runs up to the car, but I tell her to stand back and call 911, just to give her something to do because now isn't the time to be hysterical. The other car hit the driver's side door, but I can't open the back door. The only thing I can get to is the back window. I tell Sean to look the other way and I punch the glass until it breaks, and I'm able to get him out without cutting him by using my arms as his safety shield. As I hand him off to T, the smoke starts getting out of control. I can't get Sky out from her door or the window. Not having any other choice, I jump on the hood to see if I could break the windshield and pull her out, as Sky calls out to me.

"Dad! Dad! Please help me!" I try to punch the windshield but it's way too thick and I only make a few cracks in it, so I try to kick it in. Sky is coughing and trying to hang on as the smoke continues coming in heavy, but I keep kicking until my foot breaks through the glass. I'm able to kick the passenger side of the windshield in, but then my Jeep catches on fire under the hood I'm standing on. I don't have time to worry about where the damn fire trucks are; there is only one thing I'm focusing on and that is to get my daughter out by any means necessary.

"Sky! I need you to crawl over to the passenger side and push the window out. Can you do that for me, baby?" I yell to her. She says yes and tries to get out, but her seatbelt is stuck.

"Dad, I can't! I'm stuck!" She says while crying out for me.

"Baby girl! My keys! My keys have a pocket knife on them. Take my key out the ignition and use it to cut your belt!" I tell her.

"Okay, got it!" she replies as she quickly cuts the seatbelt. We are losing time, so I reach in the hole I made, pull the glass out, and slip into the Jeep to help her out.

"Hold on to me. Watch the glass, and don't touch the hood," I say. As I pull her out the fire, police, a fire truck, and an ambulance shows up. I pass her to them and she runs over to T. They clear the area and push us back while they start pulling the other person out the car that T boned them. Instead of going over with T and the kids, I walked over to the other car because I want to see who hit my kids. While the cops pull the woman out, about three liquor bottles fall out the car. In a rage, I lift the yellow tape and race over. This bitch had been drinking and driving and almost killed my kids. The cops cuff the drunken bitch on the ground, and when they pick her up, I'm mortified.

It's Makayla.

Instantly, I feel an enormous amount of pain.

"That was your son!" I screamed at her. I want to run, but suddenly, I can't move. Something is wrong with my legs and my body feels cold and wet. I look down and blood is pouring down my arms. I fall to my knees and a faded voice calls out my name. Soon, everything fades until all I can see is black.

The next day, I wake up in the hospital in so much pain. My leg is in a cast and so are both of my arms.

"Bae? He's awake!" T says to Twin as T comes running to my bedside.

"I'll go and tell the doctor he's up," Twin says.

"What happened?" I ask.

"You lost a lot of blood," she explains as she cries. "You passed out. The doctor said you must have been running on adrenaline to have been able to keep going and get the kids out the car."

"Where are the kids? Are they all right?" I try to sit up, but T stops me.

"Stop, Bae. Lay down. They are okay. Besides a few cuts, they are perfect because of you." Twin walks back in the room with the doctor and holds my hand.

"Hello, Mr. Johnson. I'm glad to see you're awake. Some kind of hero you are. You had one hell of a night." I try to lift my arm

"Yeah, I can see that. So, what's the damage, doc?" I ask.

"Well, like I was telling your fiancé and sister here, you broke both of your hands, you have a few deep lacerations on your right arm that needed 15 stitches, you fractured your lateral cuneiform bone in your left foot, tore your right ACL, which we conducted surgery on when you came in. Your fingers were reset and should heal up nicely in the cast. In addition to that, you also have a deep two inch laceration on your calf that cut into the muscle, but you only needed eight stitches for that, and last, both of your knees suffered second-degree burns."

"Fuck," I say.

"Yeah, you got pretty banged up, but you saved your children's lives last night, and for that my friend, you are a superhero," Doc says.

"Yeah, well I wish I had superpowers because this pain is intense," I reply. The doctor tells me to hold tight while he gets me some pain meds.

"Where are the kids at, anyway?" I ask.

"Joe took them to get something to eat," Twin replies.

"What time is it? How long have I been out?"

"It's 5 p.m. on Sunday, Bae," T responds.

"Damn. So, Makayla tried to take me out, huh," I say as I try to sit up, but T stops me again and tells me to stop trying to do too much.

"I don't know what she was trying to do. The police haven't really said much, but she was arrested and is being charged."

"Well, they better keep her in there for a long time because if she gets out any time soon, y'all won't have to worry about bailing me out this time," Twin says.

"You mean bailing both of us out," T adds.

I spend a week and a half in the hospital recovering. I'm finally able to bend my knees better, but everything else is still out of commission. T is there with me night and day and doesn't leave. I couldn't have chosen a better woman to spend the rest of my life with. She feeds me, cleans me, and wipes my ass. She took FMLA and set me up to get out on disability. For that, she gets my deepest love and the utmost respect.

Lil Sean and Sky stay with Twin until I get home. As for Makayla, she takes the plea deal for a crime of passion instead of being tried for intent to commit murder. She got eight years for that and three years for drunk driving.

When I get home, my friends and family throw me a big surprise Superman-themed party. It's great; everyone is there, even a few of my co-workers, including Cody, Rachel, Oliver and even big boss Tracey. It's a good time and everyone that is there also gets a surprise from us when we tell them we are engaged and having twins.

T and the kids get me a big comfy recliner, so I don't have to go upstairs and sleep. Of course, Mally gets me a few gag gifts like Depends and diaper rash cream. That dude is something else.

About a half an hour into the party, T taps her glass. "I just want to raise my glass to the man of the hour, my love, my superhero. Without you, Bae, we wouldn't be where we are right now. You are the best father anyone could ask for. You risked your life for our children." She starts crying and apologizing to the crowd.

"Take your time!" Twin yells out.

"There is no other man on this Earth I would rather raise and have my children with than you."

"There better not be," I say and everyone laughs.

"Here's to you. My best friend, my heart, my soul, the father of all my children, and my future husband!" Everyone screams out, "Aye!"

"I love you, Bae." She wipes her tears.

"I love you more," I say and she gives me a kiss.

When the night is done, I sleep in my recliner, and T and the kids sleep next to me on the sofa. It's been one hell of a few weeks, but it was all worth it. I wake up in the middle of the night and just watch them sleep.

My family. I finally have my family. I watched T sleep so peacefully, drooling and with one hand on her stomach. Lil Sean sleeps with his legs wide open and arms hanging off the sofa and Sky with her head on the arm of my chair and mouth wide open. None of us could fill the hearts of the people we wanted the most, but it was only a matter of time for all of us to find what we really needed–each other.

-ding ding- Incoming Call from Twin

It's three in the morning. I wonder what's up.

Me: Twin? Are you all right?
Twin: Sean… Makayla committed suicide.

To Be Continued...

About The Author

Born in Philadelphia, PA and raised in Elkins Park, PA., C.N. Johnson hopes to inspire people with her dedication to never giving up on their dreams, no matter how old they are. She hopes her willingness to take a leap of faith to find her purpose will give others the motivation to do the same. Johnson graduated from the Community College of Philadelphia and as of 2019, is studying English at Arcadia University.

"Fear not God's guidance… for belief is to trust the unseen."

– M. Brown

Made in the USA
Coppell, TX
22 January 2021